Danielle Ramsay

Danielle Ramsay is a proud Scot living in a small seaside town in north-east England. Always a storyteller, it was only after pursuing an academic career in literature that she found her place in life and began to write creatively full time after being shortlisted for the CWA Debut Dagger in 2009 and 2010. She is the author of four previous Jack Brady crime novels, *Blood Reckoning*, *Blind Alley*, *Broken Silence* and *Vanishing Point*.

Always on the go, always passionate in what she is doing, Danielle fills her days with horse-riding, running and murder by proxy.

DANIELLE RAMSAY

The Puppet Maker

First published in Great Britain in 2016 by Mulholland Books
An imprint of Hodder & Stoughton
An Hachette UK company

1

All characters in this publication are fictitious and any resemblance to real persons, living or dead is purely coincidental.

A CIP catalogue record for this title is available from the British Library

Paperback ISBN 978 1 473 61147 4
eBook ISBN 978 1 473 61148 1

Typeset by Hewer Text UK Ltd, Edinburgh
Printed and bound by CPI Group (UK) Ltd, Croydon, CR0 4YY

Hodder & Stoughton policy is to use papers that are natural, renewable and recyclable products and made from wood grown in sustainable forests. The logging and manufacturing processes are expected to conform to the environmental regulations of the country of origin.

Hodder & Stoughton Ltd
Carmelite House
50 Victoria Embankment
London EC4Y 0DZ

www.hodder.co.uk

To Mum and little sis – for always being there

‘Every passion borders on the chaotic, but the collector’s passion borders on the chaos of memories.’

Walter Benjamin

‘It is a man’s own mind, not his enemy or foe that lures him to evil ways.’

Siddhartha Gautama

Prologue

Saturday: 9:33 p.m.

The basement was dark, damp and cavernous. It suited its purpose as a graveyard of sorts. Forgotten about. Filled with ghostly objects and questionable medical implements. Brady shone his torch across the discarded equipment, some dating back to when the Victorian mental asylum had first opened. The security guard had left him to it. Unnerved by the old psychiatric chairs with their leather restraints and other paraphernalia left to rot in the blackness. Brady couldn't blame him. He was equally uncomfortable down here. Then he heard *it* again. A doleful booming.

That noise . . . What is that noise?

He stumbled over something on the floor. *Shit!* Whatever he had tripped over rolled away, clattering into another item. The sound echoed around him, reverberating off the high brick walls. He flashed the torch into the deep recesses of the basement. Not that he could make anything out: the blackness was impenetrable.

He was starting to get jumpy. He needed to focus. There was a reason he was searching the bowels of an abandoned and boarded-up mental asylum late on a Saturday evening – James David Macintosh; a serial murderer who was still at large. Brady had found himself unable to ignore the gut feeling he had; one that was telling him that the old psychiatric hospital was somehow significant.

He heard it again. A dull thud. It seemed to boom around him. Echoing off the high cold walls.

Fuck!

He turned around, stabbing at the shadows surrounding him. He couldn't figure out the direction of the noise, let alone the nature of it. He listened again.

Bang . . . bang . . . bang . . .

It was then he knew. He was not alone. Something – or someone – was down here with him. His mind raced with thoughts of James David Macintosh as the banging – low, dull and repetitive – filled the chilling blackness around him.

Shit! What if . . .

He pulled out his mobile. No signal. What did he expect? He thought of yelling out for the security guard. But he dismissed the thought. It was crazy. He was overreacting. He flashed the torch around the basement again, but the space was so large that he could not make out where it ended. Then the thought came back to him.

What if he is here?

Macintosh. The suspect he was looking for. A serial killer who had axed his victims to death. First, his psychiatrist and his family in 1977. Then, when he had finally been paroled for that crime, he had murdered his probation officer and *his* family. But he had left one survivor. A three-year-old girl, who for whatever sick reason only Macintosh could answer, he had taken with him when he fled the murder scene.

Bang ... bang ... BANG.

Cold sweat ran down Brady's back. He held his breath and waited, trying to ignore the loud, accelerated thundering of his heart. He wondered whether he had foolishly walked into a trap. Had Macintosh lured him here? Had he followed unwittingly? Images assailed him of the axe the killer had used so indiscriminately.

BANG ... BANG ... BANG ...

The booming intensified. He had no choice but to find out. He kicked random objects out of the way as he walked into the endless darkness ahead of him. He shone his torch, swiping at the shadows and ominous black shapes. Then he understood. Saw it. At the other end of the basement.

Brady held the torch as steady as was physically possible. He stared at the brick monstrosity that had revealed itself to be an industrial-sized furnace. It was twelve foot wide and ran up the entire height of the basement wall.

The banging began again. Louder. Uglier.

He walked over to the disused furnace, discounting the idea that Macintosh would be in there. Why would he be? No. Brady was now thinking about the infant girl he had taken with him.

He dropped the torch and started struggling with the large furnace door. It seemed to take forever before he succeeded in freeing it. The hinges groaned and creaked in resistance as he swung it open.

It took him a moment to register.

Annabel?

A girl. Thin. Small. Crouched over on scabby knees. Dirty. Covered in dried blood and . . .

Fuck . . . No . . . Brady steadied himself, not quite trusting what he was seeing.

Hair filthy. Matted. Her eyes. Black. Stared back at him. Unresponsive.

Oh Christ! What's happened to her? What the fuck has someone done?

All thoughts of James David Macintosh and the three-year-old girl disappeared. He was too thrown by the young victim facing him. *Someone had locked her in there. With . . . Oh God . . .*

Shocked, he stared past her. Past her undead eyes to the others.

So many of them . . .

He stood still. Mesmerised by the horror. They were dead. All of them – apart from her.

Why were they like that? Identically dressed. Long dark hair. Perfect faces. Painted. Heavy red lipstick – each one of them. All turned to face him. Watching him.

Grotesque. Horrific. Dead.

Then the screaming started. The girl. Her black eyes now filled with terror. Staring and staring at Brady, screeching a cry so inhuman, it was as if she had lost her mind.

DAY ONE
SATURDAY

Chapter One

Saturday: 3:01 a.m.

Shit . . . shit . . . my head . . .

She struggled to open her eyes – to keep them open. The pain in her head was unbearable. She closed them again, willing the pounding to subside. Minutes passed. Torturously slow. Any kind of movement racked the pain up to a level that was insufferable. So she lay face-down on the hard, cold floor and waited. Not moving – breathing as shallowly as possible – she remained there.

She had no idea how long she had lain there for, but finally, she was able to open her eyes and turn her head. The room was so black it was impossible to see anything.

That smell . . .

The still, heavy air was nauseating. It smelt of vomit combined with an astringent odour of stale urine. She could feel herself starting to gag. Fear snaked its way through her cold body, coiling itself into a tight knot in her queasy stomach. It brought with it a sudden acknowledgement. A hard slap that jolted her back to reality.

Last night . . . Oh God . . . what happened?

Then she started to remember. First one image, then another and another. Lurid, debasing snapshots assaulted her senses.

Him . . .

Her stomach started to churn. He had drugged her. She was certain of that. He had taken her to his place . . .

Oh fuck . . . where am I?

'Help? Help me?' she suddenly cried out. But her voice was barely audible.

Her throat hurt. It felt raw and swollen. Then she remembered why. She did not need to see the mottled purple and bluish bruising left behind by his hands. She could feel them encircling her neck and squeezing: slowly, surely, mercilessly. Her stomach tightened as she recalled the satisfaction he gleaned from strangling her while he— She stopped. She couldn't bring herself to think about what he had done.

She now understood why the room smelt of vomit. She had been sick, but her stomach could only retch up bile. Not that he had cared. He was only interested in raping her.

She could taste him in her mouth and smell him on her skin. A vile, distinctive odour that reminded her of bleach. She swallowed.

She tried to block out the thoughts. The brutal, sick images that kept replaying over and over again on a self-destructive loop.

She needed to pull herself together. She didn't have time to be weak and self-pitying. If she did, then she wouldn't leave here alive. She had to focus on one thought – *getting out.*

She listened for a noise. Something that could give her a clue as to where he had brought her. But there was nothing but oppressive silence. Then she heard it; a dripping noise. Faint but constant. Scratching . . . Something or someone was scratching. It was barely audible. But she could make out what sounded like nails dragging against metal.

Terror gripped her as she tried to discern the direction of the scratching. But it had stopped. Tears started to spill down her cheeks. She was desperate for a drink. It felt as if tiny shards of broken glass were lodged in her throat. She willed herself to get up. To move. She needed to find that water – *and a way out*. But her body felt as if it belonged to someone else. The smallest movement was an effort. Her head was still pounding and her limbs felt too weak to comply. She tried to push herself up from the mattress.

She cried out. Her knee exploded. The pain, blinding.

Then the panic took over.

I don't want to die. Not here. Not like this.

She needed to focus. Get herself thinking straight. He had left her – *for now.*

She forced herself to fight the panic. Managed somehow to pull herself up. Exhausted and light-headed, she leaned back against the cold, damp wall and sat for a moment steadying herself against the screeching pain in her knee.

Had she fallen? She couldn't remember . . .

She breathed out slowly, trying to stop herself from retching. She had no idea what time it was, or how long she had been here. It was then that she became aware that her ankle hurt as well. More than hurt, it was burning with a cold feverish intensity. She pulled her leg in towards her body and heard what sounded like metal being dragged. Something was clasped tightly around it, cutting into the flesh. Panic-stricken, she felt her way down her leg.

Panic took hold again. She tried to fight it. A metal cuff was secured around her ankle. Desperate, she grabbed at the chain attached and yanked as hard as she could. It was futile. It didn't move.

Fuck! I'm trapped ... Oh fuck, why? Why has he done this to me?

Then she understood – *he's planning on coming back and ...*

She stopped herself. She didn't want to think about him coming back. The thought of *him* filled her with dread. Those eyes filled with contempt. No remorse, shame or empathy. Nothing but disgust for her.

The things he had done to her ... He had hurt her in a way that was inconceivable. And that was just the beginning. He had told her he had plans for her.

She tried to stop herself trembling. Whether it was fear or cold that had taken over her body, she couldn't say. All she knew was that she was terrified. Terrified of him coming back. There was no mistaking the fact that he had *hidden* her.

She wrapped her arms around her chest in an attempt to warm herself.

The darkness surrounding her had started to become claustrophobic. She could make nothing out. Fear of the unknown was threatening to unhinge her. She had always been terrified of the dark. It was something that she had never grown out of – that irrational feeling that something or *someone* was lurking in the shadows waiting for you.

For fuck's sake, keep it together and think ... think it through. Try and remember what happened ...

She shut her eyes tight as she tried to recall the events that had led her here. Slowly, pieces of memory, sketchy and hazy, started to come back.

Last night. Then ...

The memory jolted her. Him. The car. What happened next? She couldn't remember.

She couldn't fucking remember!

Then she was here.

Wherever here *is ...*

She had woken up in a cellar of sorts – some underground basement. But she couldn't be sure. All she knew was that it was black in here. So black. She couldn't see anything. Nothing. But she could feel the damp everywhere. The wet cold embraced her bare flesh. Clung to her hair. She used her fingers to feel the ground. It was nothing more than dirt. The wall behind her was stone. Damp and mould covered.

She shuddered involuntarily as she thought of him. For all she knew he could still be in here, waiting in the blackness for his next move. His touch had been hard, aggressive. His breath sour and filled with longing.

'Help? Help me? Please?' she called out. But her voice was nothing but a whisper. 'Please . . . please . . . someone help me . . .'

For some reason she knew it was pointless. That he had hidden her some place where no one would hear her. After all, how loud had he made her scream out? And no one had come then. So what were the chances of someone hearing her pathetic cries now?

Tears started to fall freely at the realisation of her situation. She had had a crap life. Been through shit, much more than your average teenager, but she had coped. Survived. Even started to make something of the hand that life had dealt her. And now . . . She clenched her fists as anger coursed through her. She was under no illusions. She had watched enough TV crime series to know that her outcome didn't look good. Worse still, no one would realise she was missing. She trusted no one and consequently kept herself to herself. How long would it take someone – *anyone* – to realise that she wasn't around? Terror sliced through her like a searing blade. The likelihood of her ever being reported missing was remote.

An overwhelming sense of alarm took hold. How would the police find her if they had no idea she had been abducted? Did *he* know this in advance? Had he stalked her? It seemed more than probable that he had been watching her; for this was not some random abduction – it had to be premeditated. Otherwise, how would he have known that she was going to be there last night? She hadn't told anyone her plans. No one knew her personal life. And that was the way she operated. She had trusted people in the past – and what had it got her? Nothing but pain. So she had shut people out. And now, it seemed that the isolated sanctuary that she had created for herself had imploded. Because now no one would be aware that she had disappeared.

Oh God!

Then she heard it again. The hairs on the back of her neck stood up.

A rasping, grating high-pitched noise – as if something or someone was trying to claw their way out. But it was not the scratching that scared her. No. It was something much more sinister.

Breathing. Someone was in here with her.

Chapter Two

Saturday: 6:42 a.m.

The headlines screamed at him: '*Police Incompetence*' – followed by his name: '*Detective Inspector Jack Brady.*' He picked up that morning's edition of the *Northern Echo*, scrunched it into a ball and threw it at the overflowing bin.

Fuck you, Rubenfeld!

Brady would not have called Rubenfeld a friend, but he still didn't expect to be betrayed by him. Yet he knew the hardened hack well enough to know that he would cross anyone if it meant a front page headline and a ticket out of Dodge. To say that Rubenfeld had outstayed his welcome in the North East was an understatement. His unorthodox journalistic ways had earned him some impressive enemies. Rubenfeld and Brady's relationship had been one of *quid pro quo*. In other words, he was a snitch when it paid him to be and a tight-lipped bastard when it didn't. *But this* . . . Brady shook his head. He knew the score. Rubenfeld, like every other scavenging journalist, wanted to make headline news. Which he had – at Brady's expense.

It had happened less than thirty-six hours ago; not that it felt like that. Brady could have sworn it had happened days ago. But then, he had literally worked straight through since the night of the crime, grabbing a couple of hours sleep here and there, as had the rest of the team. He thought of James David Macintosh again . . . he had done nothing *but* think about him. There was a massive national police hunt for the murderer.

Macintosh had recently been paroled to Ashley House in Whitley Bay. However, old DNA evidence had conclusively identified him as The Joker – a serial killer from the seventies. One who had gone on a rampage and raped, tortured and gruesomely murdered seven victims. All men. All homosexuals. He had eluded the police for decades, his killing spree suddenly ending in the summer of 1977 as abruptly as it had started. Then he had disappeared. Dropped off the radar. The reason being, it turned out, that he had been incarcerated for a completely unrelated crime.

At the time of the Joker killings James David Macintosh, a twenty-one year old medical student, had voluntarily admitted himself as a private patient into St Nicholas in Gosforth – a psychiatric hospital. Whilst under the care of a Dr Jackson, he had surreptitiously succeeded in terrorising the streets of North Tyneside and Newcastle as The Joker. From what Brady had gleaned from Dr Jackson's old transcripts of his sessions with Macintosh, it seemed that his patient had inadvertently revealed too much about his abusive father's homophobic physical attacks. Whether Dr Jackson had made the connection that his young patient was responsible for the sadistic killings, Brady would never know; but clearly Macintosh believed he had said enough to incriminate himself. Enough for him to follow his psychiatrist after work to his leafy suburban home in Jesmond and wait for darkness to fall. Then, he had entered Dr Jackson's home, carrying an axe, and had savagely murdered him. The doctor's mutilated body had been found floating in the bath. The worst was yet to come. Macintosh had then tied the psychiatrist's heavily pregnant wife face-down on their bed and had swung at her. Then he had killed her infant twin sons.

Brady closed his eyes and breathed in deeply. He knew each detail of the seventies case. Every nuance. He had spent the past thirty-six hours trawling through every piece of information they had on him from the original multiple murders trying to figure out where he would have gone. And where he would have taken a three-year-old girl. That question tortured Brady. He knew the statistics. With each passing hour, the chances of finding Annabel Edwards alive were becoming less and less likely. He felt sickened by the knowledge of what Macintosh had done. Of what he was capable of still doing.

What had seemed an anomaly at the time was Macintosh's decision to abduct the psychiatrist's three-year-old daughter, Ellen Jackson. The reason was beyond the original seventies investigative team. As much as it was beyond the current one. For James David Macintosh had repeated history – thirty-seven years on. But this time his choice of victim was Jonathan Edwards, his probation officer. Thirty-six hours ago he had absconded from Ashley House and had entered Edwards' home. Again with an axe. And again with the intention of obliterating Jonathan Edwards' skull, before turning his attention to Edwards' wife and newborn son. His methodology was identical to his seventies killing spree; including the abduction of the Edwards' daughter.

Brady had turned up at the crime scene too late. Macintosh had already left, taking with him the Edwards' three-year-old child. Brady still had no idea where Macintosh had taken her. The first location that was searched was Mill Cottage; a property situated beyond Hartburn village in the wilds of Northumberland. Macintosh had taken Ellen Jackson there. The police had tracked it down in the seventies because the empty property had belonged to his mother.

However, back then when the police had arrived at Mill Cottage the psychiatrist's three-year-old daughter was already dead. Macintosh had strangled her. That morning's front page of the *Northern Echo* came to Brady's mind. The *Northern Echo* had done their own research into Macintosh and the seventies murders. Enough for them to go into macabre detail about the killing of Ellen Jackson and the fact that the police had been too late, then as now. A gut feeling had driven Brady to turn up at Jonathan Edwards' home on Thursday evening. But it had been too little, too late. The media were not the only ones accusing Brady of not doing enough. His own mind tortured him with thoughts of *what if?* But he knew he had to remain level-headed and focused. There would be plenty of time for recriminations later.

The *Northern Echo* journalists weren't interested in the truth. The fact that Brady had no authority to detain Macintosh longer than he had – let alone press charges against him for a crime he had not committed – did not matter to the press. The *truth* was lost amidst the media hysteria. It was the principle that a notorious serial killer had been released on parole. Worse still, he had been released from police custody – Brady's custody – and had then gone on to murder his probation officer and his family.

It was simple maths. Someone had to be held accountable.

Brady breathed out slowly as he looked towards his office window. The dusty wooden blinds were still open. The burnished orange glare of the street light below bled in. Soon it would be daylight. Then all hell would break loose.

Where are you Macintosh? Where are you hiding?

Brady turned his attention back to his desk. It was covered in files. He had spent the last day and night trawling through every piece of information they had on Macintosh, trying to figure out where he could have gone. And crucially, where he would have taken a three-year-old girl. That question tortured Brady. He knew the statistics. With each passing hour, the chances of finding Annabel Edwards alive were becoming less and less unlikely.

A dull knock at his office door shook him from his compulsive thoughts.

He turned his head and called out wearily: 'Yeah?'

He wasn't in the mood for talking.

The door opened. Conrad walked in. He looked as tired as Brady felt.

'Sir?'

He was early. Brady assumed that Conrad had seen the front pages of the Saturday papers. They didn't make good reading. Not if you were DI Jack Brady – or anyone associated with him.

Conrad cleared his throat. A sign that he was nervous.

Despite the fact that he looked exhausted, he was still impeccably dressed in a dark tailored suit, a crisp white shirt, cufflinks, an Italian tie and expensive handmade English leather brogues. This was typical of Conrad. He was always professionally attired. Unlike Brady. A beat-up old, black leather jacket that he had for too many years, accompanied with skinny black jeans, black T-shirt and heavy black Caterpillar boots was Brady at his best – and worst.

'May I?' Conrad asked as he walked over to Brady's desk and pulled out the chair opposite.

He was five foot eleven, muscular, with short blond hair; good-looking when he wasn't looking uptight – which was most of the time. Today was no exception. If anything, Conrad looked even more wound up than usual. His steel grey eyes were narrowed and his square jaw clenched.

'Do I have a choice?' Brady asked as he watched Conrad sit down.

'Do you know who would have leaked this?' Conrad asked as he handed Brady a selection of that morning's newspapers, all leading with the same headline – Brady's incompetence and Macintosh's unknown whereabouts.

Brady looked over the front pages. The tabloids and broadsheets were following the same hysterical rhetoric as the *Northern Echo*.

Conrad waited. He wasn't sure whether Brady was aware of what had been printed about the investigation – about *him*. But it was his job to make sure his boss was aware. Conrad could see it in Brady's eyes as he scanned the front pages – the torment and feelings of guilt. Conrad realised that he was taking this personally. Too personally. He clearly felt responsible for the murders. After all, Brady had interviewed Macintosh. Brady had had a hunch that Macintosh was the original Joker, despite evidence to the contrary. But he had refused to give up until he had something conclusive to substantiate his gut feeling. And then it was too late. Once he had confirmation that Macintosh was the seventies Joker, the man had already disappeared with his hostage.

Thirty-six hours had passed and there had been no conclusive sightings of Macintosh. The station was packed. Extra officers had been called in from other Area Commands. Every officer had had their holidays and days off suspended. The entire country was gripped, waiting with bated breath for news on the serial killer's whereabouts and the fate of the victim Macintosh had abducted: petite, pretty, blonde, and three years old. Annabel's face and Macintosh's had dominated the papers and news channels. Worse still, the newspapers and TV stations needed someone to crucify. The fact that Macintosh had had the freedom to murder again posed some difficult questions; and in a time of mass hysteria, someone had to pay. And that someone had been Brady. Simply because mistakes had been made and instead of looking higher up the food chain, Brady had been an easy target. A piece of meat to throw at the dogs, to keep them off the people who really were in charge. But they were savvy enough to make sure there was some distance between them and the orders they passed on. Consequently, there was nothing Brady could do about it.

Conrad had heard from certain sources that there would be an investigation into the handling of James David Macintosh's release from police custody. Questions needed to be answered. And Brady was the one who was being called into account. Simply because he was good at his job and didn't give a damn what anyone else thought – including his superiors. He was the ideal sacrificial lamb. Too maverick in his ways to be liked from above, despite getting much-needed results. Brady had virtually single-handedly solved Alexander De Bernier's murder; despite it being a copycat killing designed to foil the police. That crucial fact had now been forgotten. *Less than two days later . . .*

The macabre killing of Alexander De Bernier, a twenty-two year old politics student, had been identical to the Joker's seventies murders.

Brady had not only solved De Bernier's murder, he had also identified the Joker: a serial killer who had gone on a killing spree which had escalated in the summer of 1977. His target – young, gay men. But it was the fact that he had identified Macintosh as the original Joker that had crucified him. The *Northern Echo* wasn't alone in its damnation of Brady. In its denouncement and vilification of him – or to be precise, as the Senior Investigating Officer who had had James David Macintosh within his grasp. The journalists weren't interested in the truth. Brady had no evidence against Macintosh, and hadn't been able to detain him any longer. The crucial forensic results proving he was the Joker had come too late to stop him going after Jonathan Edwards and his family. But the facts were lost amidst the media hysteria. It was the principle that a notorious serial killer had been released on parole. Worse still, he had later been released from police custody – Brady's custody – and had then gone on to murder his probation officer and his family. That had happened on Thursday evening – less than thirty-six hours ago.

Brady could see from Conrad's expression that even his deputy was having a hard time accepting the turn of events. The fact that they had had Macintosh in their grasp – in custody – wasn't worth thinking about.

Brady sighed. Exhausted, he sat back and ran a hand through his long dark hair. He looked back down at the newspapers in front of him. Contemplated Conrad's earlier question about who could have leaked the information on the Macintosh case to the press. Information that could be his downfall. He had his suspicions. But nothing conclusive. He looked back up at Conrad.

Realised it was better to keep his doubts to himself. 'No. I have no idea who would have leaked these details.'

'What are you going to do about it?' Conrad asked.

Brady suddenly laughed. 'Are you serious? There's nothing I can do. I just have to accept it. They need someone to kick, that's all there is to it.'

Conrad frowned. 'But . . . this isn't just a kicking, sir. Is it? The national papers are all running with the same story.'

'It's me the press are holding accountable. Not the police, Conrad.'

Conrad didn't say a word.

Brady knew there was nothing he could say. It was the truth; he was being persecuted by the news channels and the papers. Macintosh's crime was so heinous, so depraved that the public needed to be reassured that someone had fucked up. That it could have been prevented.

'Maybe if you gave a statement to the press? Explain the fact that you had no grounds to hold Macintosh? That by the time the laboratory results came back it was too late?'

Brady looked at Conrad. 'It's too late. The damage has already been done. The only thing I can do is find that bastard and bring him in.'

'I had an update on my way in, sir. Nothing. They still have no reports on the car he stole. He's just disappeared.'

'How the fuck does someone disappear with a three-year-old kid?'

Conrad shook his head.

'I'll find him, Conrad . . . No matter what happens, I'll find him.' Brady clenched his fists. 'And in the meantime I don't give a shit what the media throws at me. They need someone to blame, so it may as well be me. I don't give a fuck what they print.'

'I just wanted to make sure you were aware of what had been printed before the briefing later.'

'Yeah . . . thanks for letting me know.'

Conrad nodded and stood up. 'If I were you I'd try and get a few more hours' sleep before the briefing. And a shower and a change of clothes might be advisable.'

Brady didn't have the energy or the inclination to tell Conrad to *fuck off.* That it wasn't his place to be telling a senior officer to sort himself out. He already knew he looked like shit. He *felt* like shit! But he knew that Conrad was looking out for him. His way of damage limitation. But being dressed in a designer Italian suit wouldn't help Brady where his boss DCI Gates was concerned. Brady still had to hear Gates' take on that morning's headlines.

He watched as Conrad headed for the door.

'Harry?

Conrad stopped. He turned around.

'Do you think we'll get him?' Brady asked. 'You know . . . before . . .' He left it unsaid. The words were too difficult to utter.

Conrad looked at him. 'I . . . don't know, sir. All we can do is our best.'

'And what if our best isn't good enough?' Brady asked.

Conrad did not answer.

Brady waited. He needed more. But it was clear Conrad wasn't going to give him more.

'Briefing's at eleven.'

Conrad nodded and walked out.

Brady watched Conrad leave. His deputy was right. He could do with a few hours' sleep before the briefing. He needed to have his wits about him. More now than ever.

Brady lay on his back with his hands behind his head, staring blankly at the ceiling. The office was in shadow. Outside the day was emerging. Bleak, grey and pissed off.

He forced his eyes closed. He needed to sleep. Had no choice. Otherwise he wouldn't be able to function. But . . .

James David Macintosh.

Whenever he closed his eyes, the serial killer's face haunted him. Somehow Macintosh had evaded the police and the public. His face and crimes had gone viral. The world was now watching the events unfolding in Whitley Bay.

Brady sighed heavily. He was exhausted; both physically and mentally. He tried to block *him* from his mind. He had to.

Eventually he started to feel drowsy. Relief coursed through his tired body as he felt himself drifting. All external noise – traffic in the street below, distant phones ringing, hurried footsteps and hushed voices – faded into a serene blackness.

Suddenly his heart was racing. Threatening to rupture. His mouth dry. Fear held him tight, restricting his breathing. Brady sat bolt upright. Panting, short, shallow gulps of air.

Shit!

His hands were trembling. He desperately needed a drink. But the stabbing bursts of daylight through his Venetian blinds brought him to his senses.

Saturday. It's Saturday morning. Shit . . . She's been gone since Thursday evening.

He rubbed his tired face. He just wanted it to be over. But he knew it wouldn't end. Not until . . .

Until you find the girl. That is . . . if she isn't already dead.

Chapter Three

Saturday 10:05 a.m.

Shut up! Just shut the fuck up or I'll kill you!

'Help? Please ... I know you're there. I can hear you breathing ... Please help me?' she whispered, desperate. 'Just talk to me? Please? I hate the dark and ... I ... I ...' She faltered.

Stop talking! Just STOP!

'Help!' she hoarsely shouted. 'HELP!'

'Shut up! Just shut up, will you?' she finally hissed from the blackness, venomous and deadly.

'Who are you? I ... I need help ... He ... he ...' she stopped.

I don't care. I don't fucking care what he's done to you. Just stop talking to me.

'Talk to me? Please?' she pleaded.

'Shut up! He'll hear you. Don't you get that, you stupid bitch!' she spat.

'I ... I'm scared ... I just want to get out ...'

Boo-fucking-hoo! You're not the first and you won't be the last.

'Please? I just want to go home,' she persisted.

'Yeah? Well, rule one, shut the fuck up! If he hears you kicking off he'll kill you. He doesn't like it if you cause a fuss. So don't give him a reason to hurt you more than he needs to. Get it?'

'Are you hurt?' she asked her, keeping her voice as low as possible. 'You sound hurt. Your breathing . . . It sounds as if you're in pain. Did he do that to you?'

Deathly silence.

'What's he done to you?'

Everything imaginable . . . and more. She was done with talking. She just wished she would go away with her fucking questions. Soon enough she would give up. Accept her fate. She tried to remember if she had been the same when he had first brought her here. But it had been so long ago now that her memory couldn't be trusted. Not anymore. The blackness seemed to have seeped under her skin and taken everything that had once been bright and full of life. All she knew now was him. She lived for the moments when he would return. To her. For her. But she didn't want the new girl here. She didn't want to share him.

It was simpler before. Now she *was here it complicated things. Just as she herself had fucked things up for the girl before her.*

She had a vague memory of the girl who was there when she had first arrived. The one she had replaced. The one who had been sat in a wooden hospital chair, unable to move. Or talk. He had . . . *What had he done to her?* She didn't want to remember. But soon afterwards she had disappeared. And then it had just been her on her own. In the damp, cold darkness. Alone for what felt like an eternity.

Until now …

'Please? Talk to me … I'm Emily. Emily Baker. What's your name?'

She was about to say but then the footsteps distracted her. *He's coming back* … Her initial flush of excitement was soon replaced by fear. *What if he doesn't want me now he has her?*

'Help me? Please help me? I'm chained up down here … PLEASE!' Emily Baker hoarsely called out. 'PLEASE! Help … help me … us. There's two of us down here. Help!'

She tried to block out Emily Baker's shouts. She listened as the door that led down to the basement was opened. Followed by the overhead light being switched on. Harsh. Blinding.

'Help! Help us … please …' Emily Baker cried out, hopeful.

She heard him climbing down the stairs. Wondered what he would do to the new girl. He didn't like them to make a noise. He was very clear about that.

She tried to look up to see him but the light still hurt her eyes too much.

But she heard her. Emily Baker and her annoying whining. Then, when her eyes had stopped watering, she saw her. Sat on the mattress in front of her struggling to get free from the chain that was secured around her ankle. She didn't see him. And when she did, it was too late.

‘They’ll be looking for me. Please? I just want to go home . . .’ Emily pleaded as he stood over her.

She watched his reaction. He struck her face with enough force to knock her unconscious. She watched silently as Emily’s body slumped onto the mattress. *Good. Maybe he will get rid of her now? Better her than me*. ‘I told her to be quiet. I told her that you would be angry.’

He turned.

She watched him study her; as if he had forgotten that she was there. He then smiled. ‘You’re a good girl. You know that? That’s why I’ve kept you the longest.’

She nodded. It was a weak and weary acknowledgement. ‘I know . . . I’m a good girl.’

‘I’ve brought you something . . .’ His voice trembling with excitement.

She didn’t ask what he had brought her. She had soon learned that he did not like questions. She had only survived by adapting. Learning to keep her mouth shut and accepting the rules – no matter how cruel. Sometimes he brought her gifts. Like now. But it depended upon his mood. She was hoping that the arrival of the new girl would make him treat her better – for a short time at least. That the new girl would get the violent and erratic treatment instead of her. She knew he was crazy. That he heard voices. Sometimes he even argued and screamed at them out loud. Those were rare occasions, but when it did happen, she knew that something dreadful would follow. So far, she had been lucky. So far, the voices hadn’t told him to kill her. *At least, not yet.*

A familiar feeling of fear stirred as she felt his finger trail down her long dark hair. Then he kissed her head. It was gentle. Delicate. So unlike him. She knew something was wrong. That her time had come.

She felt him place something on her lap.

She couldn't look at it. Her head was secured so she could only stare straight ahead at the wall above the mattress. But she did not need to see it to know what he had brought her. It was a white ankle-length nightdress; old-fashioned and ugly. She had watched, silent and obedient, as he had forced the girl before her to wear a nightdress identical to this one. That was when she had slept on the mattress with her ankle chained to the ground like the new girl. Now he kept her strapped to this chair. It was his way – his '*process*', as he called it.

'You are so beautiful.' He tilted her head up towards his face. 'Look at the bone structure in this light. Perfect. You do know I have an eye for detail? And you . . . you are quite exquisite.'

She attempted a smile as she looked into his cold eyes, but failed. Icy fear had now gripped her from the inside. It was screaming at her that she had to do something – *anything*. That this was her chance. She had been waiting for this moment for months . . .

Or was it years?

She had lost track of the days, weeks and months. Her clock was ruled by him. She had come to welcome the noise of the door being dragged open. The metal scraping in protest against the stone floor. Whether the outcome would be good or bad, she always felt the stirrings of hopefulness. For sometimes he brought her real gifts. Unlike today. What he had brought today was not a gift for her – *it was for him*.

Ordinarily he would bring her food. Disgusting food. And if she had refused to eat it in the earlier days, hunger had soon won out. But sometimes – if she had shown willing and had been good – he would bring her chocolate and a can of Coke. The real Coke with sugar. His only condition was that he had to feed her. He liked to keep her restrained in this chair when he brought her gifts. He called it his mother's chair, which used to creep her out. But now it didn't bother her. In fact, not a lot bothered her now. Apart from this new girl showing up, shouting and screaming. She knew it would upset him. And she didn't like to see him angry. When he got really mad he forgot about her. Sometimes for what felt like days and days. She would wait for him, silently praying that he would come back. That he would remember her. Remember that she was *his* good girl.

'Are you going to behave for me?' he asked as he bent down. His face was now level with hers. He gently brushed a loose strand of hair away from her eye and tucked it behind her ear. But his voice betrayed him. It was heavy with malevolence. 'Mmm? Because I need to know that you're not going to do anything stupid when I remove these restraints?'

She shook her head. 'No . . . promise . . .'

'Good girl,' he said, letting go of her chin.

Her skin felt pinched, bruised; his grip too tight. She looked at him. The smile had gone. He looked distracted.

Irritable, even. She knew this was a bad sign. She watched, scared, as he began to unbuckle the leather cuffs.

'I'll dress you,' he told her. 'Then I'll photograph you.'

She stared at him. She had witnessed this procedure – his '*process*' – just the once. But it was enough.

'You know you have nothing to be scared of, don't you?'

She didn't respond. Instead she let her eyes focus on the wall above the mattress. It was covered in Polaroid photographs. Bleak, ugly, lacklustre faces stared back at her. She didn't see it as '*art*' – his term for it. All she saw were the faces. All much of a likeness: young, long dark hair, starved and half beaten to death. But each one shared a common trait – their eyes. He had altered their eyes forever.

'They look perfect. So at peace,' he mused as he looked proudly at the wall covered in photographs. He smiled as he looked from one photograph to another. 'Perfection immortalised. Do you not agree?'

She kept quiet. To her they looked like those macabre Victorian photos of dead loved ones. She had seen the photos – dead people – staged to look as if they were alive. Posed sitting, or bizarrely standing, all looking straight at the camera but with one obvious difference; most had their eyes closed. The ones that had their eyes open looked like the faces on the wall ahead of her – blank. Staring at nothing.

He turned to her. 'And you will be the most beautiful one.' His smile had returned.

'Promise?' she asked as she stared at the wall; fixated. *They horrified, yet fascinated her … They had been photographed – sat in THIS chair – dressed in a white Victorian-style nightdress, staring out with those dead eyes.*

She knew the reason why they looked like *that*. And that was what terrified her.

He nodded. 'Yes.'

'And then you'll let me go?' She asked, trying to keep her voice steady. She didn't want him to know that she was scared, for fear of angering him. He liked her to be compliant. It had not taken her long to realise that being complaisant guaranteed her survival. *But now?*

'Of course. After I've finished with you, then you can go.'

She nodded. She was too weak – or perhaps the better word was too *institutionalised* – to cry or object. She had been hoping that this day would never come. Now it had. Maybe it was the arrival of the new girl that had prompted the change? Maybe . . . or maybe not.

'Ready?' he asked as he started to unbuckle the leather restraint that secured her head.

'Yes.' But it was a lie. She wasn't ready. She thought of the unconscious new girl sprawled on the mattress, oblivious as to what was about to happen.

This girl was her replacement. She had watched while he had performed his '*art*' on her predecessor. And now it was her turn. How she wished she was lying on that mattress, unaware of what was about to happen. That it was her who was still chained to the ground.

'Good. Now arms raised so I can put this over your head.'

She obeyed. The material felt odd. Prickly and coarse against her naked skin. She couldn't remember the last time she had worn clothes. It was before he had brought her here. That was another life – a life she had long given up on.

'Now stand up so I can pull it down,' he instructed.

She did as she was told. The pain in her knee, her crippled leg, unbearable. She put her weight on her good leg. Bit her lip. Held it in. He didn't like her to complain.

She looked down as he slipped it over her waist. It fell down to her ankles. She couldn't help thinking it looked like a shroud.

'Perfect . . .' he murmured as he stepped back to admire her.

She stood as still as a mannequin and waited for him to tell her she could move.

'You really are perfect . . .' he repeated, smiling at her.

She stared at him, willing herself to do something – *anything!* She had her chance. She wasn't restrained. She could make a move if she wanted to. Surprise him. Throw herself into him. Catch him off-guard. Then get out. Escape. It was that simple. Up the stone steps towards the door at the top. Then out. Freedom.

Then do it . . . Do it now!

'Sit down.'

Without thinking, she automatically did as she was told, despite the voice screaming frantically in her head to do something; anything, rather than accept this fate.

All thoughts of escape disappeared when he started strapping her to the chair.

'I won't hurt you . . . I promise,' he said as he took his time securing her head in place.

She didn't say a word. *He was lying – they both knew it.*

She fixed her eyes on the wall ahead. *At them. Their faces. Soon she would be just like them. She would be identical.*

She had witnessed what he had done to the girl before her. She had screamed. *Oh God how she had screamed ...*

'You will let me go when you've finished?' she asked again, her eyes never moving from the photos. She was searching for her. The girl she had replaced.

'Of course ... Didn't I promise I would?' he replied.

'Yes ...' she whispered. *But I'll never know whether you do or not.*

She watched, mute as he swung a delicate gold pendant in front of her. She knew it would have her name on it. She wished she could look away. But she couldn't. Her head was fixed.

'This is for you when I've finished. So you will be just like them.'

Her eyes darted beyond the dangling pendant to the young women in the Polaroid photographs on the wall ahead. They all wore gold necklaces with their names engraved on them. Soon she would be identical to them.

She suddenly couldn't breathe. She felt as if she was going to choke. She couldn't bring herself to look at their eyes, knowing that soon that would be her. She had never felt so alone. So scared. No one even knew she was here. Or that she was missing ... Why would they?

Chapter Four

Saturday: 10:43 a.m.

Brady looked at himself in the mirror. He had caught up on a couple of hours sleep. Not that it had made much difference. He still looked like crap. His naturally tanned, olive-skinned complexion had an unhealthy greyish pale pallor to it. His eyes were bloodshot and the skin below, dark and puffy. He looked as if he had been on a bender for a week. But nothing could have been further from the truth. He had spent the last God knows how many hours working, like the rest of his team.

He bent over the sink and splashed cold water onto his face. He had showered and shaved but from the state of his face it hadn't had the desired effect. Then again, he accepted that he was not the only one who looked like crap. The pressure of the case had affected every officer working on the investigation.

He had taken Conrad's advice. Luckily, he still had a spare change of clothes in his locker for such occasions. But it wasn't every day that the station was thrown into mayhem because a serial killer was loose on the streets of Whitley Bay. Not that Brady expected him to be anywhere near this small, family seaside resort. Or at least, it was once known as a family holiday destination in its heyday. Now it was hailed for its coachloads of binge drinking lads and lasses booking in for a weekend of debauchery equivalent to Magaluf without the sunburn.

Brady leaned over and splashed his face again. But he knew that no amount of cold water would work. He looked down at his hands. They were trembling. He put it down to the two cups of black coffee he had downed in an attempt to wake himself up. He couldn't remember when he had last eaten. He still felt sick to his stomach; the memory of what Macintosh had done to the Edwards' family too fresh, too raw. Alcohol was a different story. If he didn't need to be on the job, he would have sought comfort from a bottle of scotch. But he didn't have that choice. And he knew that getting drunk wouldn't help him. It would feel good. That warm buzz that spread through your body. The lightheaded numbness that came with it, dissipating all tormented thoughts. That was, until he sobered up. Then he would still be faced with the same problem – James David Macintosh.

He turned the cold tap off and pulled out some paper towels. He dried his face and hands and stood back to appraise himself. Black T-shirt and black skinny jeans. By no means as smart as his deputy, but at least they were clean. He would never be Conrad. Brady was savvy enough to understand that his dress code was unconventional. It wasn't liked from above. Not that he cared. It was the job that mattered. And the job didn't give a crap what clothes you wore, as long as you got the results at the end of the day. Brady hit the much-needed targets; that was what counted and that was the reason that his unorthodox dress code was overlooked. But Brady wasn't a fool. He knew that today his appearance would count. The way he looked would matter for the first time in his career.

When he walked into the briefing he knew that everyone would have seen the news. That he was being held responsible for Macintosh being able to kill – *again and again.*

The door to the changing room opened. He turned round to see Tom Harvey walk in.

'You all right?' Harvey asked, concerned.

It was clear Harvey had seen the news.

'Never been better.' Brady couldn't help himself. But then again, this was Harvey. He was a long-standing friend. Brady had known him from when he first started out in the force. They had climbed the ranks together. However, Harvey had stopped at detective sergeant. Brady had gone on that one step higher. Not that it had made a difference to their friendship. Harvey was better than that.

What Brady liked about Harvey was that he always spoke as he found. He always knew that Harvey would tell him the truth; even if the truth was something he didn't particularly want to hear. Then again, Harvey had his own issues when it came to the truth. Particularly in relation to his personal life. Harvey was lousy at relationships, yet didn't want to face the reality of his situation. He was a middle-aged, unmarried fool currently being played by some twenty-two-year-old Thai internet girlfriend for his wallet and his wallet alone.

'You know it's all a crock of shit!' Harvey said now, shaking his head.

Harvey wasn't often right, but he was this time.

'You know everyone else thinks the same?' Harvey reassured him. 'Nobody is taking the bullshit they've printed about you seriously.'

Brady looked at him in the mirror with a raised eyebrow. 'You sure?'

Harvey shook his head. 'You're a dick! You know that?'

'Well if I didn't, I do now,' Brady answered, turning to face Harvey. He leaned back against the sink. 'How are the team holding up?'

'You know . . .' Harvey shrugged. 'Some are finding it difficult.'

Brady nodded. The events of Thursday evening had hit them all hard.

'But that shit that's in the papers has wound them up some,' Harvey added.

Brady didn't reply. But he was quietly relieved to hear that he had their support. For a moment he had been worried it might have gone the other way.

'I mean for fuck's sake! Those scrotes are making out you're responsible. And you saw him for how long?' Harvey asked, shaking his head.

'Long enough.'

'You're over-reacting. You couldn't have done fuck all, Jack. You know that it's all lies they've printed about you, so don't start thinking anyone here thinks otherwise.'

'Thanks Tom.'

'Don't thank me. I'm just telling you how it is.'

Brady gave him a half-hearted smile. 'Come on then, the briefing starts in fifteen minutes. Reckon we better get there before Gates.'

Harvey looked at himself in the mirror as he straightened his tie.

'Yeah . . . yeah . . . You look shit hot, Tom. But it's wasted on Kodovesky. She's not interested. I'd stick to internet dating if I was you.'

'Fuck you!' Harvey said as he followed Brady out of the Gents.

Brady was waiting for the room to fill up. Gates hadn't shown yet, so the atmosphere was still relaxed and casual. Brady had taken a position against the wall at the back of the large room. Harvey was stood next to him talking his usual crap. Brady was feigning interest while noting who was in the room. Some faces he recognised. Most he didn't. Under the circumstances support had been called in from all other Area Commands. But they also had detectives from as far afield as the Met who had had more experience in dealing with this kind of situation. After all, this was Whitley Bay: a small, run-down seaside resort that had its fair share of crime but serial killers were something entirely different. The last time Whitley Bay had been thrown into this sort of frenzied panic was the summer of 1977 – when Macintosh had first terrorised the streets of North Tyneside.

Five minutes had passed and in that time the room had filled up. It was the largest conference room in the building. Now its role was as an Incident Room for a major multiple murder investigation. There must have been over forty officers and detectives; some were sitting, others stood where they could. All focused on DCI Gates who had just walked in. Brady watched his boss stride to the front of the room. He didn't bother with any pleasantries. Instead, he began by updating the room on the progress so far. But Brady had heard it all before. They had nothing on Macintosh's whereabouts. Nothing. That was all he needed to know. Not the speculations or theories as to why Macintosh had committed such a heinous, inconceivable crime. The simple fact was that they were still no closer to apprehending him. Or saving the life of a three-year-old girl.

'We know Macintosh stole Jonathan Edwards' car. We have CCTV footage of him driving through Whitley Bay town centre heading in the direction of the Coast Road on Thursday at 11:02 p.m. We do have more CCTV of him heading South on the A1 and then, six hours later, driving towards Watford. It is believed that Macintosh is now in London. So all our efforts are on narrowing down exactly where in London he is hiding. Consequently I and a few members of the team here will be heading down to London later today. Our problem is that we are running out of time. He has Annabel Edwards. And if we look at past history as a predictor of future behaviour, we have a finite amount of time to find her alive. He took her on late Thursday evening. This is Saturday.'

No one said a word. But the room bristled with discomfort. Unease. These were facts. Nothing more. Nothing less. But this was a three-year-old girl's life in Macintosh's hands – *their hands*. The feeling of rising panic was palpable. Brady knew that every resource had been used to try to find Macintosh. Anyone who had come into contact with the man in the past thirty-seven years had been tracked down and contacted. Inmates, prison guards, ex-probation officers. Anyone who might have had some kind of relationship with him. Any kind of understanding where he might have absconded to with Annabel Edwards. The result? Nothing.

Brady was acutely aware that the Met were also looking for Macintosh. The last sighting of the stolen vehicle was early yesterday heading for London. It also explained the two detectives that had been assigned to Whitley Bay from the Met. It was a nationwide police effort. But he was surprised to hear that Gates was going to London. He hoped that he wouldn't be expected to join him. Brady's gut feeling was that Macintosh wasn't in London. That they were wasting time focusing the search on the wrong location.

'Sir?'

Brady watched, curious. It was Kodovesky who had just interrupted Gates. She was part of his team. Someone he could rely on to do the job. No questions asked. She was in her late twenties, and as such, was one of the youngest detectives stationed at Whitley Bay.

'I understand that we have CCTV images of the car as far south as Watford. But what if he then turned back and headed North in a circuitous route to elude us? Either in the same car, or a replacement vehicle.'

'Where do you think he would be heading?' Gates asked, unconvinced.

'Hartburn village, six miles west of Morpeth. What if he returned to the Mill Cottage where he—'

Brady waited. It was unlike Kodovesky to falter. But then these were exceptional circumstances. The room was packed. Like Brady, Kodovesky would not be familiar with all the faces staring at her. The majority of them, male.

'Where he was arrested in 1977?' Gates asked.

Kodovesky nodded.

To Brady she seemed relieved that Gates had omitted the gruesome nature of why Macintosh had been there.

'The cottage is personal to him. That's why he took his psychiatrist's daughter there,' Kodovesky continued.

Brady couldn't help but notice that she couldn't say the victim's name. Perhaps because Ellen Jackson had only been three years old. Murders were always bloody. But children were different. The brutality never left you.

He suddenly caught Dr Amelia Jenkins watching him. Brady imagined that she would be wondering how he was bearing up after his monumental kicking from the press.

He gave her a slight nod. To let her know he was fine. He then broke her gaze and turned his focus back to Gates.

'And?' Gates asked Kodovesky. Irritation flashed in his eyes.

Brady waited. Kodovesky had interrupted Gates. It was clear that he didn't like that. Especially from such a junior officer. He was a man who liked to feel in control. The problem here was that he wasn't in control. None of them were. Only Macintosh – for now. Everything about Gates was regimented and exact. His dark hair was cropped short. His face, clean-shaven at all times, regardless of the hours he had put in on the job. Gates kept a tight rein on his feelings, no matter what the situation. But to Brady's eye, Gates looked under pressure.

'Well sir, the murders were premeditated. That suggests that he would have had plans in place—'

Gates stopped her mid-sentence. Cold. Incisive. 'Tell us something we don't know, DC Kodovesky. Time is of the essence here and we don't have the luxury of thinking aloud.'

Brady could feel everyone in the room take an intake of breath. But his junior officer continued, unabated.

She nodded. 'I'm sorry, sir. All I wanted to point out was that I think he would have revisited Mill Cottage. With the victim. It was his childhood home. There is something there that compelled him to return in 1977 with his first victim. I think he will repeat this behaviour.'

'We have already searched the premises. It is also under surveillance. He's not a fool. His face is on the front page of every newspaper.' Gates paused. His eyes suddenly turned on Brady. He then fixed his irritated gaze back on Kodovesky. 'On every news channel. So do you really think he would return to his original crime scene?'

'Yes,' Kodovesky said. Short and succinct.

Brady had already suggested to Gates in private that Macintosh would return to the scene of his original crime. But Gates had batted him off with the same answer. The focus was entirely on London – where his car had last been sighted. But Brady's feeling was that Macintosh had found somewhere close to Mill Cottage. That there was something that tied him to it. Something that the police knew nothing about.

'I think that we need to narrow the search down to within a ten-mile radius of Mill Cottage, sir. We need to be checking all the properties within that area and to establish whether he is hiding out in a property or outbuilding there.'

Gates shot her a look. It was enough. Kodovesky had over-stepped the line. Brady could see that. It wasn't her place to be telling a senior officer how to handle a major murder and abduction investigation.

'Before the start of this briefing I had received conclusive evidence that Macintosh is within the London area. I was about to share these new findings before I was interrupted.' Gates then turned his attention to the rest of the room. 'A member of the public reported the car used by Macintosh abandoned at Heathrow Airport's Terminal Four long stay car park. CCTV footage is now being examined but we know for definite that he hasn't left the country. He's still here. In the UK.'

Suddenly the room was electric. Gates had thrown them some much-needed hope.

Brady leaned back against the wall. He didn't buy it. He was certain that Macintosh was still in the area and that this was some foil to throw the police off his trail.

He watched as Gates handed the briefing over to the police forensic psychologist – Dr Amelia Jenkins. She was now at the front of the room. To her side the white-board now showed graphic crime scene photographs from both the 1977 family slaying and the recent one. Officers and CID alike stared uneasily at the brutal images next to the psychologist.

Amelia Jenkins' dark brown, almond-shaped eyes suddenly rested on Brady, taking him by surprise. They looked puzzled, if not disturbed by what she saw. He watched as she tucked her sleek, black, razor-sharp hair behind her ear as she talked to the room – to him. Her red lipstick was as deep and bold as ever. Tom Ford lipstick. It was an irrelevant detail but one he remembered. Her clothes, sophisticated with a classic retro feel. She was dressed in a three-quarter cut black wool skirt suit; complemented with a pair of black patent leather classic Jimmy Choo heels. Everything about her was still reassuringly the same.

He watched her. She had turned her gaze back to the room as she continued talking. She was still only in her early thirties, with a career that was going somewhere. She had originally worked for the force as a forensic psychologist. But something had happened. Brady didn't know what, but it had been enough for her to quit her role and turn to practising clinical psychology. It was Gates who had managed to persuade her to come back. Supposedly as a favour to him. A one-off. That had been nearly eighteen months ago.

'We have confirmation that Macintosh was also the serial killer known as the Joker,' Amelia said as she briefly turned her attention back to Brady.

'Why the radical difference between the Joker killings and the way he murdered the psychiatrist's family and his probation officer's?'

Brady looked to see who had asked the question. It was someone he didn't recognise. A white man in his early forties. Tall, muscular and good-looking. His accent indicated that he was from the Met. Brady watched as Amelia nodded at him. Something in her eyes told Brady that she found him attractive. Not that anyone else would notice anything different about her demeanour; she was as cool and professional as ever. But Brady recognised that look. It was the way she had once looked at him. Inquisitive, with a subtle hint of playfulness. He could feel the jealousy, a tight knot in his stomach, start to stir. To awaken. But he had no right to feel anything. Not anymore. He had well and truly fucked that up.

Amelia broke free and quickly looked back across at Brady. It was awkward. As if she knew what he was thinking.

'We have Dr Jackson's transcripts from when Macintosh was a patient at St Nicholas' Psychiatric Hospital. It details the systematic and homophobic abuse that he suffered as a child at the hands of his father. He would make James stand naked in front of him and threaten to cut his penis off. You can see the clear connection between the Joker killings and Macintosh's abusive childhood?'

The detective nodded.

'As for the reason he killed his psychiatrist and his family? I assume it was because he had realised he had said too much. That what he had revealed to his doctor would tie him to the Joker killings. The exact details were never revealed to the press. But his psychiatrist would have soon realised that Macintosh could be connected to these seven young men's murders. The way he killed Dr Jackson and his family typifies the anger and betrayal he felt. These killings were personal. For all we know, maybe he also revealed something incriminating to Jonathan Edwards that he later regretted.' Amelia paused as she looked at the whiteboard behind her showing photographs from both crime scenes. 'The extent of the injuries to Dr Jackson's body, in particular his head and his face, is typical of an emotional attachment to the victim. Macintosh completely eradicated any trace of his victim's features. And he continued with his attack long after Dr Jackson was dead. As for the torture of his wife . . .' Amelia faltered as she looked at the graphic scenes of torture documented in the crime scene photos. 'He despises women. Hates them. An absolute misogynist. He played with her. Enjoyed the power he had over her.'

Brady tried to block out the mental images of the crime scene he had witnessed first-hand. To stop them blurring into Edwards' body. His wife's. Their son's. But there was no disputing what Amelia had surmised. Macintosh hated women. But why?

'But notice the difference. Her face is left untouched. Unlike her husband's. His anger was focused on her body and her body alone. He had no personal interest, no attachment to her. She was just sport for him. Part of the pleasure of torturing and killing. A pattern we see evolving in his childhood when he reportedly tortured and killed animals.'

'Why does he hate women?' It was the same detective.

Amelia looked back at him and shrugged. 'You would have to ask his mother that question. His childhood relationship with her will have influenced his attitude towards women. And from what we see here, I would suggest it was not a particularly healthy mother-son relationship.'

'And the mother? Where is she?' he asked.

'We don't know, as yet,' Amelia replied looking to DCI Gates for confirmation. 'We understand that the family home in Jesmond was sold and the equity put into an offshore account. But we have been unable to trace the account or Eileen Macintosh. She disappeared thirty-seven years ago and no one has seen her since.'

Brady had been looking into the whereabouts of Macintosh's mother for the past twenty-four hours. But he and the investigative team had found nothing. No trace of her since Macintosh's arrest in 1977. She had never visited him, nor corresponded with him during the past thirty-seven years of his prison sentence. The likelihood of her showing up now? Zero. The odds were stacked against them. Given Macintosh's age, there was a chance that she was already dead. She had disappeared after his arrest. If she was still alive, Brady couldn't blame her for wanting to disappear. Who wouldn't? The press would have hounded her to her grave if given half the chance. A social leper who had had the misfortune to have a sadistic serial killer as her only child.

'If she's alive, he will try to find her,' Brady stated. All eyes turned to him. But he knew he was right. Macintosh would be looking for her. Hunting her down. She wouldn't be able to hide from him. No matter how hard she tried. After all, she had left him to rot in prison for thirty-seven years with not a word.

Amelia raised an eyebrow at him. 'How can you be so sure?'

'I just am. What he did to Ellen Jackson was different. Her death was an aberration from his typical killings. Yes, his MO as the Joker is radically different to the signature he exhibits with the families he has killed. But the one detail that no one is looking at is the fact that both Dr Jackson and Jonathan Edwards had a relationship with him. He had won their trust. I would even suggest earned their respect.' Brady paused as he gauged Amelia's reaction. He wasn't bothered about the other forty members of the team. It was the police forensic psychologist's opinion that mattered. And Gates'.

Intrigued, Amelia nodded for him to continue.

'They must have told Macintosh about their families. The investigation notes from the case recorded that Dr Jackson had a black and white family photograph on his desk. Suggesting that Macintosh would have seen it.'

Amelia looked at him, as if surprised. 'Perhaps . . .'

'Maybe this isn't about Edwards or Jackson. What if we are looking at the wrong motive here? That their murders were simply a means to an end. What if this is about these men's daughters?' Brady said as he gestured to the two photographs of the girls on the whiteboard. Both girls looked Nordic. They had long whitish blond hair that hung in ringlets, dark brown eyes and petite, perfect features. 'If I'm not mistaken, they are virtually identical.'

Brady caught Conrad's eye. Brady could see from his expression that Conrad understood what he was suggesting. 'Dr Jackson wasn't murdered because Macintosh was scared he had revealed too much to him. I think Macintosh is too clever to accidentally reveal anything other than what he intends. This is about him targeting his psychiatrist to get to the child. That's why the brutal murder. The anger and rage exhibited is classic overkill. And yes, it's personal. But not in the way you suggest,' Brady said as he looked from the crime scene photos back to Amelia.

'How so?' she asked, curious.

'These family killings are to do with his own family dynamics. Something happened to him as a child. An emotional or physical trigger that set this time bomb of a serial killer off. I'm not saying that he wasn't already predisposed. But something happened to him that gave him that extra push. Not just to murder . . . ' Brady shook his head. 'It's no coincidence that he slaughtered his probation officer and his psychiatrist. Both male and both in positions of authority over him. Both judging and assessing him. Absolute patriarchal power; just like his father. That's why he butchered them like that. Destroyed them so they were unidentifiable. Because he was killing his father. Again and again and again.' Brady stopped. He had said too much. This wasn't the place. But he knew in his gut that if they didn't understand Macintosh's motive for taking Annabel Edwards, then they had no chance of finding her alive.

None at all . . .

'So what is his relation to the girls? If he, as you propose, is metaphorically killing his father, why kill the infant boys? And not the girls? Why abduct them?' Amelia asked, frowning.

'I think the infant males are representative of him as a child. He hates himself. A voice inside him – his father's voice – hates him. The girls . . .' Brady paused and shook his head. 'He's trying to repeat something. Why? I don't know. But it's crucial that we find out if we're to have any chance of saving Annabel Edwards.'

Amelia didn't look convinced. Neither did DCI Gates, who looked like he had better things to be doing than listening to Brady psychoanalyse the suspect. Time was running out.

Brady looked back at the crime scene photographs of Ellen Jackson. They still jarred with him. As he was sure they did with every other member of the team. He had spent hours staring at all the crime scene photographs. Trying to glean something – anything that would hint at why Macintosh had done this. Because that was what this was about – *the girls*. Why had he kidnapped both girls? That was the question that tormented him, because he still didn't have an answer.

The room was deathly quiet. Unease had settled over everyone.

Brady stared at the sickening images of Ellen Jackson. He could feel the anxiety building. The tension. *This could soon be Annabel Edwards.*

The crime scene photographs showed the three-year-old victim sat on a chair. Perfectly posed. Her long blond hair hung in neatly arranged ringlets around her pale, cruelly pretty face. Her clothes stiff. Old-fashioned. A starched white dress with a frilly petticoat underneath, white tights, small black patent leather shoes. She had been dressed to match the old Victorian porcelain doll she clutched in her hands. But it was unnatural. Unnerving. Her dark brown eyes staring. Open. Blank. Dead.

Brady swallowed. Hard. He still couldn't get his head around what *he* had done to her. Or why.

Chapter Five

Saturday: 11:20 p.m.

When she came to, the overhead light was on.

The sudden glare surprised her. Blinking, she forced herself to sit up. As she did so, her headache notched up a gear and the dull thump became a deafening noise. She then remembered being hit so hard that her head had ricocheted backwards, knocking her out. She fought the instinct to lie down again. She couldn't do that – wouldn't allow herself to do it. Her primary focus was the fact that the light was on. How long for before *he* turned it off, she had no idea. But she needed to see exactly where he had brought her. And if there was any chance of escape.

Keeping her eyes closed, she succeeded in leaning back against the cool wall and caught her breath for a few moments while she waited for the pain to lessen. Finally, feeling less likely to retch, she opened her eyes.

Shocked, she felt herself lose control of her bladder.

Oh God ... what did you do? What the fuck did you do?

The image in front of her was cruel, twisted ... barbaric.

Her mind had gone blank. She couldn't believe what she was looking at. Her brain refusing to process it. She closed her eyes, squeezing them tight. She counted to ten. Tried to calm herself down. Rationalise. Then she opened them again. It – *she* – was still there. Unmoved. Unchanged.

The girl . . . the one I was talking to. It had to be her. But . . . what has he done to her?

She forced herself to breathe. Slow deep breaths. For a second it felt as if this was some horrific nightmare. She closed her eyes again and willed herself to wake up.

Come on . . . make it end. WAKE UP!

Nothing. She could feel, even with her eyes shut tight, that *she* was still sat there – staring at her. Blindly, she grabbed the flesh on her left arm and twisted it as hard as she could. Again and again.

The pain jolted her eyes open. Nothing had changed.

Tears slipped down her cheeks as she hugged her knees to her chest. She wanted out. Wanted to go home. Anything but ending up like *that*.

She tried to make sense of what she was seeing. She forced her eyes to look. To understand what had happened and what kind of crazy person was holding her captive.

The girl was in a chair directly under the bare light bulb. She looked no older than twenty but she was so emaciated that she couldn't weigh more than five stone. Her bones protruded from her parched skin; skin that was an unnatural sickly pale colour – as if she had been locked in the dark for months and months. She looked like a Holocaust victim. Bruises and cuts sporadically decorated her bony body and her dark, long hair hung in greasy clumps around her face. Her head was held in place by a heavy brown leather restraint that secured her forehead in position. But on either side of her head her hair had been shaved. And . . .

She swallowed.

She realised with horror that this was more than an old wooden chair. It looked like some kind of torture chair out of a horror film. Thick leather ankle and cuff restraints were fixed to its arms and legs, securing the girl in place.

Without warning, the light went out.

No . . . no . . . NO!

Overhead, footsteps could be heard walking away.

What do I do? What do I do? What do I do?

Short, sporadic gasps suddenly filled the blackened room. She tried to block the disquieting noise out, along with the disturbing mental picture that she had of the girl shackled to the old psychiatric chair. Positioned so she was staring straight at her. The thought turned her stomach.

Oh God . . . Oh God, help me. Please help me . . . I don't want to be left like that. Please God? I . . . I would rather die . . . Those eyes . . . lifeless. He has . . . has . . .

Chapter Six

Saturday: 12:24 p.m.

Brady knocked on Gates' office door and then walked in.

Distracted, Gates looked up from his desk. He didn't look happy to see him. Not that Gates ever looked happy to see Brady, but his expression was worse than usual. On his desk were copies of that day's newspapers. Broadsheets and tabloids. All with screaming headlines about police incompetence – *Brady's incompetence*.

'Sit.'

Brady did as instructed. There was something about Gates' mood that warned Brady not to push him. Not today.

Gates studied him.

Brady noted that Gates looked as tired as he felt. Gates would be under even more pressure than Brady. He had to deal with the political bullshit that came with the job. Brady was certain that Gates was being raked over the coals when it came to the media frenzy over Macintosh's release from police custody. It was one of his officers that had let Macintosh go. The same man who somehow knew where Macintosh had taken his axe.

Gates cleared his throat as he clasped his large hands together. Brady couldn't help but notice the neatly manicured nails. Even his desk was ordered and clutter free. Everything about Gates was regimented. And that was the problem. Gates couldn't quite get Brady to fit within his strict, controlling, exacting ways.

'Jack,' Gates began. His deep voice was cold, detached. Unnervingly so.

Brady waited, nervously. A lot had happened to him in the past few days, both professionally and personally; including his ex-wife leaving him without any warning. She had checked into a private psychiatric hospital after five or so months of living with Brady. It was either that, or she would have taken her life. She had survived being held hostage by two extreme Eastern European gangsters – unlike her boyfriend, DCI David Jameson, who had been in the wrong place at the wrong time and had been tortured and murdered. Not surprisingly, Claudia suffered from survivor's guilt. Brady had done everything to help her, but it had not been enough. Then there was James David Macintosh. If he was honest, it was the Macintosh case that was keeping him together. Without it, the reality of Claudia's sudden disappearance from his life would cripple him.

'Is there anything you want to talk about?'

Brady was surprised. That was one question he had not anticipated. 'No, sir.'

'What about your personal life? Are there any problems that you want to discuss with me?' Gates continued.

'No. Everything is fine,' Brady lied, feeling Gates' eyes scrutinise his every word and movement. He knew exactly where Gates was heading and the outcome didn't look good – not for him. He could feel the anger rising within him, combined with the fear of being taken off the case and not being able to find Macintosh and Annabel Edwards. He had a bad feeling that Gates was looking for a reason to remove him. But he found it hard to accept that Macintosh would be in London. And Gates knew that. Brady had made it quite clear to him that he believed Macintosh would remain within the North East. Not that Brady had had a chance to discuss the new evidence tying him to London with Gates. He had kept his thoughts to himself during the briefing. But it didn't make any sense to him. The recent murders were an exact copy of what had happened in 1977 which led Brady to believe that Macintosh would find a way back to Mill Cottage.

'I know about Claudia, Jack. And I am sorry. Truly, I am.'

Brady sat back. He felt blindsided. 'How? How do you know?'

'Listen . . . why don't you take some time away from the job to sort your personal life out? You look burnt out, Jack. Too much has happened to you, you need some breathing space . . .' Gates shrugged.

Brady breathed out. He needed to steady himself. The last thing he wanted to do was say something he regretted.

'Look . . . sir. I'm fine. Honestly. My personal life has no bearing on the job. I'm coping. I admit I'm tired. But that's to be expected. So are the rest of the team. Didn't I deliver on the Alexander De Bernier case?'

Gates nodded. 'You did.'

'So why take me off a case as crucial as this one? I know Macintosh. I was the one who knew where he had gone when he had absconded from Ashley House. True?' Brady fired at his boss.

'Yes,' Gates answered, nodding. But it was clear he had already made a decision.

'Trust me with this then. I know you think Macintosh is in London, but I am certain he is still here.'

'He is in London, Jack. The car has been officially identified. It has his fingerprints and DNA all over it.'

'What about Annabel?' Brady asked, not believing what he was being told.

'Yes,' Gates replied. His voice heavy. 'Hair samples and fingerprints were found inside the boot of the car. It appears that he had hidden her in there.'

Brady didn't say anything. He digested the news. It took him a moment but then he realised why Macintosh had chosen Heathrow's Terminal 4 car park. 'He left the car there to elude you. To throw you off his tracks. I suspect that he would have paid to have a car waiting for him to pick up. He would have used a pseudonym. He's planned this meticulously. Macintosh is too clever to be caught so easily.'

Gates considered Brady's comment. 'You really believe he's still in the North East?'

'One hundred per cent, sir.' Brady answered.

Gates sighed heavily as he deliberated his next move.

'I know him. Better than anyone else on the team. I understand that you have forensic evidence that he is in London. But that is what he wants you to think. It is all part of his plan.'

Gates studied him with narrowed eyes. 'Why would he still be here? And more to the point, where?'

'He's here because he has a personal attachment to the area. To Mill Cottage. I don't know why, but I just have a feeling that he will take Annabel Edwards there. Just as he did with Ellen Jackson.'

The expression on Gates' face told Brady he disagreed. 'Come on, Jack. Seriously? The place has already been searched and we found nothing. No trace of him. He hasn't returned there. And he certainly won't be returning now. It is under twenty-four hour surveillance. Macintosh is anything but stupid. He will have known the first place we would search would be Mill Cottage.'

'I am not disagreeing with that. But I think he will wait. He wants you to think that he is in London. As soon as the investigation becomes focused on finding him there, that is when he will return to Mill Cottage. I guarantee it.'

Gates clasped his hands together as he weighed up what Brady had said. 'All right. I am going to trust you on this, but do not, under any circumstances, fuck up.'

'I won't, sir.'

'While I am in London, you continue as acting SIO here. But you keep your head down and stay out of trouble. Understand me?'

Brady nodded.

Gates leaned forward. 'My reputation is on the line here, Jack. And I am sure you're aware of what the press are reporting,' he said, gesturing towards the newspapers on his desk.

Brady nodded without looking at them.

'Your bloody name and face is over all the front pages. And on the news channels. They're holding you responsible for releasing Macintosh so he could kill . . .' Gates waited for a moment before adding: 'Again.'

'But you know I had no grounds to detain him.'

Gates nodded. He looked weary. Reluctant even to continue. 'I know that. But they don't. And until we apprehend Macintosh you will be held responsible by the press. Christ knows what they would print about you if he murders Annabel Edwards. Believe me, Jack. You would become the press's most hated figure. They'll dig up every piece of information they can get on you and run with it. It wouldn't take them long to suggest that you're a bent copper with friends on the wrong side of the law. You seriously want to think about what you've got to lose before you start following some inexplicable hunch of yours which could be to the detriment of this case. We already let Macintosh slip through our hands once before and I damn well will not allow it to happen again.'

Brady felt numb. How was he to know that Macintosh would kill again? He had nothing to do with the parole board and their decision to release him back out onto the streets. Brady had simply brought Macintosh in for questioning in connection with the on-going Alexander De

Bernier's murder case. A copycat killing. Identical to the Joker's seventies murders. He'd had no idea when he had Macintosh in custody that he was the original Joker killer. Macintosh had served thirty-seven years for an unrelated crime: the gruesome killing of his psychiatrist and his family. The three-year-old Jackson girl had been the anomaly. She had been abducted from the crime scene and later murdered at Mill Cottage; Macintosh's childhood home.

A DNA swab had been taken from Macintosh while in Brady's custody. But it did not tie him to Alexander De Bernier's murder. Consequently, Brady had had no grounds to detain the ex-offender. It was only after Macintosh had been released that Brady learned that Macintosh's DNA sample conclusively matched forensic evidence found on one of the victim's T-shirt's from the seventies Joker killings. But by then Macintosh had already killed his probation officer, Jonathan Edwards, and his family.

All Brady had done was his job. And all he could do now was his job. There was no other alternative. At least not one that he would consider contemplating.

Otherwise you'll never be able to get him. Because they won't find him. And then . . . Then, Annabel Edwards will die.

Brady walked out of Gates' office and down the corridor. He couldn't believe what had just happened. He was still trying to process it. How the hell Gates had found out about Claudia's admission into a psychiatric hospital was beyond him. At least he was still acting SIO while Gates was following up leads in London. But it was a close call. Too close. Even the mere suggestion of taking time away from the job had panicked him. Without it, he didn't know what he would do. Especially now Claudia had gone.

'Sir?' Conrad called out behind him.

It was then it hit him. *Conrad.* He must have told Gates about Claudia.

Conrad caught up with him. 'Sir?'

Brady continued walking.

Conrad realised. 'What did Gates say?'

'Enough.'

Brady reached the stairs. He ran up them two at a time, despite the searing pain in his right leg. At the top he continued at a brisk march towards his office, doing his utmost not to break into a run.

He could hear Conrad hurrying to catch up. Brady reached his office and walked in, slamming the door behind him.

A few seconds later, the door opened.

He turned to see Conrad in the doorway. 'You do know I had no choice?'

Brady shrugged. 'Do I?'

'Sir, Gates asked me about Claudia. I hadn't expected it and when I didn't come up with an immediate answer he realised something was wrong. I couldn't lie to him. You know how fond he was of her. He respected her a great deal and when . . . You know, when Claudia was held hostage and DCI Davidson was . . .' Conrad faltered, unable to say what had happened to him. 'Well, Gates was really affected by it. You do know that?'

'Do I?' Brady asked as he walked over to his filing cabinet. He opened the top drawer and pulled out a bottle of Talisker. Two-thirds of it had gone. He hadn't had a drink despite what had happened over the past couple of days. Couldn't. He had a job to do. But that didn't deter him from picking up the Che Guevara mug and pouring himself a drink now.

'You're not responsible for what has happened to her,' continued Conrad.

'Do you want one?' Brady asked gesturing with the bottle of scotch, ignoring what had just been said.

'No,' Conrad answered.

'So, what did you tell Gates about Claudia? Did you tell him what . . . what she was contemplating . . .?' Brady was unable to finish.

There was no reply.

He turned and looked at Conrad. 'Did you?' he demanded.

Conrad nodded.

'Fuck you!'

'You don't understand. I had no choice. '

Brady turned his back to Conrad. He didn't want to hear. Didn't need the excuses. He had divulged his personal life to Gates. He had told him that he had driven his wife to the brink of suicide.

'Sir?'

Brady could hear the defeatism in his deputy's voice. It made no difference. He refused to turn and look at him.

'Sir?'

Brady ignored him.

'Sir.'

Conrad's voice sounded desperate but Brady didn't respond. He had been here before with him.

'Gates called me in for a meeting early this morning. He had seen the news. Had the newspapers in front of him with you on the front pages.'

Brady listened. His hand gripped the bottle of scotch, sorely tempted to add what was left to his mug. But he didn't move.

'He suggested that I distance myself from you for the sake of my career. That with all the media fallout there was a strong possibility that there would be an internal investigation into your decision to release Macintosh. I refused. I said that I would be sticking with you regardless of what the press, or anyone else for that matter, said about you. And then I told him you were having a hard enough time without Gates expecting me to distance myself from you. He asked why. And I had said it was personal. He then realised it had to be about Claudia. So he asked and . . . I told him. I now wish I hadn't. But I did. I told him you're blaming yourself for what has happened to her. And that you feel personally responsible for Macintosh and what he did. And that . . . that you're one of the best DI's this place has ever had. Regardless of what the press are saying. And . . . well . . . you don't deserve this, sir. Any of this.'

Silence.

Brady knew that Conrad wanted him to say something. Anything to clear the air. But he couldn't bring himself to speak.

A few moments later he heard the office door close. He was relieved that Conrad had left him alone. He needed some time to absorb what had happened in Gates' office. And then, Conrad's admission. Time to just reassess everything. He let go of the bottle of scotch and looked at the mug in his hand. Swirled the golden liquid around before savouring the smell. The anticipation was always better than the actual experience itself. He swallowed the contents back in one. It felt like smooth velvet as it slipped down the back of his throat. Followed by a welcoming burning sensation.

He looked at what was left in the bottle. He wanted to finish it. But he needed to be able to drive. Somewhere. Anywhere. As long as it was as far away from Whitley Bay as possible. He knew Gates was right. He had to keep his head together and stay out of trouble. Then he thought of Claudia. How easy it was to crash. To become dependent upon alcohol after a traumatic event. It numbed the mind. Took the edge off the pain and finally, if you drank enough, blurred all the thoughts that kept coming at you.

Claudia . . . Where are you?

It seemed to suddenly hit him. The fact that she was gone. He was still struggling to cope with the fact that Conrad had known that she had left him before he did. That Conrad had asked her parents – not him – to help her. To book her into a private psychiatric hospital without Brady's knowledge or consent. Not that they needed his permission. But he had been the one who had looked after her for five months. It was him who had forced her to vomit up the prescription medication she overdosed on. It was Brady who had sat in a freezing cold shower with her to sober her up – not them. And yet . . .

He shook his head. So much had happened in the last four days.

He put his empty mug down on the filing cabinet. Then grabbed his jacket from the back of the chair. He took one final look around his office. The beat-up old leather sofa under the large Victorian sash window. The wooden blinds and the grey light filtering through. He turned back to his desk. It was as cluttered as ever, files and paper strewn all over it. He shifted the files around looking for his car keys. Finally found them. Clutching them, he stepped back from his desk, accidentally knocking over his overflowing wastepaper bin. He stared down at the scrunched up newspapers and other rubbish now on the floor. It was a mess. Just like his personal life. And now there was the threat of an investigation into his decisions about Macintosh.

He knew what he had to do. He had to get his head together. To silence the tormented thoughts he was having about Claudia. He needed to go. Anywhere, as long as it put some distance between him and his life. He pulled open the top drawer of the filing cabinet and took out an unopened bottle of Talisker. A thirty-year-old malt that he had been saving for the right occasion.

Well, this is it . . .

Brady walked down the corridor. Jacket and car keys in one hand. An unopened bottle of Talisker in the other. He didn't care who saw him.

He ignored the awkward glances as colleagues moved out of his way. He couldn't give a shit what they thought. It couldn't be any worse than thinking he was responsible for three brutal, savage murders. Or the abduction of a three-year-old girl. After all, that was what the papers were saying.

And if he kills her, what will they think then?

Brady made his way to the ground floor, heading for the double doors out onto the street. He passed the reception desk on his way out. The desk sergeant on duty was Charlie Turner. The last of the old guard. He had been stationed at Whitley Bay for years. He was due for retirement soon and he was one of the few colleagues that Brady would genuinely be sad to see go.

'Bloody hell, Jack! Where are you going?' asked Turner, his spidery white eyebrows raised in alarm.

'Nowhere.'

'Bloody hell, lad! That's exactly where you'll end up if you think the answer's in that bottle of scotch.'

Brady already had his hand on the double wooden doors. He turned back and gave Turner a tired, weary look. 'I just need to clear my head.'

'Well you won't be clearing it with scotch. I can tell you that for a fact,' Turner said shaking his head.

'Thanks, Charlie,' Brady said, suddenly walking back towards him. He knew the desk sergeant was right. He was better than this. He had a job to do – regardless of whether his personal life had disintegrated in front of him.

'What for?' Turner questioned, frowning at Brady.

'For telling me when I'm being a jackass. That's what! Here. You have it. It's a bloody good bottle of scotch, so don't waste it,' Brady said as he put the bottle on Turner's desk.

Turner inspected the bottle of scotch. 'Nah, lad. I can't take this. Save it for another time.' He looked up as Brady was heading out the doors.

'I'm too bloody old for this malarkey, Jack Brady!' Turner shouted after him.

But Brady was gone.

Chapter Seven

Saturday: 1:03 p.m.

The BBC twenty-four news was on the television. It was about him. He expected no less. He listened with interest, then disdain, as the newsreader interviewed a criminal psychologist. Middle-class, middle-aged and getting off on being on TV and making his name, making his career, out of Macintosh. His proffered opinions trite and nonsensical. He picked up the remote and was about to turn it off, then stopped. He smiled on hearing DI Brady's name. Pleasure rippled through him. They were *still* discussing the fact that he had been released without charge. Set free to kill – again. He watched as Annabel Edwards' name was mentioned and a recent photograph put up on the screen. Questions asked, answers given on what was happening – would happen – to the three-year-old girl.

Only he knew what was going to happen to her. He was the one in control. Not fucking DI Brady. It had pleased him to know that Brady was being torn apart by the media. His actions or inactions being questioned and speculated over. He doubted DI Brady would have a career left by the time he had finished with him.

That thought made him feel good. He wondered how it felt right now for DI Brady. How he was coping under the media spotlight. It had gone better than even he could have imagined. He wanted Brady's name tarnished. His professional judgement questioned. Simply because Brady was the one who posed a threat to him. It was DI Brady who, if he had the chance, could foil everything he had planned. And if he did. Then— He stopped himself. *It is not necessary. Not yet . . .* For now it seemed that the police had taken his bait. Followed his lead to London. And that was what he had planned. He wanted their focus to be anywhere other than here.

He turned his attention back to the news. To the missing girl.

They could speculate and speculate but it would make no difference to her outcome. He remembered the first time Jonathan Edwards had shown him a photograph of his daughter. She was so much younger then. But still, she had looked so much like her . . .

He had to stop himself. *Not now.* He turned and looked out the window. It was a panoramic view of the Northumberland countryside, dominated by the Cheviot Hills. He had rented this place two months earlier, paying up front for a six month lease. The owner, who lived in New Zealand, had been more than happy with the arrangement. Money was a very persuasive weapon. After all, this was a holiday let and he was paying a premium weekly rate for the privilege. But it was worth it. The isolation alone was priceless. As was the location. It was close to the only place that interested him.

He turned away from the window, his gaze falling on the child opposite him. That comatose look on her face. Acting as if she was not really a part of all this. But hers was a significant role. It would not be long now. And then it would finally be over. He blocked out her gabbling. The words she babbled over and over again. She didn't understand that what she wanted no longer existed. That they were gone. But he could feel her words poisoning him. Making him doubt himself. Doubt everything he had done.

He had done all of this for her . . . He had planned meticulously. Waited for so long. And now she was ruining it by not wanting to be here. With him. But she was with him now. It was her . . . her who had driven him to do this. HER.

He looked at her. Anger welled up inside. She was still crying. It made no difference what he did. He had given her the doll.

The special doll. The one he had searched and searched for until he had found it.

An identical one to *hers*. But she continued to blankly stare at nothing in particular. Still crying. Ignoring him. Ignoring what he had done for her. He could feel the memory stirring somewhere in the deep recesses of his mind. He didn't want to go back there. *Not again.* The pain too raw. Too intense.

Her cries . . . He could hear her crying out. Begging. Her words jumbled up. Muddled. Inaudible sounds. NO. Stop it! Stop hurting her . . . STOP IT!

Chapter Eight

Saturday: 2:43 p.m.

Brady was parked up by the wild, overgrown lane that led to Mill Cottage. Hidden off the beaten track, it had taken some finding. The secluded three-bedroomed stone cottage had been left derelict for years, the broken windows boarded-up long ago. He knew that the last occupants were the Macintosh family. They had lived there in the fifties and early sixties when James David Macintosh was a boy. Then they had moved out. To Jesmond; a suburb on the outskirts of Newcastle-upon-Tyne.

He studied the cottage. It was over 200 years old. Externally it was still in reasonable condition. It had been built from stone. Intended to last Northumberland's wildest winters.

This was Macintosh's childhood home. But it was more than that – this was where three-year-old Ellen Jackson had been murdered.

His phone vibrated, suddenly making him jump. *Shit!* He looked at who was calling – Conrad. Again. He left it. Whatever Conrad wanted could wait. Brady had more important things on his mind than easing his deputy's conscience.

He looked back up at the house. He was certain that Macintosh would come back here. If he hadn't already. He just knew it. Could not explain how or why. But the gut feeling was there none the less. And it wouldn't be silenced. Which was why he had driven the twenty-four miles out here to Mill Cottage. It was situated on the outskirts of Hartburn village; six miles west of Morpeth. Further up the A1 and you hit Alnwick, followed by Berwick-upon-Tweed. This area of Northumberland which stretched up to the Scottish borders was known for its rich and savage history. One that included the Border Reivers; lawless clans – both English and Scottish – who ruthlessly and mercilessly raided the entire border country as a means of survival. They had no allegiance to anything or anyone, other than their own kin. No regard for their victims; age, sex, nationality irrelevant. Violence, treachery, rape, arson and murder, merely a way of life.

Brady got out the car. He shuddered involuntarily as he stared at the derelict cottage. It had seen its share of violence and murder. That had been in 1977. Brady tried to imagine the house then. Surrounded by police. Macintosh had eluded them. He had been arrested hours later heading north, towards the Scottish borders. But it had come too late. Macintosh had left behind a disturbing scene inside the house. The officers had hoped to find the three-year-old girl. *But not like that.*

Brady checked the time: 2:45 p.m. He felt restless. Uneasy. As if someone was watching him. He had already announced himself to the two plain-clothed coppers parked up at the bottom of the lane. They had been assigned surveillance duty. Not that they really expected anything to happen. Let alone for *him* to turn up. There was one access in and out.

Unless you came through the woods.

The place was surrounded by acres of woodland. Trees and bushes lined the winding lane and surrounded the house. There was a large overgrown garden at the front with a broken, sun-blistered wooden swing still hanging from a large elm tree. Brady wondered why the cottage had never been sold on. Or demolished. The place had a history; an ugly one that had been left to fester.

But now Macintosh had reopened old wounds. He had started to play his sick, twisted game again.

What the fuck do you think you'll find, Jack, that no one else has found?

It didn't matter. It was his time to waste. Gates had granted him that. At least he was doing something. What was the alternative? There wasn't one, other than focus on finding Macintosh in London. But Brady knew he wasn't there. He might have left evidence to suggest that he had been. But that was a foil. Part of whatever game Macintosh was playing with them.

Brady walked through the hallway and shone the torch into the living room. Stabs of light penetrated through the partially boarded-up windows. But it wasn't enough to properly see the room. He swept the light over the faded, deteriorating walls. Pastel floral wallpaper had peeled away, taking with it chunks of flaking plaster. He knew what he was looking for, but it wasn't there.

Evidence of what he had done to her.

He shone the torch over the furniture that still remained. Two shabby-looking Queen Anne chairs sat on either side of the fireplace. A small table with a lamp. Two other antique wooden chairs had been shoved up against a wall next to an empty drinks cabinet. He turned and looked behind him. A large bookcase had been fixed in place along the entire length of the wall. It was stuffed with old, damp-ridden books left to rot, the pages stained dark yellow. They were mainly large hardbacks on war. The choice of fiction was eclectic. There was Proust's novel, *Remembrance of Things Past*. Then the complete collection of George Orwell's work as well as Boris Pasternak's *Doctor Zhivago*. Even a copy of C.S. Lewis' *The Lion, The Witch and The Wardrobe*. Despite their damp condition, Brady could see that they had been well-thumbed and not just there for decoration.

He turned his attention back to the fireplace. It had a large stone hearth and open grate. A coal scuttle and poker remained, covered in cobwebs and dust. The grate itself was filled with debris: bird feathers, skeletons belonging to small rodents and dried, shrivelled-up insects. But there was nothing else here. No evidence of what the police had found in 1977. Yet the room made him feel uneasy. Whether it was the knowledge that the police had finally tracked Ellen down to this cottage – this room – he couldn't say. When they did find her, they had been too late.

But there was something else. Something inexplicable that made him feel ill at ease. It was the smell. An overpowering stench: dank, musty, rotting. *Like death.*

He backed out into the hallway. Welcome daylight streamed in from where he had kicked in the front door. He headed down the corridor towards the kitchen. The room was equally cold, damp and dark. He shivered involuntarily as he shone the light over the old double cast-iron range situated under a large chimney breast. A pan still sat on the range. Beside it, a black cast-iron kettle. Brady glanced around. He was surprised by what had been left. A large wooden Welsh dresser stood against the wall opposite the boarded-up kitchen window. A delicate bone china dinner set covered in a thick layer of dust and grime sat on display. Brady walked across the stone flagstones to the dresser. Curious, he opened the drawers. Neatly arranged silver cutlery with ivory handles lay untouched.

Why had it been left behind?

Brady turned to the door in the corner of the room. It was a walk-in pantry. He shone the torch around. Rows and rows of tins of produce, jars of homemade pickles, jams and nibbled bags of stale flour and sugar were still there. Decades later.

Again, why had they left the food? It was as if they had just left overnight . . .

He felt someone watching him through the slats in the boarded-up kitchen window. He turned quickly around and flashed the torchlight across the window. *Fuck!* His heart was pounding. He had seen a face. He was certain of it.

He ran to the back door and tried to pull it open. It was locked. He shook the door knob but it wouldn't budge.

He turned and flashed the torch back over the window again – nothing. He ran to the window and leaned over the sink in an attempt to look out between the gaps in the boards covering the window. No one was there. But he was certain he had seen someone. He sighed. Too tired. Too on edge. Maybe he was letting the house get to him. The knowledge of what had happened here.

He turned on the taps to splash water over his face. To bring him to his senses. But the water had long since been disconnected. He looked down at the bottom of the sink. It was a bloody rust colour – the result of a constant leaking tap.

He looked around at the large wooden kitchen table that dominated the room. Six wooden chairs were still around the table. In the centre sat a pile of newspapers dating back to 1963. It was eerie. Brady couldn't shake the feeling that the house was waiting for its rightful owners – *owner* – to return. The thought of the face at the window came to mind.

He needed to check the back garden. Just to silence his unease. He had already noted that there was access from the front garden round to the back. He made his way to the back of the house. The grass was wilder there. Nature had ferociously reclaimed what had once been hers. Then there were the woods. The dense trees encroached closer than he expected, throwing the back of the house into shadow. He walked towards the back kitchen window and door. It was clear from the freshly trampled grass and weeds that someone had just been there.

Relief overwhelmed him. But it was soon replaced by questions. *Who was it? Could it have been Macintosh?*

Brady spun round, certain that he had heard what sounded like twigs snapping. Suggestive of someone lurking in the woods. He ran in the direction of the sound; straight ahead into the woods. Then stopped. He couldn't hear anything. Nor could he see anyone. The woods seemed to be filled with a disquieting unease. The air, heavy and still. Fragmented fading light stabbed through the trees but the woodland was still dark and overbearing. Even the unending sea of bluebells that covered the woodland ground did nothing to dispel the atmosphere. Brady looked around. Nothing. He turned and looked back at the boarded-up cottage. No one was there.

He decided to shrug it off. For all he knew it was just kids. Macintosh's name was very much in the public arena. It wouldn't take much to realise that Mill Cottage was where Macintosh had murdered three-year-old Ellen Jackson in 1977. Brady started walking back. As he did so, he spotted something unusual to the left of him, partially obscured between trees and sprawling bushes. Curious, Brady walked over. Foliage had covered most of it, but it was there; a small, four foot by four foot brick structure that stood two feet above the ground. Sinewy knots of thick ivy and sodden decaying leaves and other foliage acted as a camouflage disguising what looked to be an opening leading below ground. Brady pulled back some of the ivy and bushes revealing steep concrete steps that led deep below the ground's surface. He could see that the steps made their way to a cast-iron door situated deep underground. He went down to check it out. The door had been bolted shut, then padlocked. He shoved his weight against it. But it didn't budge. Not that Brady thought anyone was inside. The heavy, old padlock was rusted in place; and the steps leading down to the door had been covered over by decades of woodland decay, wild ivy and bushes. No one had been here for a long time.

But just to be certain, Brady banged on the door. 'Hey? Anyone in there?' he shouted.

Nothing. Not that he expected a reply but he just wanted to reassure himself. After all, Annabel Edwards was still missing. He assumed that this was one of many Second World War air raid shelters that had been left, unused and abandoned. Someone had locked it against trespassers or vandals.

But it's the perfect location to hide someone . . .

Brady headed back to the cottage. He walked through the open door and straight up the wooden stairs zigzagging the torch across the dilapidated walls. He was preoccupied by what he had found hidden nearby in the woods. It obviously belonged to Mill Cottage; or at least the occupants who had lived here during the Second World War. He was aware that the North East of England – known for its industrial production – had been raided by German bombers. Brady knew that there was no point calling it in. No one had been near it in years. Yet, even with this fact, Brady still felt uneasy about it. He decided that he would come back later with bolt cutters to check out what was inside.

Brady reached the first floor landing. It was shrouded in blackness. He shone the torch up and down and counted; four rooms. Doors all shut. He stepped into the bathroom first. Shone the torch around. Nothing. He looked in the mirrored medicine cabinet on the wall. Empty – apart from an old cut-throat rusty razor. He turned and looked at the deep enamel bath. Around the plughole rust had bled into the enamel, discolouring it a burnished orange. But again, nothing unusual.

He made his way to the largest bedroom first. An old, rusted double bedstead had been left. Pillows and thick blankets lay neatly arranged. Bedside cabinets with lamps sat either side of the bed. A book, half read, had been left on one of the cabinets. A large Indian rug was spread over the wooden floor. If the windows had not been boarded-up Brady would have believed that someone still lived here. But the thick layers of dust and chunks of chalky white plaster that covered everything told a different story. He looked up at the ceiling. Part of it had collapsed from rain damage, letting in stabs of fast fading daylight where roof tiles had slipped or broken.

A feeling of disquiet had taken hold again. He looked around the room. A lopsided picture of a landscape still hung on one of the peeling walls. It was eerie. He still couldn't shake the feeling that Macintosh's parents had just walked out one day and never returned.

A large wardrobe stood opposite the bed. Tall and imposing. Brady walked over and opened it, expecting it to be empty. He was wrong. The smell hit him first. A pungent, musty waft of moth balls. Then he saw the clothes. Clothes dating back to the Fifties. Men's suits neatly arranged. Women's floral dresses. Skirts. Coats. Even shoes.

Why leave them here?

He walked to the adjacent room. It was the smallest one, and was completely empty. He then made his way to the final room at the back of the house. He immediately realised that this must have been James' room as a boy. The wallpaper was a faded blue decorated with fighter planes. There was a child's bed, again with pillows and blankets neatly folded. A chest of drawers and a small wardrobe filled the rest of the space. Brady pulled open the drawers but they were empty. The same with the wardrobe. He walked around the room looking for something – anything. But it was empty. There was no trace of Macintosh as a boy.

He wasn't sure what he thought he would find. An insight into Macintosh's mind. A clue as to where he could be hiding. But there was nothing.

He sighed. He had to concede that Gates could be right after all. Maybe Macintosh was in London. Why would he come back here? There was nothing left for him.

Brady decided enough was enough. He would go home. Force himself to eat and then get some much-needed sleep. Maybe then he would start to think straight.

He turned to leave. As he did, something caught his eye. There was a small door fitted into the low wall on the landing opposite. Brady walked over and tried it, expecting it be jammed shut, but it opened. He bent down and shone the torch inside. It was a small room under the eaves which had been boarded out. He somehow managed to crawl in to get a better look. Trying not to breathe, he shone the torch around. The air was dry and stale and his eyes and nose itched from the years of undisturbed dust.

Then he saw it.

He managed to force it out from where it had been hidden behind one of the rafters. It was an old, beaten-up leather suitcase. Dragging it with him, he shuffled backwards out of the cramped space onto the landing. Hands trembling, kneeling over the torchlight, he pulled on a pair of blue latex gloves from his back pocket. Trepidation filled him as he questioned what could be inside. It was heavy – heavy enough for a young child's body.

Steeling himself, he opened it. Disappointment hit him hard. Or was it relief?

The case was filled with layers and layers of clothes. Children's clothes. But these were girls' clothes. Brady picked up what looked like a sailor's dress. It was old – dated. He would have hazarded a guess that it was from the late fifties, early sixties. But what was clear was that it was for a very young child.

As young as three-years-old . . .

He rummaged through them. All the same. Petite dresses with matching wool pastel coloured cardigan. Even nightgowns, white cotton slips and laced socks. Carefully – *lovingly* – folded and arranged in order. There was even a pair of black patent leather shoes made for tiny, dainty feet. The bottom of the suitcase was weighted down with a substantial collection of children's illustrated nursery rhymes and fairy tales books.

But there was something else buried along with the books. Something wrapped in a quilted baby blanket: an antique Victorian doll. Brady looked at the grotesque doll's heavily painted face.

It was identical to the doll that Ellen had been found holding. But this one was old. Worn. *Used.*

Brady stared at it. *Why?* He couldn't quite understand. The information the police had on Macintosh said he was an only child.

So, who did the clothes and the doll belong to?

Macintosh had been born in 1957. A period where gender identity was still very fixed. Gender fluidity was a recent acceptance and would certainly not have been openly discussed, let alone understood in the late fifties and sixties. Brady was also aware from Macintosh's psychiatrist's transcripts that his father had been an officer in the army. He had been the victim of considerable homophobic abuse meted out by his father. Brady seriously doubted that he would have allowed his son to play with dolls.

Unless it was the mother?

Macintosh's mother was an enigma. The investigative team still knew very little about her, yet Brady was certain that Macintosh's relationship with his mother was essential to the abduction. That they were missing something crucial. But Brady was still at a loss as to what it could be.

He had noted that during Macintosh's sessions with Dr Jackson, his mother had never been discussed. If questioned, Macintosh would change the subject – or remain silent.

He placed the doll back down and picked up the small biscuit tin which had also been wrapped inside the blanket. He prised up the lid, revealing a collection of black and white photographs. He picked them up. It was a family – *of four.* Mother, father and *two* children. A boy who looked roughly six or seven years old and a much younger girl. Brady recognised the dress the girl was wearing in the photograph – it was the dark navy blue sailor's outfit from the suitcase. He flipped the photograph over. On the back someone had scrawled something – *'The Macintosh family. James aged six. Lucy aged three. July 1963.'*

Shit! James David Macintosh had a sister . . .

Brady turned the photograph over and stared and stared at the stark, frozen image. It felt as if his blood had turned cold. The girl in the photograph – Lucy Macintosh – was pretty, with blond cascading ringlets and dark, inquisitive eyes. Brady could feel his heart accelerating. His mouth felt dry. One thought kept repeating itself – they look just like her.

Annabel Edwards. Ellen Jackson. Oh Christ!

Then a question hit him.

Where is Lucy? What happened to her? And why the hell did no one know she existed?

James David Macintosh had a sister. *Or had had a sister.* One who looked uncannily like Ellen Jackson – the seventies victim. The one Macintosh had brought here. Brady tried not to think about what he had done to her in this house. Instead he turned his mind to Annabel Edwards. The victim who was still alive – he hoped. The photograph of her that had dominated all the newspapers and the TV channels came to mind: blond ringlets and dark brown, trusting eyes. It was those eyes that Brady couldn't get out of his mind. He knew if he didn't find her – *alive* – they would haunt him to the day he died.

Out of the two victims, it was Annabel who most resembled Lucy Macintosh. And that scared the hell out of him.

What are you planning to do to her, Macintosh?

Brady's blood ran cold. *Or have you already done it?*

Brady was sitting in his car waiting for Amelia to answer his call. The light was fading. Fast. The gloomy air of the derelict cottage intensified as the sun set lower and lower in the bleak March sky.

Finally she rang. 'Jack?' Her voice sounded unusually concerned.

'Yeah—' but before he had a chance to speak, she cut him off.

'Where exactly are you? You do know Harry's been trying to contact you?'

'No . . . I mean yes,' he corrected. He knew there was no point in lying to her.

'So, where are you?'

'Mill Cottage.'

'Do you really think he will return there?' Her voice had an unmistakable edge of scepticism.

'Yes,' Brady replied.

Amelia did not respond. But her silence was enough for Brady to know that she was not convinced. However, Brady wasn't bothered. Nor was he in the mood to explain his reasons for believing that Macintosh had never left the North East.

'Did you know Macintosh had a sister?'

'Sorry?'

Brady could hear the surprise in her voice. 'He has a sister. Lucy Macintosh. From what I can gather she was born in 1960, or thereabouts.'

'Wait a minute. Run that by me again?'

'Macintosh has a younger sister. We somehow missed this fact. It's crucial to the investigation. To the reason why—'

Amelia abruptly stopped him. 'How do you know that he has a sister?'

'I found old photographs hidden in the eaves of the cottage.' Brady paused for a moment as his eyes dropped to his knee. On it he had placed the photograph taken of the Macintosh family in 1963. Lucy Macintosh's curious, upturned face was staring at the camera. It still made him feel uneasy just looking at her. The resemblance between Macintosh's sister at the age of three and the Edwards' child was uncanny.

Brady swallowed. He didn't want to think about Annabel Edwards. Couldn't. 'This ... this whole thing with Macintosh is all about his sister. We need to find her. ASAP.'

'Listen, Jack,' Amelia's voice had changed. The scepticism gone. Filled now with concern for him. 'There's no mention of any siblings in Macintosh's medical history. Or even prison records for that fact. Nothing.'

'So?' Brady sighed. 'I have evidence to the contrary.'

Amelia didn't reply. Her silence said it all. But Brady knew that once she had seen the photograph she would be convinced. 'I'll copy the photograph and send it to you. Then you can tell me I've got it wrong.'

'Look, Jack, that's not what I am saying. But you've been under considerable stress.'

'So has everyone else. It doesn't mean that I can't do my job.'

'Come on, Jack. You know what I mean . . . With everything the press are saying about you and—'

Brady had heard enough. He wasn't sure whether she knew about Claudia's sudden disappearance. But the last thing he needed was her acting like his shrink. 'I don't want to argue with you, Amelia. Just do as I've asked. And get Conrad to run a check against that name.'

Brady waited. The resistance in her silence was palpable.

'Fine,' she finally agreed. 'Maybe if you had answered your phone you could have asked Conrad yourself. He wanted to tell you we have a new lead.'

'Go on,' Brady said, ignoring her jibe.

'A witness has come forward.'

Brady held his breath. Waited.

'An elderly woman named Barbara Houghton. She knew Macintosh personally. Thinks she might be of some help.'

'When?' Brady asked.

'She contacted the helpline earlier today.'

'I don't mean that. When did she know him, Amelia?' Brady asked, trying to keep the frustration out of his voice.

'Well, she knew him as a young boy. When the family moved to Jesmond. She lived next door at number nineteen. Is still living there now.'

The disappointment was bitter. Brady had been hoping against the odds that she had known him recently. That she might have some idea of where he was hiding.

'She knew him from 1963, right up until he was arrested and charged in 1977. For all we know she could have some information about him that could be crucial to the case.'

'Do you think you and Conrad could interview her today?' Brady suggested. He was tired. All he wanted to do was get back to the station with this new evidence and find out what he could on Lucy Macintosh. And he wanted to increase the search for Macintosh's mother Eileen.

People just don't disappear. Or do they? Lucy Macintosh . . . Then Eileen Macintosh.

'Look, I would if I could but I've been asked to go to London with . . .' she left it unsaid. 'I'm sorry but I leave in literally ten minutes. When Conrad said he couldn't get hold of you, I wanted to check in with you myself.'

'Great!' Against his best intentions, it sounded truculent. 'I mean, that's great. London. Right . . . So, she wants to give a statement, does she?'

'Yes. She specifically asked for you. Has seen your face on the news. She was adamant that she could be of some help.'

Brady was keenly aware of the amount of calls coming in from the public. Most were a waste of police resources. But there was a reason why the public had been thrown into a frenzy: a three-year-old child had been abducted by a serial killer – after he had savagely murdered her family. It couldn't get worse than that. So, the nation – *the world* – watched and waited.

'Conrad can do it. He'd be better suited to take her statement than me. Especially with all the bad press, the last thing I should be doing is dealing with members of the public.'

'No chance. Gates has him chasing something else up. The same with the rest of the team. Kenny, Daniels . . . Harvey . . . they've all been assigned jobs. The investigation is starting to pick up momentum. A new lead has come in about Macintosh's potential whereabouts in London and Gates has everyone focused on that.'

Suddenly the photograph on his lap seemed inconsequential. Pointless. He didn't even bother asking how they had got this new information. Or even where they believed Macintosh to be. It didn't matter. Gates and the team were convinced Macintosh was in London and were doing their utmost to find him, whereas Brady had remained behind chasing what now seemed to be ghosts.

Brady's silence forced Amelia to speak. 'Think of it as good PR going to see this woman. You could do with some right now, Jack.'

‘Fine . . . I’ll drop by on my way back.’

‘Good,’ Amelia said. ‘And Jack?’

‘Yeah?’

‘Some advice. After you’ve got her statement, go home. Get some rest. If Macintosh is in London, there’s not a lot you can do here.’

Brady didn’t bother to reply. Instead he cut the call. He couldn’t take any more well-intentioned crap. Not any more. He was still a copper. One with a gut feeling that Gates was off on a wild goose chase.

Which is exactly what Macintosh wanted. Them searching in the wrong place for him and Annabel Edwards. While Brady was isolated and working alone . . . Brady breathed out slowly. He couldn’t shake the feeling he had that Macintosh was playing them – *him*. But why?

Chapter Nine

Saturday: 4:54 p.m.

'Honestly. I'm fine.' Brady smiled as he shook his head. It was the third time Barbara Houghton had offered him a drink. She had just made herself a gin and tonic. A generous measure at that. First of the day she had said.

'Are you certain you don't want something, DI Brady?'

Brady nodded. Smiled. Tried to look relaxed, even if he was anything but. He was in a large 1930's detached house on Jesmond Dene Road. The spacious living room was surprisingly minimalistic and contemporary. It had a Scandinavian feel to it. One wall of the room was made of glass which faced directly onto a large, well-established garden. It was clear that Barbara Houghton was comfortable in her retirement. What wasn't so clear were her objectives.

'So . . . what is it exactly that you want to tell me about James David Macintosh?' Brady asked.

'Well,' she replied, finally sitting down across from Brady. 'He lived next door to me for fourteen years. Came when he was six. Sullen, quiet boy.' She shook her head as she remembered him.

Brady waited. She was well into her eighties so would have been in her late twenties back then. Not that she looked her age. She was a small-framed woman but she still had fire in her sharp eyes. When she had told Brady that she had been a headmistress at one of the all-girl private schools in Jesmond it hadn't surprised him. Regardless of her build, she would have been a formidable woman in her day. Barbara had short white hair. No make-up. She wore a woollen check skirt and jacket with a white blouse underneath accompanied with simple, but expensive jewellery. She had a no-nonsense appearance which matched her no-nonsense attitude.

'You really should join me in a gin and tonic, DI Brady,' she scolded. 'You could do with some colour in your cheeks.' She shook her head. 'Then again, I imagine it must be very difficult for you. I still can't believe what the papers are publishing. That they're even allowed to print such things is beyond me.'

Brady smiled. It was a pained one. Barbara Houghton was more interested in Brady's infamous career than in offering any information on the suspect.

'I understand that you don't want to discuss it.'

Brady nodded. Attentive. Polite. He had a bad feeling that this was going to take some time.

'Right!' She took a sip of her iced gin and tonic and then looked him straight in the eye.

Brady waited.

'As I said, James was a sullen, uncommunicative boy. He wasn't much liked by the other children in the street. Or at school. So I was told. That continued up until the age of eleven. Then things got radically worse. His poor mother Eileen was beside herself. Her husband, Raymond, had recently died of a heart attack. Went to work one morning and didn't come home. Polite man. He was an officer in the army for years, then took up a post as a civil servant. Worked in London during the week and commuted home every second weekend.' She looked at Brady, her intelligent blue eyes gauging whether he was interested. Satisfied, she continued. 'Always got the feeling Raymond didn't like the boy. And after what James did, I can't say I blame him.'

'You mean his psychiatrist?' Brady asked.

'Oh no! This happened years before that. If someone had done their job properly, then James would never have been let out to attack again.' Her small, delicate hands remained clutched around her crystal tumbler. She took another sip.

He leaned forward, keen to hear more. 'I don't follow?'

'I don't suppose you would do. No charges were ever pressed. But then Eileen Macintosh sorted it before anyone had a chance to do anything. The boy was gone as soon as she found out. Overnight bag packed and taken immediately to St George's.'

Brady shook his head. 'As in the psychiatric hospital?'

'Yes, in Morpeth. It used to be called St George's mental asylum back then. Nor was it the first time he had been placed there.'

Brady frowned.

'Raymond and Eileen arrived here in autumn of 1963. Remember it well. They had rented a house in Whitley

Bay for a few months before buying this house. When they moved in, they didn't have James with them. He didn't arrive for another six months. Pale, sickly looking boy. Felt sorry for him to begin with. What with Raymond's draconian strictness and Eileen's remoteness with the child. I would spend time with him. I never had children you see, DI Brady. Too busy with my teaching career. But not too busy after work or at the weekends to entertain young James.'

'Where had he been?'

Barbara raised her eyebrows at Brady. 'Good question. They had said he had been convalescing with relatives in the South. But it later transpired Eileen had had him admitted to St George's, that he had already spent eight months there when he was six years old. That was how she was able to get him institutionalised so quickly the second time when he was eleven. No fuss. No police involvement. He just disappeared. He was gone for four years. And when he returned he was never the same.'

Brady absorbed this information. He realised that when the Macintosh family suddenly left Mill Cottage in Northumberland, James David Macintosh must have been immediately placed in St George's psychiatric hospital. But why? He then thought of the girl in the photographs he had found. Whether there was a connection he couldn't say. At least, not yet. He accepted that the Macintoshes would not have wanted to divulge such sensitive information to their new neighbours and understood why they would have lied about their six-year-old son's whereabouts.

'Did James have any siblings that you knew of?' Brady asked, even though it was clear that Lucy Macintosh had never made it here. But then again, neither had James Macintosh until much later. If Barbara Houghton was correct, he had been placed in a psychiatric hospital for eight months. Could the same have happened to his sister?

He watched, disappointed, as Barbara shook her head. 'No. They never mentioned any siblings.'

'What about James? Did he ever mention having a younger sister?'

Again she shook her head. 'No. Never. Not that he talked much about his family.'

Brady waited while she took another sip of her drink. He was suddenly overcome with the desire to have a scotch. But he resisted. The temptation was outweighed by the consequences. He was already being castigated as being professionally incompetent. Throw into the mix drinking on the job – while interviewing a witness – and he would be finished. He needed to focus. 'What happened for him to be sent to St George's when he was eleven?'

Barbara nodded. Her eyes narrowed as she looked at Brady. 'His behaviour had been escalating. Started really a few months after he first arrived. He would have been seven then. Fights at school. He would come home with his clothes torn and his face covered in cuts and bruises. Wouldn't talk about it of course. But that didn't worry me. It was his interest in animals. *Unnatural* interest, I should add. His parents had bought him a tortoise. Quite an exotic pet in those days. I think they were concerned about him as well. Anyway, Raymond had been burning some garden waste. I then heard a commotion in their garden and I went out to see what was wrong,' she paused for a moment as she looked out at her garden. 'James had thrown his tortoise on the fire. Alive.'

Brady nodded. Not that he was surprised. Torturing and killing animals was a typical psychopathic trait. The question was how far did he escalate to warrant being locked up in a mental institution for four years?

'What happened next?'

She shook her head, a look of sadness in her eyes. 'Well . . . James was severely beaten by Raymond. I heard it. James' screams. Him begging. And then the silence. The other neighbours heard it. It was hard not to. But in those days . . .' she faltered. 'Well, parenting was different back then. And it wasn't your place to get involved. But the amount of times I wished I had reported it. Don't get me wrong. I was a stickler for corporeal punishment in my day. But this was different. Raymond nearly killed the boy. Broke his arm and two ribs as well as dislocating his shoulder. The child was unrecognisable when his father had finished with him.'

Brady couldn't hide his surprise at this news. 'And this wasn't reported to the authorities?'

'No. He was admitted to hospital with the story that he had been climbing a tree in the back garden and had fallen. But maybe Raymond knew what his son was capable of? Maybe that was why his punishment was so . . . so extreme.' She could see the disbelief in his eyes. 'As I said, Detective, it was different back then.'

Brady resisted the urge to reply that it wasn't that different now. He had dealt with child abuse cases. Arrested parents, step-parents, boyfriends. The evidence typically horrific. It still continued, regardless of the scathing media and press coverage. People knew it was wrong. But it was not enough to deter them from such cruel abuse. Drugs, alcohol and poverty had led to what seemed to be a rise in child abuse. Factors often overshadowed by the brutal consequences.

His mind went back to a case years ago. He had been a young copper then. But the extreme physical abuse that he had witnessed on the eight-year-old's murdered body had been an all-too-familiar sight. He was the only officer who had not been visibly traumatised at the scene. The numbness he had felt at the time had shocked him. Shocked his colleagues. However, his own father – then spending time in Durham gaol for murder – had attempted to kill him as a child. Many times. His drunken rages had suddenly ended one night when his mother had intervened. She had saved him and his brother, Nick. But she had paid for it with her life.

But he had been saved. Unlike the eight-year-old boy he had found. Too late. Again, too late.

Shame and guilt consumed him, but Brady made himself focus on the present. On Barbara Houghton and whatever information she still had to divulge. The past needed to remain where it was – buried.

'Are you alright, Detective?' enquired Barbara, her sharp eyes missing nothing.

'Tired. That's all,' Brady reassured her. 'You were about to tell me the reason James was sent back to St George's?'

'Yes I was. Well, the tortoise was just the beginning. When he came out of hospital he seemed more determined. Focused even. Cats would go missing from the neighbourhood. Owners would put up "*Lost*" posters. But to no avail. My Persian cat disappeared. Missing for three days. Then I heard her cries coming from the shed at the bottom of the Macintosh's garden. I presumed she had accidentally been locked in. I knocked at the house and James answered the door. His parents were out. He refused to let me in but said he would check the shed for me. A few minutes later, he returned with my cat wrapped up in a towel. Her body was still warm.' She stopped for a moment. Took a sip of her drink, then another, before continuing. 'She had been grotesquely tortured. Patches of her skin had been removed. Not accidental. Cut by a knife. Her ears were both missing and all four paws had been removed. Brutal, it was. And cruel.'

Brady looked at her. 'I'm sorry.' He genuinely meant it. He could see the pain in her eyes.

'Oh I'm fine now,' she said, batting him off. Her voice was level but her distressed eyes contradicted her calm tone. 'I just wished I had acted upon it. I . . . knew he had tortured her. Killed her. But I was worried about what Raymond would do to him. He nearly killed the boy when he had thrown his tortoise onto the bonfire. Can you imagine what he would have done to the child if he had known James had killed my cat? Anyway, James had said he had found her in this condition when he opened the shed. Suggested rather lamely that the cat must have been attacked by a fox or something.'

Brady waited. It was pointless explaining to her that this was very typical behaviour for someone like James David Macintosh.

'I kept my distance then. Had nothing to do with the boy. Until a few years later. His mother was out. His father had not long since died. He was eleven then. I saw him playing with a five-year-old girl in his back garden. I didn't recognise her as one of the neighbourhood children but I didn't think any more about it. An hour or so passed before I realised I hadn't seen or heard them for a while. So I stopped weeding and looked over the garden fence and saw that the shed door was open. I could hear him talking in there. To her. But I didn't hear the little girl. And that's when I started to worry.

'I shouted out to James. Asked him what they were doing. He didn't reply. That's when I knew something was wrong. I went round to the front of the house and tried the door. It was unlocked. In those days that was usual, unlike now. So I walked through to the back garden. And that's when I found him. Them. In the shed. He had . . .' she shook her head at the thought. Her hands gripped the tumbler. 'He had his hands around her neck and he was choking her with such fury. Such hatred. Such . . . such pleasure.'

He thought immediately of Ellen Jackson. But that time there had been no one around to stop him strangling her to death.

'What colour was her hair?' Brady suddenly asked.

Barbara Houghton looked surprised by the question. 'Blond. Why?'

'I was just curious,' Brady lied. He could see in Barbara's eyes that she knew he was lying. But she didn't challenge him. His mind went back to the photographs of the blond-haired Lucy Macintosh that he had found at Mill Cottage. Then to the victim murdered in 1977 and to Annabel Edwards. 'What else had he done to her?'

'He had taken her clothes off and had made her lie down. When I walked in he was straddled over her body. His hands lifting her head. His face so close to hers. As if he was trying to breathe in her last breath.' She shook her head, disturbed. 'God only knows what would have happened if I hadn't walked in when I did.'

'What did you do?' Brady asked.

'I screamed at him to stop.'

'Why weren't the police called?'

Barbara sighed as she looked at him. The horror in her eye gone. Replaced by a defeated acceptance. And a profound sadness.

'I hate to think of what he's doing to that poor Edwards girl. It turns my blood cold. You see, I've looked in his eyes. There is nothing there. Nothing.' She took a drink. Her hands trembling as she did so. After a couple of meditative mouthfuls she looked back at Brady. 'Eileen Macintosh begged me not to say anything. That she would deal with it. With him. From what I understood she paid the girl's mother off. Silenced her with money and the assurance that James would be removed. That he wasn't well and needed medical help. The girl's mother, a cleaner for someone in the street I think, agreed.'

Brady frowned at this.

'Eileen Macintosh could be very persuasive. And she remained true to her word. James left that evening. And I didn't see him again until he was fifteen.'

'And what was he like when he returned?'

Barbara smiled. 'Complete transformation. I don't know what sort of treatment he received inside St George's that time, but it worked. He was polite and even . . . well, *charming*. It was as if he was a different person. He had even changed physically. He returned an attractive young man. Tall, athletic. So when he was arrested and charged with killing his psychiatrist and his family I could not have been more shocked.'

Brady sat back for a moment and contemplated what he had just been told. He wanted to check out St George's to see whether they still had Macintosh's medical records. If they did, then they might mention Lucy Macintosh. He knew it was a long shot but it was worth it if it helped him get a better understanding of Macintosh's mind.

'Thank you, Mrs Houghton. You have been a considerable help.' Brady stood up.

Barbara followed suit. 'I hope so. I wasn't able to sleep last night knowing he has that poor child. I knew I had no choice but to talk to you. I . . . I still feel guilty for not phoning the police when I found him with the cleaner's little girl.'

Brady gave tried to reassure her. 'It wouldn't have made any difference. I promise. James David Macintosh would have gone on to kill regardless. He's just hard-wired that way.' But he could see that she wasn't buying it. 'What happened to Eileen Macintosh when he went to prison?' Brady added as an after-thought.

'She left. Had no choice really. The press were camped outside her door hounding her. But that wasn't what made her leave. Nor was it the hate mail and phone calls she started receiving. No. It was the fact that the neighbourhood had ostracised her. No one looked her in the eye. Or talked to her. She was even getting dog faeces pushed through her letter box. Then the bridge club she belonged to turned their back on her. So she left.'

Brady couldn't imagine how difficult it must have been to be related to such a high-profile murderer like James David Macintosh. 'Where did she go?'

Barbara shook her head. 'She moved as far away as possible. To the other side of the world. Sydney, Australia, I think. She wanted to start over. Not that I could blame her.'

Nor could Brady. He just hoped he would be able to track her down in time. He needed to understand why Macintosh had abducted Annabel Edwards. Before it was too late.

'Conrad?' Brady asked as soon as the call was answered. Again, he was sat in his car, down by Jesmond Dene Bridge. A five-minute walk from Barbara Houghton's house. It was dark now. The orange glow of the street lights along the bridge did nothing to disperse the disquiet he felt. Below, the Dene was blanketed in darkness. He looked to his right and sought solace from the burning lights emanating from Dene House, a nineteenth-century mansion now converted into a luxury hotel. Brady fought the compulsion to go in. Have a few drinks and forget everything. That wasn't an option.

'Sir?'

There was no mistaking it. Conrad's voice sounded strained. It was clear that he still felt uncomfortable about disclosing Brady's personal life to Gates despite the circumstances.

'I need you to do something for me.'

'I'm under strict orders from DCI Gates to get this information he's requested back to him ASAP. He's got us all running around here.'

Brady needed this information. 'It's to do with Macintosh.' He heard Conrad sigh. Then silence. Awkward silence.

'It's just that Gates has threatened me that if I don't get this back to him—'

'I don't give a shit what Gates has threatened you with or what the hell he even thinks right now. I will square it with him. All right? All I'm bothered about is finding some psychotic serial killer who has the life of a three-year-old literally in his hands. This isn't a bloody game. Nor is it about keeping your promotion options sweet. This is someone's life. A child's life. For fuck's sake, Conrad. Gates and those wankers from the Met are so busy chasing their own tails that they don't see that Macintosh is playing them. He's not in London. He's bloody well here in the North East!' Brady breathed out, realising that getting angry with Conrad wasn't the answer. He was angry at himself for not realising that by releasing Macintosh from custody, he was setting him free to kill. Again. And again. He knew he should apologise to Conrad for his unfair outburst but couldn't bring himself to swallow down the anger still lodged at the back of his throat.

'Amelia mentioned something,' Conrad began.

Brady reined in his reaction. Lucy Macintosh's name – existence – wasn't '*something*'. But pissing off Conrad wouldn't be a wise move, considering that he was the only person involved in Annabel Edwards' abduction prepared to talk to him right now. 'Lucy Macintosh. Born around 1960 in the Northumberland area,' Brady added for clarification. His voice was strained, but non-combative.

'I'll see what I can do.'

'I appreciate that. One more thing,' Brady began knowing that he was pushing it. 'Eileen Macintosh—'

Conrad cut him off. 'We've already run checks on her, sir. Nothing. She just disappeared. And there has been no communication between her and James Macintosh from 1977 after he was arrested and charged.'

Brady steadied himself. Conrad was being atypically belligerent. He didn't like going against orders. And right now, it was Gates' orders he was following.

'I talked to Barbara Houghton, the Macintosh's neighbour. She said that Eileen Macintosh left the UK for Australia soon after Macintosh was imprisoned. If she's still alive, we need to talk to her.'

'Why? If she's relocated, why involve her? Maybe she doesn't want to be found?' Conrad asked.

'Trust me here. I just need you to check up on her before Macintosh does.'

'Where are you?'

Brady paused before answering. 'I'm on my way to St George's Psychiatric Hospital in Morpeth.'

'Sir . . .'

Brady could hear the unease in Conrad's voice. He realised that Conrad must have immediately assumed that he was trying to track down Claudia. He still had no idea which psychiatric hospital she gone to or when, she would be released. 'Barbara Houghton said that when James Macintosh was a child he spent some time in St George's. He attacked a five-year-old girl when he was eleven and his mother had him placed there. For four years. But he was also there for at least six months when he was six years old, directly after the family left Mill Cottage. I want to see if any of Macintosh's psychiatric records still exist in case there is a correlation between Lucy Macintosh and Annabel Edwards.'

'I see,' answered Conrad, the relief in his voice palpable that this was not some hunt for Claudia.

'So, will you run those checks for me?' Brady asked.

'Yes, sir. But . . .' Conrad faltered.

Brady didn't bother asking what he was about to say. He had the answer he wanted. 'Thanks, Harry. I owe you.'

Conrad didn't reply.

Brady listened to the dull tone. Conrad had hung up. He breathed out. Relieved. He knew Conrad would run those checks for him. Had his word. It was enough.

Brady knew he should have gone home. He didn't know what he had expected to find. But definitely more than what he did. Which was nothing. He had shown up at St George's Psychiatric Hospital. It was an unorthodox visit on a Saturday evening. He had called the reception in advance and used his police status to get in. But they had no patient records in the new building dating from before 1995 – the year the original St George's Hospital had been closed down.

Brady walked over to his car, his eyes automatically drawn to the monolithic, sprawling building that had once been the original hospital. It remained standing – just. It had been sold off. The site a valuable commodity. The old buildings – for the original hospital had been added to over the years – now a liability, with a history no doubt including barbaric and questionable practices that the new owners would rather remain buried. Mesmerised, he walked over to the main building of the old hospital. It had an ominous feel about it. The windows and doors had been sealed off years ago. An added measure against public curiosity. The extensive land, which backed onto fields and woodland, now guarded by fences. Blackness engulfed the surrounding grounds and the access routes between the various Victorian buildings. Brady noted the gaps in the fences along the perimeter where they joined hedges, realised it would be all too easy to climb in and have a look around.

Brady mulled over what the receptionist had told him about the old Victorian building. Opened in 1859, it had originally been known as the Northumberland County Pauper Lunatic Asylum. Later renamed the County Mental Hospital and finally in 1937, St George's Hospital. It had housed men, women and children. He found it hard to even contemplate a six-year-old child being placed in such a place. He had heard enough accounts of psychiatric hospitals to make him feel uneasy about it. The treatment of mentally ill patients had been barbaric and cruel. He couldn't imagine what a child would have suffered in such arbitrary conditions.

What could you have possibly done at the age of six for your parents to have left you here, Macintosh?

Brady shuddered. He put it down to the cold March air. He was about to call it a night when he thought back to what the receptionist had suggested; that some outdated patient files might still be stored in the basement in the main building of the old hospital. She knew that most of them had been destroyed. But some of them remained. The receptionist had stressed that he needed to check with the security office, once Rose Cottage, located opposite the main entrance to the old hospital.

Brady looked over at the security office. The small cottage was brightly lit. Twenty-four-hour security was in place to prevent trespassers from entering the grounds. Numerous signs had been erected warning that the old hospital buildings and grounds were unsafe. Not that people took heed, Brady included. He played with the idea of breaking in and thought better of it. Gates came to mind. His boss definitely wouldn't be impressed if he got caught breaking and entering. Brady turned and headed for Rose Cottage. He knew it was the right decision to clear his entry with whoever was on duty. He had no choice but to check out the old hospital, just in case Macintosh's medical records were still there.

Brady had an inexplicable feeling that he was going to find something. And with that knowledge came a sense of dread and foreboding. Part of him wanted to just run. To forget about Macintosh and what might – or might not – have happened during his childhood. But he knew he had no choice. He had come this far. He might as well see it through to the end. Regardless of the outcome.

Chapter Ten

Saturday: 7:09 p.m.

Emily opened her eyes. Blinking, she tried to adjust to the glare of the light bulb directly above her. Her eyes felt heavy and the desire to drift back to sleep compelling. But it was her aching body that had nagged her awake. And the cold. She was so, so cold.

Shit! I can't move . . . I can't move my head!

It was then that it hit her. *No! God no!*

She remembered the thick leather restraints that had held the other girl. Adrenalin coursed through her at the thought of what had happened. She listened. Hard. Straining to hear the laboured, punctuated breathing. Nothing. She had disappeared. It was now her who was shackled to an old, battered psychiatric chair.

She had no idea how long she had been like this. Nor did she have any memory of being placed in the chair. She knew he had to be drugging her.

Otherwise, why couldn't she remember?

The inexplicable tiredness that overwhelmed her, saturating through to her bones, said it all. Every particle of her body felt heavy and weighted down.

Oh God ... what am I going to do?

She needed to fight the tiredness. She needed to stay awake so she could figure out how to get out. She chewed her dry, cracked lips as she tried to swallow down the panic.

Think ... come on, think ...

She was certain he would be back soon to drug her again. She had to be smart and outwit him if she was going to survive this. She had no choice.

It was then that her eyes registered what was on the wall in front of her.

Fucking hell!

It was covered in Polaroids of women. All young with long dark hair and brown eyes. Each one had the same blank, lifeless expression. She searched from one photo to the next, to the next. All of them had been strapped to this chair when photographed.

They looked like they were already dead when he had photographed them. As if they had been poised with their lifeless eyes open, staring blankly straight ahead.

She shuddered at the thought.

It was what he had done to them before he had photographed them that horrified her. The blood dripping down their necks from ... from ...

She couldn't let herself go there. If she did, then she might lose her mind. And she needed to be strong if she was going to get out of here alive.

She flinched at a sudden noise above her. Then she recognised the ominous dragging of a door being pulled open.

A knot of fear unfurled in her stomach. She clenched her body, balling her hands into fists. Her eyes stared at the wall. She didn't want to end up like them.

God, no . . . please, no . . .

Then she heard footsteps. He was coming down the stone steps. Slowly. Deliberately. She couldn't see him. She couldn't turn around. She was strategically positioned so she faced the wall covered in photos of *his* victims. She felt like some freak exhibit sat there, waiting. Waiting *for him.*

Gripped with terror, she listened to his footsteps as they closed in. Then, she felt him standing behind her. Followed by a burning prick in her neck. He held it there, the sharp tip threatening to pierce her skin. *Teasing, threatening, terrifying.*

'No . . . please . . . I don't want to be drugged—'

His hand covered her mouth and nose, preventing her from breathing. 'No talking.'

She tried to object.

He pressed the needle harder against her flesh. 'Understand?'

She didn't answer. Didn't struggle.

'Good girl.' He took his hand away from her face. 'Now, you need to do *exactly* as I say. Exactly.'

She felt sick when she heard those words.

Tears began to flow down her cheeks as she looked at the other victims' faces. She closed her eyes against them. Against the prospect of what could become of her.

I don't want to be drugged again. I don't want to fall asleep . . . What if I wake up like them?

'Shhh . . .' He caressed her hair.

His touch was surprisingly gentle. She recoiled in disgust. 'Don't fucking touch me!' she hissed through bared teeth.

She felt the cold air first, followed by the stinging burn of his hand as it hit her face.

A deafening ringing filled her ears as blood began pooling at the back of her throat. Her cheek stung as if acid had been thrown at her face. Her tongue tentatively touched the inside of her throbbing mouth. The impact had knocked her teeth into her cheek, gouging out a chunk of flesh.

Shit! That hurts . . . you fucking crazy bastard!

Her bottom lip was throbbing. She could feel blood ebbing down her chin and realised it must have split open.

He came into her vision.

She winced, expecting him to hit her again.

The blow she was expecting didn't come. She opened her eyes to see him knelt down in front of her, staring at her. Or to be exact, studying her face.

'Why am I here?' she mumbled. Her words felt awkward. Her mouth thick and swollen. But her eyes were defiant.

He studied her. Disappointment flashed across his face, quickly replaced by irritation.

She stared belligerently at him, taking in every detail of his features. She needed to memorise it so when she did escape she could identify him.

It's him . . .

She couldn't bring herself to admit it.

'I need you to eat for me,' he said as he reached on the ground for something. His voice lacked any compassion or empathy. It was simply a fact. Without food she would die.

She couldn't see what it was that he was picking up, but realised it had to be a tin of something when she heard the click as the ring pull released and he opened it.

He moved a spoon of congealed brown lumps towards her mouth. She closed her lips tight. She felt nauseous at the thought of eating. She had no idea what he was trying to feed her, and her mouth and lip throbbed where he had hit her.

'Eat!' he ordered.

She refused, keeping her mouth firmly shut against the spoon that he was forcing between her sealed lips.

He pinched her nose between his thumb and forefinger and waited. His piercing blue eyes intent on making her comply.

I can't breathe . . . Shit! I can't breathe . . .

She lasted less than a minute before she gasped for air. Before she could react the spoon was rammed into her mouth. She spluttered and coughed as she gagged on whatever suspect meat was hidden in the cold, congealed gravy.

She looked at him, her eyes filled with hatred.

He smiled in return.

With as much strength as she could muster she spat the mouthful of food in his face. 'Fuck you!'

He didn't react. Didn't flinch, even. Instead he reached on the floor for a hand towel. He wiped his face. Slowly, deliberately, ensuring that every trace was gone.

'Let's see how long you last in the dark without food or water. Because I can guarantee that you will be begging for me to come back. But right now . . .' He faltered as he looked at her, eyes filled with disgust. 'I'm not so certain that you're worth the wait.' He turned his back to her.

The knot of fear tightened in her stomach. Whatever bravery and defiance she had had was now gone. His words had hit her. Hard. 'What are you planning to do?' she asked, unable to disguise the terror she felt.

He turned and looked at her. The smile gone. 'I am going to make you better.'

'No! You can't touch me. Please don't . . . They'll be looking for me. My family and friends will have already reported me missing. The police . . . the police will be searching for me.' Tears slipped down her face as she stared at him, willing him to believe her. But she knew from his eyes that he saw it for what it was; an empty, pathetic attempt at saving herself.

He reached into his pocket and took out a full syringe.

'Midazolam hydrochloride. So you don't feel anything,' he explained.

'No . . . Please no . . . You know me. My name is Emily . . . Emily Baker. Remember? You must remember me?' Tears fell, hot and salty down her pale cheeks as she tried to persuade him not to inject her.

'Shhh . . . Who you were is not important anymore. The past is irrelevant. It is what I am going to do for you that matters now. Think of me as doing you and society a favour. I rid you of the disease that riddles your body and mind and at the same time, I rid society of the scum that plagues the streets,' he said. 'You see, I'm a philanthropist of sorts. My calling is to cleanse society by taking your body and ridding it of the sickness that contaminates it. Then,' he smiled benevolently at her, 'I will immortalise you.'

'But . . . but I . . . I have a family. They'll be worried. Please . . .' she pleaded.

He paused for a moment, disappointed. 'I know all about your background. I've read your records. So don't lie to me.' The smile returned. 'You see? You need me to protect you from yourself.'

'NO!' she yelled and felt an intense burning as he stabbed the needle into her neck.

She knew it wouldn't take long before she lost consciousness. And there was one question that had been troubling her . . . *What had happened to the other girl? Where had he put her?*

'The other girl . . .' But before she could finish the sentence she could feel herself drifting, her mind starting to get hazier and hazier as the drug coursed through her veins.

'She's where she belongs . . . with the others. You see, I released the demons from her head. I set her free,' he replied smiling benevolently as her heavy eyelids finally acquiesced.

He caressed her hair. His touch delicate. His fingers lingering. 'Shhh . . . Emily. There . . . Doesn't that feel better? Soon all those tormented thoughts and evil desires will be gone. Replaced by . . .'

When Emily came to she was surrounded by blackness. She tried to move but couldn't. She was still shackled to the old psychiatric chair. She had no idea what had happened to her. All she knew was that her body hurt. But the memory of what he had done to her was non-existent. He had drugged her. And then he had . . . She had no idea what he had done. She bit down hard on her lip to prevent herself from crying. She didn't want to give him that. Not when he had everything else. She tried to at least move her head. But she couldn't.

Then she heard a noise. Faint. But it was there. She held her breath so she could hear. And it was coming from above her. It sounded like footsteps. And someone talking. A man's voice. But not *his* voice. She was certain it was someone else. Adrenalin coursed through her. Maybe this was her chance to get out? Had someone found her?

'HELP!' But she didn't recognise the sound that came out. The word was lost. Slurred. Not her own. She tried again. 'HELP!' But it made no difference. It didn't sound like her voice. Whatever drug had been used on her was still in her body.

She waited, silent. Desperate to hear the sound again. It was gone. Replaced by what sounded like fingernails furiously scratching against metal. It was then followed by a thumping sound. A loud, ominous banging which reverberated around the damp stone walls. It was in that moment that the panic took hold. She recognised the sound. It was familiar. The first time she had woken up down here she had heard what sounded like fingernails being dragged across metal. Then it had suddenly stopped. She hadn't heard the noise again until now. She squeezed her eyes tightly shut as she tried to block out the frenzied scratching, intermittently broken by a dull, foreboding thud. Whoever or whatever it was sounded desperate. Frantic.

Chapter Eleven

Saturday: 8:40 p.m.

Brady was freezing. He had been hanging around waiting for Dave the security guard to get his shit together. There was a reason he was a security guard and not a copper.

'You ready, mate?'

Brady looked up at him. He was six foot four. In his mid-thirties. Overweight, with a flabby stomach that hung over his too-tight trousers. His sandy-coloured hair cropped short. His shapeless face, bloated. Brady wouldn't be surprised if he had a drink habit. Then again, working the graveyard shift in a place like this would drive even the most hardened temperance followers to drink.

Weary, Brady nodded at him. He'd been stood around freezing his bollocks off for nearly an hour.

'Yeah, sorry about that. Have to do my job. Sure you understand, being in the police an all?' he said as he switched his flashlight on. 'Laser torch, this. Bought it from the States. Cost a hundred and eighty quid.'

Brady nodded. Again. He wasn't much in the mood for talking. He just wanted to get the job done and get back to his car. Put the heating on full blast. Turn the stereo up and reverse as hard as he could out the car park and off these godforsaken grounds. It was starting to get to him now: the tiredness, the cold and the feeling he was being watched. It had been with him since Mill Cottage. A disquieting sense that someone was following him – stalking him.

'Do you want me to give you an unofficial tour?' the guard asked.

'Yeah,' Brady replied.

'What are you looking for then?'

'Medical records dating back to the sixties.'

'Shit!' Dave muttered as he fumbled with the keys for the main entrance. 'Hold that, will you?'

Brady took the torch and shone it on the lock.

'Thanks, mate. This one's always been a bugger!'

He opened up the heavy door, then gestured for his torch back.

Brady looked down the cavernous hallway as Dave illuminated it with his American laser flashlight. Dilapidated didn't even come close. Chunks of plaster had fallen down from the ceiling and the crumbling walls. The floor was covered in all kinds of debris. Brady looked over at the old sixties-style reception area. Apart from a few broken chairs and the main reception desk there was nothing else there. Graffiti covered the desk and the walls behind it.

'Trouble with kids then?' Brady stated as he walked down the corridor taking in the scrawled writing that covered most of the rooms that lead off from the main hallway.

'Yeah. Little shits! They make my job hell. What they don't realise is that if one of them stupid buggers gets hurt, then it's me who gets it in the neck. Could lose my bloody job!'

Brady sympathised. He could see how difficult it would be to keep kids out. If they really wanted in, they would find a way somehow.

'Can't afford to lose my job. Not that anyone can nowadays. Came back eighteen months ago from a tour in Afghanistan to find the missus with her bags packed. She'd met someone online. Stupid fucking cow! In Turkey. Some young kid of twenty-two. So she upped and left. That's where she is now. Living in some squalid apartment with him. Not quite the life she expected. But I won't have her back. She deserves everything she gets.'

Brady glanced at him. Realised he had misjudged the bloke. But then again, he had been waiting around freezing his bollocks off for an hour. 'You got kids then?'

'Yeah. Two. Boy and girl. Benjamin's six and Olivia's four. Only fucking two when that mother of hers just upped and left her. Tell me, what kind of mother does that? Eh?'

Brady shrugged.

'So . . . I ended up taking this shitty job just to keep a roof over my kids' heads. Couldn't stay in the army, could I?' his voice filled with bitterness and regret.

'Life sucks,' Brady commiserated.

'Sure fucking does!' agreed Dave. 'If it wasn't for my mam, I don't know what I would have done. She moved in with me. Needed someone at night to look after the bairns, you know? She's more of a mam to them now than their own fucking mam.'

They walked along in silence. Brady could feel him brooding as he flicked the torch across the floor and walls. Checking out the abandoned rooms as he did so. He realised the job suited Dave. Not that the ex-soldier would admit it. But there was no need to talk to anyone. He could just keep his head down and ruminate over why his wife had left him and his kids for a twenty-two-year old Turk, and how that could have possibly happened when he was stationed out in Afghanistan risking his life for family and country.

Brady thought to himself: *Yeah . . . life fucking sucks!*

They reached the end of the corridor. It was like a maze. The corridor split off three-ways. Then there were stairs further down to the left.

'What was this building used for?'

Dave turned and looked at him. 'Mainly kids. Hard to believe really. The west wing was used for the women. Best building of the lot if you ask me. It looks out onto bluebell woods. Beautiful in the summer. East wing was for the male patients. And this one, the kids. The main staff accommodation was located here. Must have made sense considering the patients were children.'

'Where are the rooms they were kept in?' Brady asked, curious. He wanted to see where a child such as Macintosh would have been held.

'Upstairs. First floor. The second floor and the attic rooms were used by the staff.' He turned and looked at Brady. 'Why? Do you want to have a look?'

'If you don't mind?'

'It's all the same to me.'

'How do you know all this stuff about when the hospital was actually in operation?'

Dave shrugged. 'Came across some old plans of the main building, that's all. And I've walked these halls and checked these rooms God knows how many times. Reckon I could do it blindfolded by now.'

Brady followed him up the stairs to the first floor. When he reached it, he wished he hadn't asked. The hallway had an uneasy feel to it. Bleak metal doors lined the walls. Harsh. Unforgiving.

He pushed open one of the doors. It groaned, resisting the movement. He walked inside. Dave followed, moving the light around the small six foot by eight foot room. A small metal bed still remained against the wall. What jarred were the thick, unyielding leather restraints attached to the top and bottom of the bedframe. He turned to the small window. Metal bars obscured whatever view there would have been. It was a prison cell – literally. Or a torture room.

Brady looked around and tried to imagine what it would feel like to be a child left, locked, even restrained inside this room. No parents to love him. Just staff. Underpaid. Overworked. Over-zealous in their admonitions.

He shook his head, unable to comprehend what that would have felt like. To have been left at the mercy of others. Your life – *your body* – in their hands. Mental illness, until recently, was a medical condition that had been demonised. Initially by the church, then the state.

Misunderstood and misrepresented. He thought of Claudia; of the radical difference between her private psychiatric care and the brutal practices that would have been the norm when this building had first opened. And then for the decades that followed.

Techniques such as straitjackets, solitary confinement and sedation such as bromides were used upon patients deemed unruly. By the seventies and eighties many mental hospitals had closed down – St George's no exception – as political questions began to be raised of these large, unaccountable institutions.

'Had enough?' queried the security guard.

'Yeah,' Brady answered, his eyes lingering on the leather buckled restraints on either end of the bed.

'Good! Gives me the willies up here. Don't mind the adult patient floors as much as this one. Crazy to think they used to treat kids like that, right?'

Brady nodded.

'Bet they did weird shit to them as well. If you get my drift?' Dave said, walking out the room.

Brady followed. *He got his drift, all right.* It was hard not to notice the scratches dug into the walls and on the inside of the metal door. He shuddered at the thought of the desperation the occupants of this room would have felt. Never knowing when, *or if*, they would ever be released.

The basement was dank, cavernous and filled with obsolete items dating back over a hundred and fifty years. Old psychiatric chairs had been left down here to rot.

Bedpans. Countless decades of paraphernalia, stored or dumped.

For what purpose?

'This place gives me the willies as well. Never come down here out of choice,' admitted Dave. He ran a large, calloused hand over his scalp's coarse stubble. Beads of sweat were starting to run down his forehead.

Brady shot him a questioning glance.

'Shit, man! Like I said, it gives me the creeps. A couple of times I would hear this banging coming from down here. Would echo throughout the whole bloody building. Seemed as if it were travelling up through the chimney breasts right up to the attic.'

Brady smiled at him. 'Sure it's not just your imagination?'

Dave's easygoing attitude quickly changed. 'I've seen some real nasty fucking shit in my time. I reckon I know whether it's my imagination or not!'

'Yeah . . . I'm sure you have,' Brady conceded. As way of an apology he added: 'Maybe it's rats or something down here?'

'Could be . . .' Dave accepted.

But Brady could see it in the security guard's eyes. A flicker of unease. Something down here really scared the shit out of him.

'I checked it out of course,' he added. 'Came down here. But there was nothing. Then as soon as you walk back up to the ground floor it starts again. This deep, banging noise. Last time I heard it was about a year ago. Went on for a couple of nights. Like I said, it's weird shit.'

'This won't take long,' Brady reassured him. 'Just need to have a look through some patient files stored down here.'

'You don't mind if go outside and have a tab then?' Dave asked, offering Brady his spare torch.

Brady noticed the big man's hand trembling as he handed it over.

'Sure,' he answered, inwardly surprised at the ex-soldier's reaction to the room. Not that the disquieting feel about the place didn't get to Brady. But he had a job to do.

He busied himself looking through the stacks of files that had been dumped on the floor. Old wooden and metal filing cabinets stood, obsolete. There were countless patient records left down here waiting to be destroyed. He leafed through a large stack on the floor trying to make sense of their order – there wasn't one. Different patients' names, male and female, assaulted his mind. He skipped past the scrawled and typed doctors' and nurses' notes detailing patients, disorders, medications and diagnoses.

He soon realised the likelihood of finding James David Macintosh's records was next to impossible.

He stood up. Stretched his arms out and yawned. His body ached. His head ached.

He felt as if every part of him was protesting from lack of sleep. He checked his watch. He had been rooting around down here for over thirty minutes by torchlight alone. He accepted it would take days to go through this lot. Better to go home and get some rest and then re-evaluate in the morning.

Where the hell has the security guard gone? Brady was about to yell up the stairs for him when he heard it. The banging. A low resonating sound that echoed off the thick walls. He could feel the hairs on the back of his neck prick up. He didn't move, he listened. Again, the sound came.

Bang . . . bang . . . bang . . .

As if something – or *someone* – was down here. *With him.*

Then it hit him: *The security guard was trying to fuck with his mind.*

He was about to shout *fuck off* when the banging intensified. Fear gripped him. He took out his mobile in case he needed to call for backup. But there was no signal. He held his breath as he tried to gauge where the persistent banging was coming from. Flashed the torchlight around the large, dark basement. Then he understood. Saw it. At the other end of the basement. Obscured by the impenetrable blackness. The noise stopped, as suddenly as it had started.

Fuck . . .

Brady held the torch as steady as was physically possible. He stared at the brick monstrosity that had revealed itself to be an industrial-sized furnace. It was a large, Victorian structure that jutted out fourteen foot from the wall. It was twelve foot wide and ran up the entire height of the basement. It was an unsightly construction, built for practicality rather than aesthetics. Even the twin cast-iron doors looked ugly, staring at him with unblinking predatory eyes.

The banging began. Again.

He forced himself to walk over to the disused furnace. To face whatever it was responsible for that unnerving noise. His only fear; the unimaginable cruelty inflicted by people like James David Macintosh upon others. In that moment he dreaded opening the doors. His mind was racing. Questions and answers tumbling over one another.

What if it is Annabel Edwards? What if Macintosh had left her here? But how? How could that be possible?

Brady knew that in the mind of a psychopath, anything was possible.

He steeled himself. Didn't think to call for help. To order the security guard back down to the basement. Instead, Brady placed the torch at an angle on the ground so he could open the left door of the furnace. The banging was coming from behind it.

He struggled for a moment before managing to yank it open. It took a moment to register. Then he saw her. Kneeling there. Covered in dried blood. Hair filthy. Her eyes. Black. Staring. In shock. Then terror. She started to scream. A bloodcurdling, terrifying wail that sounded like nothing that he had ever heard before. He instinctively recoiled. Stepping away from it – *her*. From *them* . . .

Oh Christ! What has happened to her? What the fuck has someone done . . .

He quickly took his coat off. Wrapped it gently around her weak, bony body.

Oh God . . . how could someone do this?

He couldn't think about it. He reached in and scooped her out of the furnace. There was no weight to her. She was nothing more than a skeleton covered in taut, unnaturally pale bare skin. He held her to him. Her body pressed against his chest. Her head, bloodied, limp, cradled. She was suffering from hypothermia. He needed to get her warm. Adrenalin was coursing through his veins. 'DAVE!' he yelled as loud as he could. He couldn't get a bloody signal down here. He needed to call this in ASAP. She needed medical attention.

Fuck, did she need medical attention.

'You're going to be all right. You understand me? You're safe now,' Brady reassured her. His voice was low, gentle; as if he were talking to a child. 'You got a name? Huh?' he continued, desperate for her to respond. To acknowledge him. The screaming had stopped. But this was worse. Now she had gone deathly quiet. Her body slack and lifeless. He knew she was still breathing. He could feel the shallow lightness of her breath against his neck. 'I'm Jack. I'm with the police,' he assured her. But he wasn't sure she fully understood.

Oh God! What has he done to her?

He couldn't get the thought out of his mind. He had never encountered anything like this. In fact he had never even heard of such a horrific crime carried out on a victim.

'DAVE!' he yelled, even louder this time.

No response.

He started walking to the stairs. He had to get her out of here. She was in dire need of immediate medical attention.

'Not long now. We'll soon have you warm. OK?' Brady soothed her as he carried her as carefully as he could up the stairs. Her body was so fragile, he was terrified that she would break.

'What's wrong?' called out Dave, laughing. 'Heard that banging, did you? Hah! You sounded scared shitless back there! Ain't no rats down there making that kind of noise, I can tell you!'

Brady walked out.

'What the fuck!' Dave spluttered as he choked on cigarette smoke.

'Call an ambulance and the police. NOW!' Brady ordered. He started to make his way over to the newly built psychiatric hospital located on the sprawling grounds directly opposite the old Victorian asylum. The new build looked more akin to a contemporary motel.

'Where are you going?' Dave asked, fumbling for his phone in his heavily padded jacket.

'Where the fuck do you think I'm going? She's suffering from hypothermia!' Brady replied, his voice caustic. Not that he cared. At this precise moment he didn't give a damn about anything other than this girl's life. Which was literally, in his hands.

He heard the security guard make a frantic 999 call. His words rushed, garbled.

He then ran up behind Brady. 'They'll be here soon,' he panted. 'Shit! I'm sorry. I didn't realise. Got caught up on the phone to my mam while you were down there. Olivia's got a temperature. You know how it is . . . with kids,' Dave apologised, rushing his words. Panicking. He was jogging to keep up with Brady. Shining his torch on the ground ahead leading up to the new St George's facility.

But Brady had no idea how it was with kids. And didn't think he ever would. He looked down at her fragile face, the glare of the laser torch lighting it up. It had an eerie hue to it. As if her skin hadn't seen daylight for a long, long time.

He heard the security guard's intake of breath.

Part of her long hair had been cut and then shaved off. What was left of her hair was covered in congealed blood and . . . Brady stopped himself.

'Her head . . . It's covered in blood . . . Is she all right?'

Brady continued walking.

Then the guard saw what Brady had seen when he first lifted her out of the furnace. 'Shit! Someone's drilled a hole in her head!'

Brady didn't bother correcting him. There were two holes. One on either side.

'Fuck! Why? Why would someone do that?' Dave questioned. His voice shocked.

Brady knew she looked bad. Even a hardened ex-soldier who would have seen some unspeakable crimes in Afghanistan was disturbed by what had been inflicted upon her. But at this precise moment, Brady couldn't – *wouldn't* – allow himself to think about what someone had done to this girl. He just couldn't go there.

Brady stood at the crime scene. The site had been sealed off. Police were everywhere. Soon the media would be here. Speculating. Ruminating. He didn't want to be around when they turned up. But he had no choice. He had to wait for the Crime Scene Manager and his forensic team to arrive. The victim had been taken to the Royal Victoria Infirmary in Newcastle. She was in good hands now.

Too late though. Too damned late to prevent what had happened to her.

He shuddered. The cold was getting to him worse than ever. He didn't want to admit to himself that the physical condition of the girl had affected him. Never mind her mental state.

Why would some sick bastard do that to her?

For a short time, all thoughts of Macintosh had evaporated, replaced by something equally as sick and twisted. What were the odds of him finding her? If he hadn't been looking for old medical files on Macintosh he would never have found her. Or the others.

Christ . . . What the fuck had been done to them?

Brady was under no illusion. They had been left here to die. Locked up in a furnace, in the basement of a derelict Victorian mental institution. He imagined they had been left in the same state as she had. Starving to death.

But he does more than that . . .

Brady didn't want to think about it. He couldn't. Not yet.

He had put in a call to Gates. He was waiting for him to return it. He had already passed on a brief update. But he knew that his boss would have some hard questions. Firstly, how could a killer of this magnitude have gone undetected for so long?

Brady was still struggling with the 'what if' scenario. If he hadn't found her then she would have starved to death. And there would have been more of them. For years to come until the killer decided to stop. Or died.

'You OK?' The security guard asked as he approached Brady. He offered him a steaming black coffee. 'Added a shot of scotch. Reckon you needed it.'

'Thanks, Dave,' Brady replied. He could barely manage a weak smile. Exhaustion had kicked in. The adrenalin that had surged through him when he first discovered her had long since dissipated. Grateful, he raised it to his lips and blew on the scalding liquid. The heady aroma of coffee and scotch assaulted his senses.

'Who you waiting for?'

'SOCOs. I need to walk the Crime Scene Manager through what I found. Then I can go home. That's after I've called in at the hospital on the way.'

The security officer raised his eyebrow at this. 'Don't you reckon you should just call it a night? See her in the morning? I mean, don't take this personally, but you look really fucked, man!'

Brady certainly felt fucked, so the fact he looked it didn't come as a surprise. He'd looked a mess first thing this morning when he had showered and changed for Gates' briefing on Macintosh. That seemed like an eternity ago now. So much had happened. He had lost track of events. Everything had blurred. All he could think about was finding her. Locked in that furnace with the others. All sat neatly in a half-circle, positioned to be facing towards the door. Their hair had been brushed.

Smoothed down. Their faces painted. Heavy red lipstick. All very dead.

Brady couldn't rid himself of the image.

He shuddered. At the thought of her. Of what her assailant had taken from her. She was so young. Maybe eighteen, if that. But then, it was difficult to gauge because of the condition of her body.

'Why would someone do that?' Dave looked at Brady, unable to comprehend the horror of what he had witnessed. 'I don't get it. I get war. I understand that things happen that would never happen ordinarily. That it's extenuating circumstances and all that crap. Between you and me, I've seen shit in my time. Shit that I'm not proud to say I witnessed. But I did. I walked away and hoped to God I would never be privy to sick shit like that again. But I left the war behind. This . . .' he gestured around him. 'This is meant to be safe. Civilised. You know?' He shook his head as he looked at Brady. His eyes searching for answers. For reassurance.

Brady had none. He was as much at a loss to explain what he had uncovered tonight to himself, never mind anyone else. So he did all he could. He kept quiet and let the security guard talk.

'I'm just a goddamned security guard, for fuck's sake! Now I'm a suspect in a serial murder investigation.'

Brady didn't comment. Dave was right. He would be high up there on the list of suspects. At this precise moment, he was the only one on the list. Brady knew it wasn't him. But it wasn't his place to give him that reassurance. The security guard would be swabbed, and then interviewed. But he would be released. He was certain of that. Whether he had a job at the end of it, Brady wasn't so certain. After all, this had happened while he had been on watch. It would be for Dave to answer how that had been possible.

'I've got a little girl. You know?' His eyes filled with concern as he stared at Brady. Still looking for something to hold on to. Something to grab hold of, anything to stop him sinking.

'Yeah, you said,' Brady answered, unable to ignore the guilt in Dave's eyes. After all it had been Dave's role as a security guard to watch the abandoned hospital grounds and buildings for any unusual activity. It was evident he had failed. Brady took another drink, wishing this day would end. That he wasn't here right now. He couldn't give what he didn't have. He sorely wanted to tell Dave that everything would be all right. That his job wouldn't be affected. That his daughter would never suffer what they had just seen. That he wouldn't be a suspect in a multiple murder investigation. But he couldn't. It was that brutal. And he wished to God that it wasn't.

'It could have been her in there.'

'It could have been anyone. But it's not. She's at home. Safe. She's got you and your mam looking out for her. And a big brother. She'll grow up fine.'

Dave looked at Brady. Then nodded. Grateful. Accepting what he had been told. It was what he had wanted to hear. That the bogeyman didn't abduct and torture little girls like his daughter. That they targeted and abducted someone else's child. Like the girl in the furnace. And the others who were in there with her.

'Do you think she has a family?'

'No doubt,' answered Brady as he watched the headlights coming up the hill towards them.

'Do you think you'll find them?'

Brady shrugged. 'I don't know.'

'In a way, I hope for their sake that they never find out what has happened to her.'

Brady turned away from the hypnotic glare of the oncoming vehicles and looked at Dave. It was an odd statement. But one he understood. He had seen what the killer had left behind to die.

'I'm not a sick bastard. Or callous. But if that were my little girl, I couldn't cope. I would rather . . . rather that she was dead than have to live everyday looking at what some sick piece of shit had done to her. Had taken from her. You don't think that's wrong of me, do you?' The look in his eye was troubled. 'The others, they're already dead. But her . . .'

Brady swallowed. He didn't want to think about it. Not yet. Not until he had talked to the doctors. Until he had a definitive prognosis. Not until then would he contemplate what life lay ahead for her. Or her family. *If she had any.* For Brady sensed she might not have any. He didn't know why. It could be that no one had reported her missing. Or had they? Was she just another statistic? Another missing teenager believed to have run off to London or Manchester?

He heard dogs barking in the distant woods. Dog handlers had been radioed in. That had been Brady's call.

Her nightgown had been removed by the paramedics and bagged for forensic evidence, with the dogs allowed to pick up whatever scent there could be on her clothes. There was a chance that they would find him. He could be out there for all Brady knew. But he seriously doubted it. The fresh injuries to the victim's skull suggested that she had been dumped within the past twelve hours. He imagined that the suspect would have waited for the cover of darkness before bringing her here. He obviously had a way into the building. One that prevented him from being easily detected. Brady would find it. Or at least, the dogs would. They would track down the route he had taken. His fear was that then they would hit a dead end. That the dogs would track the scent to a vehicle which would be long gone.

'Can I ask you something?'

Brady turned to Dave. He looked pale. Brady wasn't surprised. A collection of women's tortured bodies had been found in a derelict psychiatric hospital that he was supposed to be guarding. It didn't look good. But that wasn't all. Brady knew exactly what the security guard wanted to hear from him. He wanted Brady to cover up for his ineptitude. 'Go on,' he instructed.

'You know that I heard that banging noise. I said I had heard it about three times over a week, a year or so ago. Shit!' He stopped and ran a large, trembling hand over his scalp as he thought over the ramifications of what he had done – or failed to do.

'Yeah. I know.' There was nothing else Brady could say.

'I . . . I just don't want to lose my job. I've got two kids to think of and me mam. Shit! If I lose this then I'll have no choice but to go back over there. To Afghanistan as a private security guard. It's all I know. But . . . I don't want my kids growing up without me. They've already lost their mam.' Dave shook his head. Numb at the prospect of what could happen to him.

'I'm sorry,' Brady said. And he meant it. But he could not pretend that it hadn't happened. It was crucial evidence. The timing alone. For all the security guard knew, he could have unwittingly seen something that could be invaluable to the investigation. Brady was certain that the surviving victim had been locked in the furnace within the past twelve hours. He was also convinced that the perpetrator visited his victims. Repeatedly. To relish in his work. And to add to his collection.

The security guard looked at Brady, understanding that Brady had no intention of letting it go.

Brady stood with Conrad, watching Ainsworth, the Crime Scene Manager, assess the scene that lay in front of him. It was a big job. The vast basement was filled with discarded medical equipment from its years as a psychiatric hospital. There were also countless old wooden cabinets and boxes upon boxes filled with patient files. There was a chance that amongst all this paraphernalia would be forensic evidence tying the killer to the crime scene. The law of averages were weighted in Brady's favour. After all, the unknown offender had brought multiple women to this place. The latest one was evidence that he had recently been here.

'You just found her locked in that old furnace?' Conrad asked, shaking his head at the prospect.

Brady nodded. He didn't feel much like talking. But he was relieved to have Conrad here. He had called his deputy as soon as he had talked to Gates, who had made it quite clear that he needed Brady working this new case – regardless of his personal interest in Macintosh. Gates had offered Brady his old team with some extra officers. Brady was grateful for whoever he was given. The force was already stretched in relation to the massive police hunt for Macintosh. Despite the sickening nature of the victims that Brady had stumbled across in the basement furnace, it was not the same as a missing three-year-old girl. Annabel Edwards' face and her tragic plight had caught the hearts of the nation. Brady had reined in his objection to being transferred to a new case. He had a duty to the young victim he had found. And to the others who had already lost their lives to this unknown killer.

'How many bodies are in there?'

Brady shrugged. 'I don't know. There were too many to count. All I know is that they were all identically dressed with long brown hair and these perfect faces. They were all wearing red lipstick making them look . . . I don't know . . . *life-like* somehow.'

Conrad gave him a surprised look.

'Sounds crazy, I know.'

Conrad stared at him, expecting a better explanation.

Brady shook his head. 'You need to see this for yourself. Believe me.' He looked back over at the furnace.

'Wait until Ainsworth has stopped with his blustering and I'll take you over so you can have a look for yourself. Don't want to get in the way of Ainsworth while he's setting up his office.'

Conrad didn't argue.

It was a well-known fact that Ainsworth couldn't stand Conrad. No one, apart from Ainsworth, knew the reason why. But Conrad's presence always seemed to put Ainsworth in a foul temper. He was an irascible old bugger at the best of times, but whatever effect Conrad had, it wasn't appreciated by Ainsworth's staff.

Brady turned his attention back to the crime scene. Ainsworth, like Conrad, was dressed in an all-white Tyvek suit with blue booties and latex gloves. Brady hadn't bothered. Not that Ainsworth had been overly convinced by his argument that he had already contaminated the crime scene, so there was no point in suiting up. He watched the white-clad SOCOs, also known as Scientific Support Officers. They were busy getting ready to film and photograph the crime scene before anything more was disturbed. The sexy new American term Crime Scene Investigator, or CSI, had officially entered the Northumbrian Police handbook but that was as far as it had got. On the job, officers still referred to them as SOCOs. Not once had Brady heard the term 'CSI' used; apart from when someone was taking the piss.

Brady watched Ainsworth as he started bollocking one of his team in charge of laying out forensic platforms for the team to walk on to avoid any further contamination of evidence. It wasn't a good start to the night. Ainsworth was in a dire mood – worse than usual. Whether it was being called out so late on a Saturday evening, or the magnitude of the job at hand, Brady couldn't say. But he had known Ainsworth long enough to know to distance himself from the bugger's infamous snapping.

Brady had often wondered whether Ainsworth's problem was his stature, or to be precise, lack of it. He was a short, portly man with a jowly face, known for his formidable temper and his unforgiving, caustic tongue. But he was respected for his dedication to the job and crucially, his team respected him even if they didn't necessarily like him. Brady wouldn't trust anyone else in here. If the suspect had left forensic evidence behind, then Ainsworth and his team would find it – regardless of how long it took. He had a Jesuitical eye for detail and an uncanny knack for discovering much-needed results.

The mood in the basement was sombre. The findings too macabre for even the SOCOs to trade their usual black humour. Something Brady had read about the reason behind gallows humour came to mind – *to be able to laugh at evil and error means we have surmounted them.* The reason the SOCOs were not taking the piss out of the situation was simple. Whoever had enacted this heinous crime upon these women was still out there. They had not *surmounted* this evil. And by no means were they even close – whoever had committed these atrocities had eluded the police and the public for what Brady believed could be years. It was difficult to joke about such sadistic murders when they had no idea whether this was the full extent of the killer's collection. There was one surviving victim in hospital – seriously injured. What if the killer already had a new victim? The stark truth was that they had no idea who they were dealing with, or why. And what the perpetrator had done to these women had left everyone attending the crime scene with a sense of disquiet.

Numbed by the cold and the bitter reality of what lay ahead of him, Brady watched as stark lights suddenly illuminated the monstrosity that was the old, Victorian furnace. The dumping ground for a serial killer who had completely gone undetected – until now.

Brady couldn't help but notice that Ainsworth looked more ravaged than usual, his face red and bloated. His sharp, black beady eyes were restless. Preoccupied. He was a cantankerous old sod at the best of times, but Brady could see that there was something else adding to his usual mood. And he was sure it was more than just Conrad's presence.

As if he sensed what Brady was thinking, Ainsworth turned and scowled at him. It was evident that he had better places to be than forensically examining the derelict basement of an old psychiatric hospital. Then there were the victims. They had to be filmed, photographed and documented before being bagged and then removed to the morgue for examination. It was a process that would take hours, if not days. It was crucial that no trace evidence, whether biological or fibre-based, was missed or contaminated. Brady and the security guard's DNA and prints would automatically be ruled out. Not that this took the security guard out of the equation. Dave was still a key suspect – until they found someone else. If Brady could change that fact, he would. But his hands were tied. The security guard had access – twenty-four-seven – to the sealed-off grounds and derelict hospital. He had also said that his wife had left him for a younger man in Turkey. Did that give him cause to torture and murder all these women? Brady seriously doubted it. Then there was the fact that some of the bodies looked as if they had been there for some time – perhaps years. But Brady still had to interview him nonetheless, even though he was acutely aware that the security guard had only recently returned to the UK from serving in Afghanistan.

Ainsworth walked over to Brady and Conrad, scowl still in place. But this time it was not directed at Conrad. 'Trouble has a nasty habit of following you around!'

Brady thought of Annabel Edwards. Of Macintosh. He shrugged. There was nothing he could add.

Ainsworth shook his head as he looked over at the illuminated furnace. 'You've excelled yourself with this one.'

'Like to keep you on your toes!' Brady replied.

'Well, you're bloody doing that, I can tell you.' Ainsworth's black beady eyes bore into him. 'This is some sick bastard.'

'I know.'

'Why is it never bloody straightforward? I've got better things to do than be tramping around in a basement freezing my balls off for the next God knows how many hours!'

Brady was surprised. He had always known Ainsworth to be keen, too keen if he was honest, to get his hands on a crime scene of this magnitude. 'What's wrong with you? Getting too old for the job?' he joked. But he soon realised Ainsworth wasn't laughing. His look was enough to worry Brady. 'You've still got years left in you, you stupid bugger.'

'Maybe you're not seeing what I see every morning when I look in the mirror?'

'No, I see what you see. A bad-tempered fool but one at the top of his game.'

'Am I?' Ainsworth mused.

Brady looked at him. The humour had gone. His already ravaged face looked even more haggard and aged. He wondered whether it was just the pressure of the job that was getting to Ainsworth. This was the second serious murder investigation within a matter of days. It was atypical and Brady was sure Ainsworth was feeling the strain. Policing now came down to politics and the budget. A budget that, under the current government, had shrunk by twenty per cent in the last five years. It was challenging times for police forces across the UK and Northumbria was no exception.

'Yes you are. And you bloody know it! You're the best Crime Scene Manager we have. I could have called in Matt Johnson and his team from Newcastle. Or Annette McCabe from over in Gateshead. But they're not good enough! They're not you. And I needed you here if we've got any chance of finding this bastard. All you've got to do is look at what he's done to those women. Locked up here alive until their organs fail. Then when they're dead their killer revisits them and dresses them up and arranges them like macabre life-sized puppets. And his latest victim? Who I found just in time? You tell me why I *wouldn't* want you here to help catch whoever's responsible?' Brady demanded.

Ainsworth looked at him. Brady could see he still didn't look convinced. He had never known Ainsworth to be so defeated and wondered whether there was more to it than he realised. 'We all have shit days where we wonder why the hell we bother.'

Ainsworth didn't agree or disagree. Instead, he turned away from Brady and appraised his team. 'I've seen some sick shit in my time. But . . .' he shook his head, 'nothing comes close to this. Not even what that crazy bastard did to his probation officer and his family.'

'It's all sick,' Brady muttered as he followed Ainsworth's gaze. He realised that the Crime Scene Manager and his team had their work cut out. Brady was depending on them finding something – anything – that could give him an idea as to who was responsible for this grotesque collection. He was at Ainsworth's mercy.

Brady watched Conrad's shocked reaction as he stared at what had been carefully staged inside the large furnace. Brady felt the same raw horror.

'Christ!' Conrad shook his head as he continued to stare.

'Yeah . . .' muttered Brady.

'Twelve. There are twelve of them, sir,' Conrad said.

Brady had just done the maths for himself. And it was twelve too many, in his books.

'How has someone got away with abducting women and then . . .' Conrad turned to look at Brady.

Brady was more than aware that his deputy was struggling to cope. The bright, garish crime scene lights behind them penetrated the furnace, highlighting in macabre detail the victims' remains. But it was what had been done to them that had shocked Brady. He swallowed hard. He could feel the bile still lingering at the back of his throat. When he had first seen them, he had not fully understood the full nature of what they had endured while alive and then the indignity they had suffered in death.

To Brady's eye it looked like a crude procedure. One that had not taken place under a doctor's skilled hand, let alone in a hospital. The killer had lobotomized each and every one of them. Systematically. Drilled a hole into either side of their skulls and then, Brady imagined, taken a scalpel to their brains. He had also dressed them in identical clothing. An old-fashioned, Victorian style, white cotton nightgown. The harsh light penetrated the fabric, showing them to be naked underneath. Around their necks, a white gold name necklace had been hung.

Brady turned around. 'Can I use that for a minute?' he asked the SOCO closest to him. 'Yeah . . . that Crime-lite you've got there.'

The SOCO handed it over to Brady. He then hoisted himself up into the furnace and shone the light on each victim, looking at their necklaces.

'Sir?' Conrad objected.

'I'm not touching them. I'm just getting a closer look.' He then shone the light over each victim. 'They're not the same, Conrad. I can't make out the names but I can tell that each engraving is different.'

'You think their actual names are engraved on the necklaces?' Conrad asked.

'I don't know. I can't make that out. All I know is that they are different. Whether the killer has named them individually or it is actually their real names, we will have to wait to find out.'

Brady thought back to the victim he had found. Alive – barely. But she didn't have a white gold name necklace around her neck, suggesting that the perpetrator returned to his victims. Dressed them in clean nightgowns – hers was torn and bloodied, covered in old soot and other debris from the floor of the furnace. Cleaned them up. Adorned them with a gold necklace. Then arranged them. Identical to each other.

For a moment, Brady looked at each victim. All sat facing him in a half-circle. Expectant. *Waiting . . . Waiting for whoever had done this to return.*

He shuddered involuntarily, unable to continue looking at their blank, lifeless expressions.

He handed Conrad the Crime-lite before levering himself down.

'Why do you think he has done that to them?'

'I don't know. We've just got to make sure we prevent whoever is responsible from getting their hands on another victim.'

'If he hasn't already got one,' Conrad added.

It was a scenario Brady had already contemplated. After all, the killer had no idea – yet – that the police had found his collection. There was a chance that the perpetrator already had his sights, if not hands, on a new woman. And that worried Brady. Worried him a lot.

Brady took a last glance at the twelve victims. All facing him, wearing what he could only describe as a death mask. Whether the cast of their faces were taken while they were alive or dead, he couldn't say, but what he did know was that each one was unique. The bodies may have been identically dressed and positioned, but each mask was original to its wearer. However, there was one common denominator – they were all young and extremely malnourished. The thickly applied make-up did not hide the sunken cheeks and eye sockets of each mask. If anything, the garish paint embellished the pronounced bone structure.

'Why the make-up? It makes them looks so . . . so . . . unnatural?'

Brady laughed suddenly at Conrad's comment. But he soon wished he hadn't when it echoed around the basement. A couple of SOCOs close by looked over. Young. Female. Clearly not impressed at Brady's cavalier attitude. After all, these women had been butchered. One by one, he had lobotomised them. Brady cleared his throat and turned back to Conrad. He made a point of keeping his voice low. 'More unnatural than skeletons wearing a mask and a wig?'

Conrad didn't look overly impressed. 'You know what

I mean. And the wigs and the mask? It's just . . .' he faltered, at a loss as to what to say.

'Christ! That's what you get with a bloody university education, Jack! Bloody idiots. The lot of them!' Ainsworth snapped from behind.

Brady shot Conrad a look, which told him not to react. Not that he would have expected Conrad to, but with the sour mood Ainsworth was in he didn't want to take any chances. Brady knew that Ainsworth had a gripe about the new breed of SOCO – most of them recent graduates from university. Cheaper to employ than a copper like Ainsworth who had been in the force for years. It was a career that was now seen as slick and sexy thanks to *CSI*. These graduates were now very much a part of life. *His life*. Not that Ainsworth was too happy about it.

'I have enough problems with those slow-witted idiots who work for me without you two stood around gawping,' Ainsworth grumbled. 'So if you've seen enough, I've got a job to do.'

Brady ran a hand over the new growth of stubble on his face as he took one last look at them. All he felt was horror.

DAY TWO
SUNDAY

Chapter Twelve

Sunday: 12:13 a.m.

Twelve of them; mutilated, then murdered. The thirteenth victim he had found – just in time. *Or had he?* That was the question that was plaguing him. She was the reason he had visited Newcastle's Royal Victoria Infirmary. He had needed to know whether . . . Brady stopped himself. She had been sedated and hooked up to various machines and drips in the ICU. He knew she was very ill. Expected her to be suffering from malnutrition and severe dehydration. But he hadn't quite realised how bad. Her five-stone body had suffered systematic physical abuse. She was covered in abrasions and bruises. Some were recent, others indicative of long-term abuse. She had also been examined and DNA swabs had been taken. The level of sexual violence carried out upon her body was staggering.

A wave of nausea came over him. He put it down to hunger. And tiredness.

When was the last time you slept? Let alone ate?

He decided there was nothing more he could do. He needed to drive home. While he still could. Grab something from the freezer. Microwave it and then force himself to eat. Whatever perishables had been in the fridge would have crawled out by now.

He turned the engine over. Sat with it idling while he stared straight ahead at the slick, contemporary hospital. Radically different from the mausoleum of a mental asylum he had found her in. He prayed to God that she would survive. But he knew from what the doctor had said that her prognosis for a *normal* life wasn't good. In fact it was zero. An MRI scan had shown that parts of her brain had been cut out with a sharp object such as a scalpel. Brady ran a hand through his hair as he thought about that.

Why do that first and then *kill them? It was so cruel, so sadistic . . . Why? Or was that the answer.*

It didn't make any sense to Brady. Unless it made the victim more docile, compliant? Easier to break into a derelict building with them and hide them. But why leave them to die locked up inside that old furnace? Left to starve to death, surrounded by the disturbing remains of his other victims. Some of whom Brady believed had been there for years.

He let it go – for now. He needed to sleep. He pulled out of the parking space and headed for the exit. He suddenly remembered that he had asked Conrad to run some checks for him in connection with the Macintosh case. He had asked him to find out what he could about a Lucy Macintosh born in 1960. Then there was Eileen Macintosh, James' mother, who had allegedly emigrated to Australia shortly after her son's conviction. Whether he had actually managed it before he had attended the crime scene was in doubt. But Brady had a new case. A new priority. One that would keep him too damned busy chasing his own shadow to even have time to think about Macintosh.

Brady unlocked the front door and just stood there. The house was shrouded in darkness. Behind him he could hear the roar of the North Sea as it battered the rocks down on Brown's Bay.

Finally he forced himself to walk inside and close the door. He hadn't been back since he had found out from Conrad that Claudia had gone. That was last Wednesday evening. Four nights ago and still he was reeling from the news. He stepped over the pile of mail lying in the front vestibule. Flicked on the light and walked past the answering machine on the hall table, ignoring the flashing red light. His eyes were on the kitchen. He walked into the large, contemporary space.

The coffee he had made her, still there. The note, untouched. She had already left him and he had not realised. He turned to the fridge. He needed a drink. Anything. He pulled out a bottle of Sancerre. Uncorked it and poured a generous measure into a large wine glass. Then drank a third of it straight down. The citrusy flavours didn't have a chance to hit his palate. All he knew was that it was cold and alcoholic. He then rummaged through the freezer. He needed to eat. Not that he wanted to, but he had no choice. He found a microwavable risotto. It would do. Bland, glutinous, tasteless. He set it going in the microwave, topped his wine up and then headed upstairs.

He made a point of not looking at the guest room – Claudia's room. He made his way into the bathroom and turned the shower on. It blasted out hot spray. He pulled his clothes off and dumped them in the wash basket. He turned and caught himself in the mirror. He had lost weight. Not surprisingly. His body, lean and well-muscled, was even leaner now. His dark brown eyes lingered on the scar on his chest where a bullet had ripped through, narrowly missing killing him. Two Eastern European gangsters had been responsible. But Brady would be the first to admit that he seemed to attract trouble. He thought about what the media were saying about him. In the past week his name had become synonymous with '*fuck-up*.' He sighed, dejected, then walked into the large shower cubicle. He stood for as long as it was going to take to rid him of the contempt he felt for himself right now. He bent his head down and leaned his hands against the tiled wall as he let the scalding water pummel his back. Brady remained there. Head down. And waited for the overwhelming sadness he felt about Claudia not being here to pass. He didn't hear the answer machine clicking on downstairs. Or the voice.

Claudia's voice.

Brady had lain awake for what seemed like hours before he had eventually dropped off. But at least he had succeeded in getting a few hours' uninterrupted sleep before coming back to the station. He had wanted an early start. Had no choice. He sighed and ran a hand back through his hair as he thought about the call he had just taken. It was 6:38 a.m. Early to be receiving calls. But this one was important. He thought about the relevance. He didn't want to raise his hopes. But it was definitely something.

He picked up his coffee and took a drink. He was feeling physically better than he had done in a long time. However, psychologically he still felt crap. Not that he expected any different. He thought about the security guard, Dave Baxter. He had asked him to come in to the station. Brady was sure he had done nothing. Interviewing him was simply a process of elimination. He was scheduled to take a statement in twenty minutes. Then he would release him. Let him get back to his kids where he belonged. The man wasn't a serial killer. Not to say he hadn't killed, in his time. But this was different. This wasn't a war zone.

But there was something else bothering him. He couldn't stop himself thinking about Macintosh and whether what he had found in the suitcase at Mill Cottage yesterday, in particular the photograph of his sister, Lucy Macintosh, held any significance.

There was a knock at the door. Brady looked up just as Conrad walked in.

'You wanted to see me, sir?'

'Yeah,' Brady said. He gestured towards the seat in front of desk. 'Sit.'

He waited as Conrad closed the door and then walked over to his desk. He sat down.

'I was too preoccupied last night to ask if you checked those names I gave you,' Brady said.

'I came back to the station after the crime scene to run those checks,' Conrad replied.

Brady was surprised at this, as he had ordered Conrad to go home. Then again, Conrad knew how dogged he could be and realised that Brady would still want to have verification of Lucy Macintosh's birth – despite the new case. So, he couldn't now understand the reluctance in Conrad's voice. 'And?'

'Lucy Jayne Macintosh was born on the third of July, 1960. Place of birth, Mill Cottage, Hartburn, Northumberland. Parents, Eileen and Raymond Macintosh.'

Brady sat back. He had been waiting for this news but still, he felt surprised by it.

He had been right after all. James David Macintosh had a sister . . . A sister who had an uncanny resemblance to Macintosh's two young victims – Ellen Jackson and Annabel Edwards.

'Have you seen the photographs that I found in the attic in Mill Cottage?'

Conrad nodded. 'There is a likeness between the suspect's sister and his choice of victims.'

'More than a likeness, Conrad! They're virtually identical.'

Conrad didn't agree. Or disagree. His expression remained impassive.

'What has Gates threatened you with?' Brady asked. It was clear that something was wrong with him.

'My job,' he replied.

It was an honest, if unexpected answer. 'I see.'

'And yours,' he added for clarity. 'I passed this new information on to him as soon as possible. He wasn't impressed to hear from me. Nor was he happy that I was still active on the Macintosh investigation when I had been transferred to this new case, sir.'

'Fuck Gates!'

Conrad didn't react.

Brady had handed the suitcase and its contents into the station last night on his way back home. He had to. Even he wasn't stupid enough to withhold evidence.

'I take it that Gates has seen the photographs?'

'Yes, sir. All relevant information was passed onto Gates early this morning.'

'And what did he make of them?'

'Honestly? I don't know. He didn't comment.'

'And the Victorian doll? Nearly identical to the one found with Ellen Jackson?'

Conrad looked at Brady. It was clear from his expression that he didn't want to discuss a case he no longer had the authority to be involved in. 'Again, he didn't comment.'

Brady rested his elbows on his desk and leaned forward. 'This lead they've got in London?'

Conrad shook his head. 'I know nothing about it.'

'Bullshit!' Brady snapped. 'I know for a fact that Amelia is in London with Gates working with the Met on finding Macintosh. I also know that you and she are tight. So if they had anything tangible, she'd tell you.'

Conrad shifted his body, the tension on his face building. His lips a thin, repressed line. His eyes narrowed even further as he held Brady's unrelenting gaze. 'They're raiding a house somewhere in London this morning. If they haven't already done so.'

Brady nodded. It was what he would have expected. Most police raids took place early in the morning; element of surprise. Suspects too busy lying in bed scratching their sweaty nads to even realise that the police were about to storm their premises.

'You know they won't find him?' Brady said.

Conrad didn't comment.

'What was the connection?'

He looked at Brady, obviously uncomfortable with the conversation. But he realised that Brady could be unrelenting. In these circumstances it was wiser to acquiesce than resist. 'An ex-inmate from Macintosh's time in Belmarsh.'

Brady thought it over. It was a set-up. This ex-prisoner wouldn't be hiding Macintosh. It was part of Macintosh's game plan. Only his boss couldn't see that. Nor could the rest of the investigative team. Too busy chasing shadows to actually realise that Macintosh wasn't in London.

Brady turned his mind back to Lucy Macintosh. He knew that she was crucial. It was no coincidence that Macintosh had abducted two young girls who looked identical to his sister. All three the same age. 'Where is she? Lucy Macintosh?'

'I couldn't find any trace of her apart from her birth records. I couldn't find a death certificate either. She wasn't registered at any schools in Jesmond or the surrounding area. I know that the family left Mill Cottage in 1963 when she would have been three years old but then she seems to have just disappeared.'

Brady had a bad feeling about this. People – *children* – don't just disappear. 'You're certain?'

Conrad nodded.

Brady was about to ask what Gates made of Lucy Macintosh's disappearance but then decided there was no point. Gates clearly didn't see a connection. And clearly, as he had impressed upon Conrad, they were no longer involved in the hunt for Macintosh – or Annabel.

'What about Eileen Macintosh?' She too, like her daughter, had disappeared.

'Nothing,' Conrad said shaking his head.

'Did you check to see whether she had relocated to Australia?'

'Yes. Still nothing. Nor is there a death certificate.'

Brady leaned back. It didn't make any sense. How could two people from the same family disappear without trace? 'You're definitely sure you didn't miss anything?'

'Yes, sir.'

Brady decided to let it go. He had no choice. He had tried to follow his hunch but he had hit a dead end. He still felt sick when he thought of Annabel Edwards. But his hands were tied. This was Gates' call and Brady hoped that his boss wouldn't live to regret it.

He breathed out. Slowly. Deliberately. It was time to focus on the case he had been assigned. He had no alternative but to let go of Macintosh. 'Thanks for checking that out for me, Harry. I appreciate it. And for what it's worth, I'm sorry about the flack that you got from Gates. It should have been me. Not you.'

Conrad shrugged. 'I'm fine.'

Brady nodded. He steeled himself. It wasn't his problem. Not anymore.

'I've just had a call from the hospital,' he began. He couldn't help but notice the relief on Conrad's face. Relief that Brady had moved on to something else. 'The medical staff have said that there has been no improvement on her condition. But she has been repeating the name "Emily Baker".'

Conrad raised an eyebrow.

'I know . . . I don't want to get my hopes up but we need to run a check on the name.'

Conrad nodded. 'I'll get straight on to it.'

It was obvious that Conrad wanted to leave. Not that Brady could blame him. Gates had him firmly by the balls. Conrad clearly didn't want to get caught up in any of Brady's unorthodox plans. His job was his life. The same with Brady. The difference was, Brady was prepared to risk it all.

Chapter Thirteen

Sunday: 9:22 a.m.

'I don't know what to say,' Dave said. He nervously ran a large hand over the stubble on his head. 'I mean . . . I just wish I had done something . . .'

Brady nodded. He felt bad for the bloke. Who wouldn't? He had seriously fucked up. His role as a security guard would be called in to question. A serial killer had been dumping victims, leaving them to die a tortuous death under his watch. Worse yet, the killer had been returning, repeatedly.

'I'll be in touch if I remember anything else. But honestly, the only thing I can think that stands out, is that car. The black Volvo. It stood out because it was an old Volvo. One of the 200 series from the eighties I reckon. It was in mint condition though. Beautiful car. The amount of times I would see it parked up by the old grounds. It's only now I think about it that I realise it could be significant. Christ! I wished I'd taken the registration details down.' He shook his head as he looked at Brady. 'I just thought he was a dog walker. You get a lot of them drive up that way because of the woodland next to the old hospital. I mean . . . he did have a dog. A black Labrador I think. On the back seat. Barking and jumping around. Thought it odd that it wasn't in the boot . . .' he shrugged. Realised he was rambling. Making excuses.

Brady nodded. He had taken down the details. But they were sketchy. A white male, early-to-late forties with dark hair. That effectively narrowed down one-sixth of the males in the North East. Then the car. A Volvo 200 dating back as far as thirty-five to forty years old. Registration unknown. But he had requested all CCTV footage filming the exterior of the Victorian psychiatric hospital. Whether or not they would be of any use, he couldn't say. But right now he had DC Daniels and Kenny scouring through the footage. Looking for anything – or one – remotely suspicious. If Dave Baxter was right about this Volvo, then it was guaranteed to be on the surveillance footage, along with the registration plate.

Brady watched as Dave Baxter was led out of the station. He had no reason to hold him. Brady was still waiting to hear Wolfe, the Home Office Pathologist's opinion on when the first victim had been murdered. He was certain that some of the victims had been murdered some time ago. When, he couldn't say, but it ruled Dave Baxter out. He had been serving in Afghanistan for the past five years. During that time twelve victims had been killed and dumped. Also, he wasn't a serial killer. He wasn't another James David Macintosh.

He was an ex-soldier whose life had turned out crap. Working a shitty job to keep the roof over the kids his ex-missus had dumped on him. He had been in the wrong place at the wrong time. His worst offence? Not investigating the banging when he first heard the noise. But it wasn't Brady's place to hold him accountable. Dave Baxter had made it quite clear that he would never forgive himself. He had done the maths. He had walked away from one of the victims. A victim who had still been alive – *barely* – banging relentlessly on the door of the old Victorian furnace that they had been locked in.

Brady was back in his office. He had picked up a bacon stottie from the cafeteria and a black coffee. Realised that he had to eat. Otherwise he would be of no use to anyone.

What about Annabel Edwards? What use are you to her?

Brady shook his head. Annoyed with himself. No matter how hard he tried he still couldn't stop thinking about the little girl. He had overheard the news about the raid in London in the cafeteria, but no one had mentioned it directly to him.

He took a bite of his breakfast and looked at the report Conrad had left on his desk. It was an update on the name that the victim had been repeating – Emily Baker. Whether that was the victim's actual name or someone connected to her, Brady couldn't say – yet. But Conrad had been thorough, so it wouldn't take them long to establish whether the victim was in fact Emily Baker. What Brady did know was that she had no known priors so hadn't shown up on the police database. Nor had she been reported missing. But Conrad hadn't stopped there. He searched and searched until he had something tangible to give Brady. She was just eighteen years old. Lived alone. Set up in a bedsit by Social Services. His eyes scanned down the report picking out relevant details. He realised there was a reason she had not been reported missing. She had no family. She had been removed from her mother's care at the age of two and put into emergency foster care. It appeared that her father was unknown and her stepfather, or to be precise, her teenage mother's then forty-year-old boyfriend hadn't much liked kids and had used her as an ashtray – amongst other things. The list of injuries the two-year-old had sustained even took Brady aback. He noted that her address was registered as Whitley Road, in Whitley Bay. She had left Social Services' care as soon as she had turned eighteen and had been living in a flat for the past ten months.

Brady scribbled down the address. As soon as he had finished the bacon stottie he would head over there.

There was a knock at the door.

'Yeah?' shouted Brady.

Conrad walked in.

'Good work,' Brady said.

Conrad didn't say anything.

'How did you know to check her name against Social Services?'

'I suspected that she might be a high-risk victim. She wasn't listed as missing which told me that no one even knew that she had disappeared. When I read the doctor's medical report it was clear that someone had held her captive for at least four months. She had sustained injuries as long ago as then. So then I asked why no one would know that she was missing. Or if they did, why didn't they care? I had already checked that Emily Baker, if this is the victim, hadn't been arrested for soliciting. So, I deduced that she must have come from a background that involved social care. A lot of the kids in the care system end up running away. Getting involved in drink and drugs. Some end up in prostitution. Others living on the streets. Or both. So I checked her name against North Tyneside's social services records and struck lucky. She was listed with them. Or had been, until last year.'

'Let's go along to her address and see what we can find out,' Brady suggested. He pushed his chair back and stood up. Finished off what was left of his coffee and picked up his phone as it started to ring. 'Give me two seconds?'

'Sure.'

Brady watched as Conrad left him alone.

He answered it. Then listened, not liking what he was hearing.

'Are you one hundred per cent certain?' he asked.

Again, he didn't like the response.

'So why the hell would she be saying Emily Baker's name?' Not that he expected them to know the answer.

'Yeah . . . yeah. Thanks for letting me know.' Brady hung up. He walked over to his office door and opened it and yelled: 'Conrad!'

'Shit!' Brady muttered. She was there. In the system. He looked at the priors listed on the computer screen. Then turned to Conrad. 'It's her, Harry. No question. Her DNA conclusively matches our victim.'

'Why would she be saying Emily Baker's name then?' Conrad asked as he frowned at the evidence on the screen.

Brady shrugged. He had not been surprised that she wasn't Emily Baker. The crucial question was why was she repeatedly saying someone else's name? Brady had a feeling about why the twenty-year-old victim, now identified as Hannah Stewart, a known homeless prostitute, might be saying someone else's name. But it was just a hunch. He wanted to check it out before he committed himself.

'Go check if she has any family,' Brady instructed. But he seriously doubted it. He was starting to think that the suspect was targeting high-risk, young females with no family to speak of – no one to report them missing. Hannah Stewart had been arrested as a minor for soliciting. She had just been thirteen years old. Sadly, she wasn't atypical. At the time she was in the care of the council – North Tyneside. After that, the following arrests detailed her address as '*unknown*'. In other words she was either sofa surfing, or having sex in exchange for a bed for the night. Or, worst-case scenario, sleeping on the streets or in local parks.

Homelessness was becoming an increasing problem. Especially amongst the young. He was aware that one in five people, aged between sixteen and twenty-five had sofa surfed in the past year because they had nowhere else to go. Homeless charities were doing their utmost to campaign about this hidden problem. But it wasn't enough.

'I need to contact her social worker. See what I can glean from their records. Whether she's been fostered. If she has, then we need to talk to foster carers. There might even be a connection between Hannah Stewart and Emily Baker.'

Conrad didn't look so convinced.

'Both girls were in state care. That already connects them. And Hannah Stewart has not been able to say anything other than Emily Baker's name. That's not a coincidence, Conrad. Far from it.'

Conrad didn't reply.

It was the obvious step. They had her address. Brady was just hoping that she was there. But he had an uneasy feeling. One that told him that they were already too late to have prevented Emily Baker from being abducted by the same suspect who had tortured and lobotomised Hannah Stewart. Who had then left her to die.

'Let me know as soon as you hear something on Hannah Stewart's family,' Brady said.

'You know what the press are calling him?' Conrad asked.

Brady had made a point of ignoring the newspapers. He had watched the news in the cafeteria about Macintosh but as soon as it changed to covering the victim discovered last night, he had left. Returned to his office to eat, instead of listening to the media speculate upon the victims' injuries.

'No.'

' "The *Puppet Maker*",' Conrad said.

Brady shook his head. He had no idea how they had gleaned enough details to be able to come up with that name for the unknown suspect. What he found so disturbing was the fact that the name was so apt. 'Sick fuckers!'

It had taken some time but Brady had managed to get hold of Hannah Stewart's social worker's number. He had informed her that he was investigating an attack on one of her ex-clients.

'You're serious?' Siobhan Reardon asked.

'Yes.' Brady knew she was struggling to come to terms with what had happened to her ex-client but he needed her to snap out of it quickly. Time was running out and he needed her help.

'How was she hurt?' The social worker's voice sounded nervous. Scared, even. As if she could somehow be responsible.

Brady sighed. He imagined that she was only in her late twenties herself. Recently graduated when she took Hannah Stewart on as a client. One of her first. He imagined that aside from shock, she would feel guilt that perhaps she hadn't done enough. 'I'm sorry. I'm not at liberty to say.'

'Oh . . .'

He waited. Knew what would be coming next.

'Hannah's not the girl who was found at that old psychiatric hospital? The Victorian one on the hill overlooking Morpeth town centre? It was on the news earlier.'

'As I said, I can't say.'

Siobhan was silent for a moment as she remembered the news report. Then she reacted. 'Oh God! Not Hannah! What the news reported . . . God . . . it's horrific! They're calling him "The *Puppet Maker*", which means there's more than one victim. Doesn't it?'

Brady ignored her question. He could not answer her, even if he wanted to. 'As I've said, I'm not at liberty to discuss that case. But I really do need any information you have on Hannah Stewart. Such as people she might have been in contact with?' Brady asked, in a last-ditch attempt at steering the conversation in a direction that he wanted it to go. Shock had obscured her professionalism.

'I'm sorry . . . I just was overwhelmed by what you told me. Right, let me see . . .'

Brady waited while she accessed Hannah Stewart's files. He didn't bother correcting her. He hadn't actually told her anything. She had just heard what she wanted. Filled in the blanks with her own conclusions.

'I'm sorry. There's not a lot here that I think will be of any help.'

He breathed in. Held it for a few seconds. Then let it out. 'Humour me will you, Siobhan?'

'Well, she came into authority care at the age of five. Mother was a heroin addict. Same with the boyfriend. No trace of her biological father. No extended family either. It was the school that reported the neglect. She was filthy. Also suffering from malnutrition. She was severely underweight and would steal food from other children's packed lunchboxes. And her body was covered in bruises and cuts. All unexplained, of course. So the school called us in and she was removed. Placed in emergency foster care and ultimately, in a home. Disruptive and abusive, she was moved from one foster home to another until she was permanently placed in a children's home in North Shields.'

'Why was she so unsettled with her foster carers? And why couldn't she have been adopted?' Brady asked, his mind unable to let go of the young girl he had pulled out from the furnace and carried out of the abandoned psychiatric hospital. She had had a shit life from the outset. Then someone had used that to their advantage.

'Well . . . she found it very difficult to settle in anywhere. But the problem we had was that her mother didn't want her back. It doesn't matter how badly abused these children are, the one thing most of them want is to go back home to their parent or parents.'

Brady didn't say anything.

'We gave her mother a deal. Get some help with the heroin addiction and lose the boyfriend. She couldn't do it. Said she would get help with the drug problem but refused to kick the boyfriend out of her life. Hannah had a really hard time coping with this. The sad thing is, you can't keep something as obvious as this from them. These kids are smart. They've had no choice but to be, given what they've had to deal with before they were taken into care.'

'So there was no foster carer to speak of?' Brady asked.

'No. Well . . . not a consistent foster carer. I think the longest she actually stayed with one carer was four months. Typically, she would be handed back after the honeymoon period was over.'

'I don't follow?'

'It's the same with any new relationship. These children are on their best behaviour for the first few weeks. They don't put a foot wrong. Too scared to, really. They have grown up with the threat of abandonment, amongst other issues. So, a lot of them will behave impeccably at the beginning – but then the cracks begin to show. You see, you can only keep up being perfect for a certain amount of time. Eventually, whatever behavioural problems or issues with adults that they have will finally come to the fore. That was the case with Hannah. With every placement she was the ideal foster child. Assimilated immediately. But it didn't last. You see, she desperately wanted to fit in with every new foster family, but when her challenging behaviour presented itself it proved too much for her foster carers. And sadly, the more she was returned to us, the harder it became to find her a permanent foster carer. Eventually she was placed in a children's residential home.'

'I see . . .' Brady answered. 'What happened after she was placed in a home?'

'She repeatedly ran away from the home from about the age of twelve. When she got to fourteen I didn't have a chance. She just did what she wanted. She got involved with the wrong people and things just went from bad to worse. She was being pimped by a twenty-eight-year-old boyfriend at the time. Then by the age of sixteen she disappeared. Haven't seen her since or heard from her since.'

'Do you have any contact details for the boyfriend?' He knew it was a long shot but it was worth a try.

'No. I'm sorry. She refused to give us his address or number. Worried that we might try and prosecute him.'

'What about any friends?'

'Not that I know of. She pretty much dropped out of school from about the age of ten. So as far as I know she had no school friends. Or any other friends, for that matter.'

Brady sighed.

'Look, Detective Inspector Brady, I do my job to the best of my ability on an ever-decreasing budget and increasing client list. Hannah was of an age where . . .' Siobhan faltered.

'What? Where she didn't matter anymore? She had survived in the system until her teens and that was enough? You cut her loose? For Christ's sake! She wasn't even listed as missing!' He couldn't help himself. He couldn't get rid of Hannah's dark, haunted eyes. Her body. So malnourished that he could have been carrying a young child in his arms. This had really affected him. But it was more than that. Hannah and Brady shared a childhood. One of living in care. After his father had murdered his mother, Brady and his younger brother Nick had been bandied about from one foster carer to another. Then they had been separated. It had been cruel. Painful. But very much par for the course. His childhood had been shit. But he at least had made it. Survived. Had gone on to have a decent life. Unlike Hannah. Someone had taken her chance away.

'No. It's not like that,' Siobhan replied, her voice combative. 'It's just we have our hands full. Our case-loads keep increasing. And yes, we have to prioritise. I'm sure the police force is in a similar position. It's a familiar one across all government funded resources. I am sure that in your time you have had to make choices that you wished you hadn't been forced to. Tell me what you would do when you have a wayward, troubled teenager who has a problem with authority? Finds it difficult to fit into society and refuses any kind of help from us, versus a reported case of child abuse involving a two-year-old?' she demanded, her tone caustic. 'Because I have to make that choice nearly every working day! So forgive me if we don't manage to keep track of the ones who run away for good when they reach sixteen. We've got enough to deal with trying to protect the most vulnerable children.'

Brady didn't say anything. He just kept thinking back to what he had said to Dave the security guard: *'Life sucks!'* And it did – for some people.

'I'm sorry . . . I'm just feeling overwhelmed with my workload. I didn't mean to sound so . . . so unprofessional,' she apologised.

Brady could hear the defeatism in her voice. 'It's fine. We all have difficult choices to make. But it must be harder to live with those choices that concern children.' He thought of Annabel Edwards – three years old and orphaned. What would happen to her if she was found alive and well? Would there be some extended family member somewhere who would take her in and raise her? Or would she end up in the system because of a monster like Macintosh? Passed about from one foster carer to another. Maybe she would be one of the fortunate ones. Her face would be advertised. Shown in a glossy brochure to potential adoptive parents. She was young enough and pretty enough to be chosen. Unlike the ones who were left in the system without a chance of being picked out.

That is, if you get her back alive.

It hit him hard. He was getting ahead of himself. She had been missing for over forty-eight hours now. The odds weren't stacked in her favour.

'Thanks . . .' she muttered. 'It is hard sometimes. Most times.'

Brady suddenly thought of Emily Baker. She had also grown up in care. In North Tyneside. He wondered if there was any chance that she and Hannah Stewart were friends. It might explain why Hannah was repeatedly saying the other young woman's name.

'One last question,' Brady began. 'Did you have any dealings with an Emily Baker? Eighteen years old? She went into care when she was two and remained in North Tyneside's local authority care until she turned eighteen.'

'No . . . She's not one of mine. I'm sorry.'

'Is there a chance they would have known one another?' Brady asked, hopeful. He would rather that their connection was one of a shared childhood than victimhood.

'Let me check her records. See if they were in the same home or shared foster carers.'

Brady waited. It was only a few minutes but is seemed like an eternity.

'Uhuh . . . Yeah, I've got her. She was my colleague's client.' She paused for a moment. 'No . . . No they definitely weren't placed in care together. So I can't see how they would know one another. They were fostered in different parts of North Tyneside, so their primary schools were different. As were their high schools. It looks from the updated notes here that Emily Baker was one of our success stories. She went on to study three A-Levels at Whitley Bay High and is now taking photography at Newcastle College. Registered last September. She's also living in Whitley Bay. Sandra, my colleague, set her up in a flat there.'

'Did she have foster carers?' Brady was hoping that there was someone he could talk to – just on the off-chance his hunch was right. That Emily Baker had also disappeared. Even though no one had reported her as missing.

'Yes. She had quite a few until the age of twelve. Then she went into a children's care home in Wellfield.'

'Why was she removed from foster care?' Brady asked. But he suspected he already knew the answer. He absent-mindedly picked up a pen and started scribbling while he listened to her reply.

'She wasn't coping in that environment. Complained that she didn't like her foster carers. Repeatedly moved from one fosterer to another. Last one was a woman by the name of Joyce Seaman. It seems that it was decided by everyone concerned that she be moved to a children's home. But as I said, she's one of our success stories. Much to my colleague, Sandra's credit. She knuckled down and studied hard at school. Regardless of her personal circumstances.'

Brady thought about what she had just told him. There was nothing else he wanted to ask. His main concern was tracking Emily Baker down. Just so he could scratch her off a list that already included thirteen lobotomised women. Twelve dead. One, barely alive.

'That's great, Siobhan. Thanks, and if you think of anything else, get back to me,' Brady concluded.

'Can I ask you something?'

'Go ahead.'

'Is Emily in danger? Do you think this . . . this *Puppet Maker* freak has got her as well?'

'No,' Brady reassured. 'We're just following up some leads connected with Hannah Stewart. That's all.'

'But, what if he's targeting young women who've been in care. Should we be doing something?'

'No. Seriously, there's nothing to worry about. And if there is a connection you would be the first to know about it. Again, thanks,' Brady said. He hung up before she could ask another question.

He sat back and thought about her final question.

What if he was targeting young woman who had previously been in care?

He checked himself. Realised that he had no such evidence.

Not yet, anyway.

Chapter Fourteen

Sunday: 11:37 a.m.

Brady had got word back from Daniels about the Volvo 200 that had allegedly been parked up outside the old psychiatric hospital. The security guard had been correct. It had shown up on the CCTV footage in the past couple of weeks. But they had been unable to get a visual of the registration plate. Brady had told Daniels to try harder. It had crossed Brady's mind that the driver might be visiting a relative or a friend at the new St George's psychiatric hospital and merely using the old hospital as a parking spot.

Brady looked at Conrad as he climbed into the car. 'Nothing?'

Conrad nodded. 'Afraid so. Hannah Stewart had no family to speak of.'

'Poor bloody girl . . .' Brady said as he focused and pulled out. He was heading to the Royal Victoria Infirmary in Newcastle. Not to see Hannah Stewart. But to visit the others that the aptly named *Puppet Maker* had succeeded in murdering. But their murder was perhaps the least cruel part of their fate. It was what the suspect had done to them first.

The question was, why lobotomise them first and then lock them up and leave them to slowly die? Unless it was the knowledge that they were defenceless. Unable to think coherently, strategically. To get out. Save themselves.

But the part that had struck a chord with Brady was the most obvious answer – they would never be able to identify him.

He thought of Hannah Stewart. She was one of the lucky ones. *Or was she?*

Regardless of how many times Brady visited the morgue, the smell always got to him. It was a rancid, noxious smell that permeated your skin, hair and clothes. No amount of industrial antiseptic cleaning agent could get rid of the smell of a decaying body. Yet the body on the on the slab had already gone beyond the seven stages of putrefaction. The liquefaction of the body's organs had occurred years ago. Still Brady could smell death. He accepted that maybe it was his imagination. After all, the *Puppet Maker*'s oldest murder victim had completely decomposed. All that was left was the skeleton – apart from the hair and scalp. The sight still took his breath away. It was too macabre to even understand the mentality behind it.

'Not a pretty sight, eh?' Wolfe wheezed as he looked at the damaged skull. The drill holes on either side of the skull were clearly visible. Even to Brady's eyes he could see fracture lines along the skull from the force of drilling through bone. The holes were roughly two-and-a-half centimetres in diameter. He couldn't even begin to conceive the pain the victim would have felt during such a procedure. After all, this was brain surgery without the operating theatre and Brady presumed, without anaesthetic. The victim would have been fully conscious of the procedure. Wolfe was right. It was ugly.

'Neither is that wee lassie upstairs in ICU, mind! Had a look at what's been done to her. Exactly the same process as your suspect carried out on this poor bugger here. Have to say though, I don't know who is in the better position. This one here or the one that's still alive.' He shook his bald, glistening head. 'Had a look at the lassie's MRI scan. It's not good, Jack. He's butchered her. Bloody butchered her brain. Still can't fathom out why.'

Brady didn't answer. Instead, he glanced at Conrad. He was typically pale and thin-lipped. Not an unusual look for the morgue. Or in the presence of Wolfe – the Home Office Pathologist. Wolfe and Conrad had never seen eye to eye. The reason for their mutual animosity had never been discussed. At least, never in front of Brady.

'What is it about you, laddie?' Wolfe asked as he shot Brady a questioning look. He had ignored Conrad from the moment the DS had walked into the morgue behind Brady.

'What do you mean?' Brady asked. He never failed to marvel at Wolfe's accent. His soft, well-educated Scottish lilt betrayed the fact that although he had lived in the North East for the past thirty years, Wolfe's Edinburgh roots had never left him.

'Your ability to make life difficult for yourself.' He shook his head as he gestured at the young, female skeleton laid out in front of him. 'I thought you would have had enough on your hands, what with that Macintosh killer on the loose, to warrant searching around for more bodies.'

Brady shrugged. He knew he could be honest with Wolfe. They had shared too many pints in the Stuffed Dog on Tynemouth Front Street. Wolfe knew about Brady's car wreck of a life – both personal and professional. And Brady knew about Wolfe's idiosyncrasies. Mainly his drink problem; one that had nearly cost him his job and Brady the outcome of an investigation. But Wolfe had somehow bounced back from infamy and had continued unscathed. He was still one of the best Home Office pathologists in the force. So, for the time being, Detective Chief Superintendent O'Donnell looked the other way. Not that it had curbed his alcoholism. He had just adapted. Became more adept at hiding it. More wary when it came to the jobs that counted. Some were more high-profile than others. Which meant that they would be under the spotlight. If Wolfe failed to detect something, or made an error in judgement, regardless of how small, he now knew that someone, somewhere would be watching, waiting for him to fuck up. So he made sure that on such occasions he moderated his liquid lunch.

Despite Brady's casual shrug, Wolfe still looked concerned. It was clear that he wasn't going to accept it. So Brady attempted a reassuring smile. Let him know that he was all right. Regardless of how shit his life had suddenly become. Not only that, the fact that his shit life was now under the glare of the media. But he failed. His smile was more of a grimace.

'Macintosh isn't my problem now. Finding the sick bastard responsible for what happened to her is,' Brady stated as he stared down at what was left of one of his victims.

Surprised, Wolfe looked up at him. 'Tell me that arse of a DCI of yours hasn't knee-jerked because of the crap those morons in the media have been saying about you?'

Brady felt Wolfe's assistant Harold watching. He looked across at him. Harold reacted by blushing profusely. He shifted his gaze to the female body – or skeleton. 'No. Gates has enough people working on finding Macintosh. He needed someone on this case and I'm the one who found the victims,' Brady answered as he turned back to Wolfe. He shook his head at the pathologist's scepticism. 'I'm fine. Honest!'

Wolfe wasn't buying it. 'So why do you look like shit? Eh?' He shot a scathing glance over at Conrad, as if he was somehow responsible.

'It is what it is,' Brady stated, sounding nonchalant. However, he was anything but. It still hurt. The press had got to him. Even though he didn't like to admit it. He caught Wolfe's disbelieving expression. 'It's just the way it goes. That's all. Someone's got to be held accountable and unfortunately I was an easy target. I released him without charge.'

'And from what I gathered, you had no choice. You had nothing on him. So, tell me why bloody Gates didn't have your back? Huh? You were only doing your job, laddie!'

'He did. Or at least as best he could. And if it wasn't for this new case I would still be working on finding Macintosh.'

'Aye, laddie! You believe that if you want! I wonder what would have happened if you hadn't stumbled across this serial killer's collection of victims? I imagine Gates is relieved to have you working on something else. You'll see, soon there will be some PR spin sold to the press saying that you've been removed from the Macintosh investigation. They won't say why, but they'll be hoping it will quell the baying dogs.'

Brady shook his head as he gave Wolfe a half-hearted smile. 'I honestly don't give a fuck what those bastards write about me. It's all lies, so what does a few more matter?'

Wolfe didn't look so convinced.

'I'm fine. Honest.' He had known Wolfe a long time now. Trusted him. Respected him. Worried about him.

Brady knew he was a heavy smoker and a drinker with a rather robust appetite. Not even the job got in the way of his pleasures. But what worried Brady wasn't just his unquenchable thirst, troublingly evident by his ever-expanding waistline. It was the fact that he was asthmatic. Not that Wolfe seemed to care. But Brady did. And his attacks were becoming increasingly dangerous. Asthma killed. It was simple maths; at some point his luck would run out.

'Well, Jack, all I can say is I wouldn't want to be in your shoes right now. Watch your back. For me?' He suddenly started coughing.

Brady waited. Tense. He relaxed slightly when Wolfe seemed to get it under control. He still shot a concerned glance at Harold, who looked as uptight as Brady felt. It was enough to tell Brady that this was a common occurrence – too common.

'Have you been back to the doctor yet?' Brady asked.

Wolfe shot him a wry smile. 'What? With all the bodies you keep sending my way? Tell me, when I would get the time to see a doctor?'

'Seriously Wolfe, you need to get another health check-up. You sound like crap!'

'Well, you look crap so it makes us equal,' Wolfe stated good-humouredly. He fumbled around on his person until he found his Becotide inhaler. He took three deep lungfuls of the medication, held his breath for a minute, then breathed out. 'See? Fine. Got it under control!'

'Yeah? How often are you having to use that?' Brady asked. He shot another look at Harold. Harold's expression told Brady, *a hell of a lot*.

'Not often. Now, will you stop acting like my bloody wife?' Wolfe ordered.

'You don't have a bloody wife!'

'And I thank my lucky stars every day that I don't. Because if I did, she would act just like you! Constantly nagging me about my weight, my smoking and the rest.'

Brady noted that he had missed out the drinking part of his self-destruct regime. Easier to ignore the problem than acknowledge it. Brady knew that better than anyone. His relationship with Claudia was a classic example of avoidance. Of not accepting what was staring you in the face.

And when he did, it was too little, too late.

'Right,' Wolfe began. 'You've got a problem on your hands, laddie.'

Brady looked at him. Frowned. 'Tell me something I don't know?'

'I'm serious!' Wolfe shook his head and sighed, turning away from the victim on the slab. 'I had a look at Hannah Stewart's medical records before you arrived and then managed to get hold of her consultant. And we both agreed that some of the injuries that lassie has sustained date back eighteen months—' he stopped and shook his head as Brady was about to interrupt. 'Hear me out first, laddie.'

Brady did as instructed. He waited. But he was shocked at the news. It suggested that Hannah had been held captive for eighteen months without anyone reporting that she was even missing. It also conclusively ruled out Dave, the security guard. Eighteen months ago, Dave had been serving in Afghanistan. Brady had the team running checks on the other hospital security guards, but as of yet, they had nothing.

'Hannah Stewart has a hip fracture in the top end of the femur that dates back eight months. Around the same time she suffered a fractured ankle and a patella fracture. Or a broken kneecap, in layman's terms. There is a significant horizontal crack across her kneecap which means it is impossible for her to straighten her knee. All untreated. I would suggest that they both occurred at the same time, more than likely caused by a fall.'

Brady listened. He could see from Wolfe's intense expression that there was more to follow.

'But these injuries are only the beginning. She also suffered two broken ribs. Perhaps two to three months later than the first injuries. Around this time she also had a broken left wrist. Two fractures. Then recently, she suffered a dislocated right shoulder and fractured right arm.' Wolfe looked at the skeletal remains on the slab. 'Hannah Stewart's injuries are consistent with the fractures I found on this victim here,' he said. He looked down at the remains and then at Brady. 'Again, the oldest injuries are a fracture to the hip and fractures in both kneecaps.'

Brady knew what Wolfe was suggesting. That the injuries indicated that she had suffered fractures from falling down stairs – or being thrown down.

'The reason I'm telling you this is because there is a pattern. The other eleven victims have suffered nearly identical fractures. Hip and knee or ankle fractures. Some have broken legs as well. It suggests that they all suffered significant falls.' Wolfe looked up at Brady, frowning. 'As if they've been thrown down somewhere.'

Brady nodded. He had already reached that conclusion.

'And . . .' Wolfe paused as he raised his eyebrow at Brady. 'From the condition of this poor lassie here, I would say that she has been dead for twenty years.'

'Are you sure?' Conrad asked.

Brady looked over at him, surprised. Conrad barely spoke when he was in the morgue. But Brady felt the same shock that had prompted his deputy to question Wolfe's findings – twenty years seemed inconceivable.

Wolfe gave Conrad a dismissive look. 'Not that I am a forensic anthropologist, and I must add that it is difficult to tell when all that is left is skeletal remains, but I believe that she died roughly twenty years ago. Of course we can get an expert in to examine the skeletons. Give you a more conclusive answer. But I would suggest that your serial killer has been collecting women for a couple of decades now.'

'Shit!' Brady shook his head as he looked down at what remained of one of the victims. The fact that someone had been killing for so long and had gone undetected troubled him. His choice of victim was obviously high-risk, vulnerable young women. People who society did not notice. Or chose not to notice. Whether they were the unwanted homeless who wandered the streets begging, or prostitutes who traded their bodies for money, drugs or alcohol. These were the women that society turned their backs on. Including the police. Until it was too late. Until they ended up a statistic in the morgue.

'Can you tell me anything about the wigs he used?' Brady asked looking at the long, dark brown wig beside the skeletal remains.

Wolfe looked at him. 'No, laddie. That isn't a wig.'

Brady looked at him. 'I don't understand?'

'He scalped them, Jack. That there is this poor lassie's own hair.'

'What?' Brady replied, shocked. He had come across a lot of sadistic crimes but never a killer who scalped his victims.

'Whether they were alive when he did it, I can't tell you. But nonetheless, he scalped them and then preserved the skin.'

Brady looked across at Conrad. He looked as sickened by this new information as Brady.

'How did he preserve the scalps?' he asked as he stared in disbelief at the victim's hair.

'A liberal amount of non-iodized salt to the skin. He would need to work it thoroughly through the skin, and repeat the process a couple of days later when the salt became saturated with moisture. This technique is also knowing as curing and it lasts about ten to fourteen days. From the small puncture marks, it looks as if he tacked the scalp down and stretched it while it cured, making sure he had no folds in the skin.'

'Christ! It's sick,' Brady muttered.

Wolfe shot him a droll look. 'That's one word for it, laddie.'

Brady shook his head. He couldn't believe what he was hearing, let alone seeing. The fact that the suspect had scalped all his victims, apart from the surviving victim, Hannah Stewart, left him speechless. He was trying to make sense of it. But knew that he never would. The suspect's MO was driven by some need, some compulsion, that Brady could never understand and would never want to.

'All DNA samples from the victims have been sent off to the lab. Hopefully you'll be able to identify them.' Wolfe shook his head, adding, 'at least for the sake of their families.'

But Brady didn't reply. That was the part that was troubling him. He was certain that no one knew that these victims were missing. So how could they have ever hoped to be found? If Wolfe was right, and Brady was certain he would be, then the suspect had eluded the police for two decades. If the police were unaware of the missing women, they would be equally unaware of the suspect's crimes. Not only was it the murders of these women that affected Brady, and the physical and psychological torture they would have endured while held captive, it was also the knowledge that they would have lived with every day. The fact that no one would come looking for them, because no one knew, or cared, that they had gone. Disappeared. *For good.*

'The hair will obviously be forensically examined. Along with the necklaces and nightgowns found with each victim. They've already been sent off to the lab. If you're lucky, they might be some trace evidence from the suspect.'

If we're lucky . . . Brady resisted the temptation to say it loud. At this point in his life, his luck seemed to have well and truly run out. The police laboratory had long gone. Draconian cuts in the police budget had resulted in all forensic evidence being outsourced to the cheapest private lab. In instances like this, there was no one Brady could ring to speed up the process. It was a

Sunday. He had no choice but to wait. Regardless of how crucial the evidence could be. He knew that there were fingerprints on the necklaces. He had seen it when he had shone the Crime-lite over one of the victim's necklace. But fingerprints and other DNA evidence were only helpful if their perpetrator was already in the system. If he had no priors, then they would be no further forward.

'Did Ainsworth find anything at the crime scene?' Wolfe asked him.

'No,' answered Brady as he shook his head. 'At least, not yet.'

'Like I said, maybe the lab will find something. The suspect clearly took care of these victims. He dressed them. Washed and brushed their hair. So in all likelihood he must have left some trace evidence behind.'

'Why not embalm them?' Brady suddenly asked. 'To preserve them forever? If he went to the lengths of scalping them and curing the skin, why not the bodies?'

Wolfe looked at him. 'It's not as easy as you think. You would need a machine to inject fluids laced with chemicals, primarily formaldehyde, into an artery of the body while the majority of blood is emptied from a vein. Then a chemical known as humectant is added, which helps to fill out the body and adds a degree of moisture. But then there would have to be periodic injections of humectant to keep moisture in the tissues. Make-up is also used to disguise the discolouration of the skin which would typically turn brown. But as you can see here, that wasn't necessary.'

Brady followed Wolfe's gaze. The suspect had made a face mask of each victim. Brady presumed the mould had been placed over the flesh after they had died – not before. So, they had a face for each victim. Each mask was different.

'What is the mask made out of?' Brady asked.

'Alginate mould,' Wolfe answered.

Brady shook his head. 'What is that? Some kind of plaster?'

'Alginate is the stuff dentists use to cast teeth. It's commonly used for face moulds.'

Brady stared at the mask lying on the slab next to the victim's scalped hair. He was surprised at the detail. He could make out small acne scars across the victim's cheeks.

But every mask was different. Unique to each victim, like the scalps. Brady thought of what the press had named the serial killer – the *Puppet Maker*. It fitted. Perfectly.

Brady was certain that someone had leaked details about the macabre nature of the serial murder case to the press. That worried him. A lot. But right now what troubled him even more was the fact that he had no idea who could be responsible for carrying out these unspeakable acts on these women.

He shuddered involuntarily as his mind filled with an image that would haunt him to the day he died: twelve deceased victims, all sat in a semicircle wearing hideously painted face masks and cured scalps with long dark hair was an image that would remain forever burned in his mind. They had looked eerily alive dressed in long white nightgowns. The only thing that had jarred was that all that existed beneath the clothing were skeletons.

'Don't get me wrong here, Jack. You can try and preserve a body for a long time but you need to apply highly concentrated amounts of the chemicals I've mentioned. It is also a much slower process and must be done very carefully. And it requires periodic maintenance. But I must stress that indefinite preservation doesn't really exist. Embalming a body cannot stop decomposition. And remember Jack, he would need to have the means to keep the body refrigerated.'

Brady caught Conrad's eye. He looked like Brady felt. Sick to the stomach.

Chapter Fifteen

Sunday: 1:34 p.m.

Brady had driven Conrad back to the station and left him there to deal with the media. There was a press call scheduled for 2:00 p.m. About the *Puppet Maker*. Brady didn't have the stomach or the inclination to take any more crap. Especially not from the scavenging rats that called themselves the press. TV crews were already setting up in the allocated press room. The station was on edge. Every officer worried about the next onslaught of media coverage.

He had literally dumped Conrad with a list of orders and left. Conrad was good at public relations. Brady knew his personae suited the media's perception of the police. More significantly, the public's expectation of them. Professional-looking, trustworthy and ultimately the antithesis of DI Jack Brady. He had scheduled a briefing for later – to catch up with the team and vice versa. But first he needed to cover every angle. Which meant heading off to Emily Baker's address. He needed to know whether he should be adding her to the *Puppet Maker*'s list. He had just finished a call with Gates in which he had updated him on what he knew so far. And to say that Gates was in a foul mood was an understatement. Gates' team were still no closer to finding Macintosh or Annabel Edwards. The lead that they had been chasing in London had turned out to be a dead end. There had been no signs of Macintosh or the girl in the house that had been raided. Nothing to suggest that he had ever been there. The likelihood of the police finding her alive was diminishing with each passing hour. Brady was more than aware of the pressure Gates was under, not only from his bosses, but also from the glare of the media. And now they had a new serial killer – the *Puppet Maker* – at large. Someone who had eluded the police for years, it seemed.

But Brady still couldn't let go of James David Macintosh. If only he hadn't released him. If he had somehow detained him until the forensic laboratory had come back with the DNA evidence that conclusively tied Macintosh to the seventies Joker killings. Brady's hands had been tied. Yet, he was being castigated for it. He could cope with the press and public hysteria. At times, it was part of the job description. It was your colleagues and your boss whose opinions mattered. They were the ones who would protect you when your back was against the wall. But Brady had never felt so alone. So isolated. And ultimately, held accountable by those he ordinarily counted on, for actions beyond his control.

Gates had made it clear that he wasn't interested in Emily Baker. That Brady had enough on his hands without trying to add to the victim list. His point – Brady had no proof apart from the ramblings of a lobotomised girl.

One who would be lucky if she could manage to independently feed herself one day. So he had ordered Brady to focus on the facts he knew about. And not to go looking for more trouble.

Brady's response had been to keep his mouth shut. And when he did talk, he made sure it was what Gates wanted to hear. By the end of the call, his boss had seemed confident that Brady would keep his head and follow orders. Not that Brady could blame Gates. His boss had his hands full as it was chasing false leads in the Macintosh case. The last thing he needed was to be worrying about Brady wasting time following up hunches. The ever-decreasing police budget didn't allow for the luxury of mistakes.

He looked up at the first floor flat. 12b Whitley Road, Whitley Bay. Emily Baker's address. He had thought about Gates' orders to dismiss her from the investigation and decided against it. He had a feeling that something wasn't quite right. Hannah Stewart had been saying her name for a reason. Brady was worried that just maybe, Hannah was saying her name because she had been held prisoner with her. That Emily was a new victim. From what Brady could understand, it seemed to him that the killer held these women captive for eight months and then moved on to a new victim. The time frame regarding the fractures sustained by the victims seemed to support Brady's hypothesis. And high-risk, vulnerable young women were perfect targets for his crimes, making it hard to track him down. Hannah Stewart had no family or friends that he could contact. No one to talk to who could give him a description of the victim. Where she would hang out, who she socialised with – all crucial elements in narrowing down a suspect. It was the victim's story, their life choices that could help track down their killer. Without that information, it made Brady's life as the SIO difficult, if not impossible. Because then he was reliant on DNA evidence. If he was fortunate, the lab might find traces of biological evidence that could tie the suspect to the murders. However, the attacker's DNA would need to be on the police database, or his identity would remain unknown. As for witness reports, the suspect had managed to kill over a period of twenty years and store the bodies in a derelict but guarded psychiatric hospital without ever being noticed, let alone stopped.

Brady sighed. He had instructed Harvey and Kodovesky to go through the list of missing persons in the last twenty years or so. They had photographs of the face masks that the serial killer had made of each victim. Whether it would help, Brady had no idea. He was still waiting for the lab to call back with the DNA details of each victim. If he was lucky, the victims' DNA, like Hannah Stewart's, would be in the police database. But he wasn't holding his breath.

He got out the car and walked up the short path to the dilapidated Victorian terraced house. It had seen better days. It had once been a large three-storey house. But now it had been converted into flats, accommodating some of Whitley Bay's most vulnerable. Brady had recognised the address. It was a regular dumping site for ex-offenders who had successfully completed their six-month parole at Ashley House. They needed accommodation, just like anyone else. However, most of the residents in Whitley Bay had no idea that ex-offenders of this ilk lived within such close proximity. These were rapists, wife batterers, murderers and paedophiles; some were also child murderers.

Brady rang Emily Baker's doorbell and as he did so, he wondered how an eighteen-year-old girl coped being left by Social Services to fend for herself, surrounded by hardened ex-prisoners. He had heard accounts of young girls in authority care –some as young as sixteen – being placed in bedsits along the seafront. Left indefinitely to rot. Surrounded by alcoholics, druggies and men looking to make some easy money.

No one answered. He held his finger on the buzzer for over a minute. Still nothing. What did he expect? He was certain that she wasn't there. He pressed the buzzers for the three other flats. Curtains twitched as unimpressed, scowling faces looked out at him. He slapped his warrant card on the ground-floor window next to him. Right in front of the ugly, broken-nosed occupant's face.

'Police!' Brady shouted. It got a reaction. The kind of response that told Brady that the occupant of the ground-floor flat had recently been inside.

He heard a door slamming and then truculent footsteps.

The door swung open. 'If that fucking wanker has reported me, I'll fucking do him!' snarled the scrawny bloke.

He looked wired. Nervous, antsy and paranoid. Ready to stick a knife in someone's jugular. He had clearly had his shot of whatever illegal substance had been going cheap that day. Brady noticed the nose ring and the cropped stubble that he had attempted to dye black. A pathetic but failed attempt to look younger than his years. The black – which was more blue – looked bloody unnatural. Brady imagined he thought he looked shit-hot. And maybe he did to some old granny wankered on too many shots on a Friday night in the Bedroom pub in Whitley. But in the Sunday gloom called daylight, he looked nothing more than an old bloke desperately clinging to some semblance of youth.

'Shut the fuck up or I'll arrest you,' Brady ordered. He didn't have the time or the inclination to even bother explaining his reason for being there. Not to a shitfaced ex-con with ageing issues.

'Why the fuck would you arrest me? I haven't fucking done anything!' he spat as he yanked up his dirty grey jogging bottoms. His long-sleeved white T-shirt was covered in last night's takeaway and alcohol. It was also mottled with cigarette burns. The burns on his T-shirt matched the cigarette burns between his fingers on his right hand. He was a clear liability where the other occupants and neighbouring residents were concerned. The burns evidence that he would get so shitfaced that he would pass out with a cigarette smouldering between his fingers.

'Emily Baker. Girl who lives on the first floor?' Brady asked as he stepped into the dark, dank hallway. It stank.

The smell of rotting fish hit first, followed by the acrid undertone of stale piss. The place was a dump. Battered, discarded *Whitley Bay Guardian* newspapers lay in a pile in the corner of the hallway, alongside other piles of unopened mail. Brady assumed that people moved on without leaving a forwarding address. It was the kind of place that if you somehow managed to get out, you wouldn't want to broadcast where you'd gone.

The scrawny bloke had stepped back, out of Brady's way. It wasn't Brady's towering physical presence that had made him back down. It was the mention of Emily Baker.

'Why? What's wrong with her? I haven't touched her. I swear!' he insisted.

'Did I say you had?' Brady asked.

The bloke started nervously pulling his top down over his hands as he backed away. 'I didn't touch her like . . .'

'When did you last see her?' Brady asked walking towards him forcing him even further back into the dark hallway.

He shrugged. The sweat on his forehead glistening. 'I dunno, like. Friday morning? She left for college at eleven. Bumped into her on my way back from signing on. She had all her equipment with her. Said she was doing photography.'

'Pretty girl, is she?'

He looked at Brady. Scared. Not sure which way to answer the question. 'I dunno . . . Yeah . . . No . . .' He shook his head. Agitated, he started scratching the white stubble on his face.

'Did you see her come back on Friday?' Brady asked.

'Nah.'

It was an automatic reply. No hesitation. Too quick an answer for him to be lying. 'What about yesterday then?'

'Nah . . .' He continued scratching, causing the red and raised skin to bleed slightly. 'Come to think of it, I haven't heard her all weekend. Or seen her. She's right above me. I can even hear her in the bathroom first thing in the morning having a piss!'

'Bet you enjoy that. Don't you, Johnny?' Brady replied.

'How'd you know my name like?' he asked, scratching furiously at the stubble on his cheek.

'Your mail's on the floor. Ground floor Flat 12 A. John Atkinson. But you don't look like a John so I guessed you'd be a Johnny.'

'Yeah . . . right . . . yeah . . .' the bloke answered, confused.

'OK, just so I'm clear, you haven't seen or heard from her since Friday late morning?'

'Yeah . . . that's what I said, like,' he answered, eyes darting from Brady to his flat door.

'If you remember anything, or she comes back, can you give me a call?' Brady asked him. He handed him a card from his leather jacket. 'If you see her, tell her to get in touch with me ASAP.'

'Has she done something then?' he asked.

'No, she hasn't. But someone else has. Remember, call me,' Brady reminded him.

Johnny stood for a moment, confused. He watched as Brady walked up the stairs to the girl's flat.

'You'll need keys to get in. Landlord's got a set if you want me to call him?' Johnny offered.

Brady ignored him and continued walking up the stairs.

'Are you a real copper or what? 'Cos you don't look like a copper. You ain't got no police uniform and if you're really a detective like it said on your warrant card, why ain't you wearing a suit?' Johnny yelled.

Brady blanked him. He reached Emily Baker's door. He banged on it. Waited. Banged some more. Waited. The lock was simple, a Yale. He pulled out a pick from his jacket. He had taken it from a drawer in his office before he left. Suspected he might need it. He had made it some time ago from a hacksaw blade. It was something that he had learnt growing up on the Ridges. It came in handy from time to time when he mislaid the keys for his car. It was his pride and joy; a black 1978 Ford Granada 2.8i Ghia that had a good old-fashioned key instead of a remote central locking one. The Ford Granada was Brady's connection to the past – to his younger brother, Nick. The car had been bought as a project for them both to work on. But it was Nick who had turned it around. He focused on the lock. Blocking out thoughts of his brother. Now wasn't the time to reminisce. He had a job to do. Finding Emily Baker.

Brady didn't have time to wait for the landlord to show up. He knew that he could enter the property under Section 17 of the 1984 Police and Criminal Evidence Act on the grounds of saving an individual's life. That was why he was here. He heard the lock release. The door swung open slightly. He put the pick back in his jacket pocket and walked in. He wasn't worried about Johnny downstairs reporting him for breaking and entering. He reckoned that good old Johnny would have a list of convictions as long as his arm. Not to mention the stash of drugs he was using. The last thing he would want was the police around here.

Brady called out: 'Police!' But he already had a feeling that the place was empty. That she had left, as Johnny had said, on Friday at 11 a.m. and not returned since. His next move would be Newcastle College. His problem was that it was the weekend and staff wouldn't be around until Monday. He decided to check out the flat first and if there were definitely no signs of the teenager, he would get either Daniels or Kenny to get him a contact for one of her tutors. He needed to know whether she had turned up to college on Friday. And if she had, who she had left with.

He walked around the living room. It was basic, but Emily Baker had made it her own. A large photographic canvas dominated the chimney breast above the sixties-style tiled hearth surround and gas fire. The photograph was of wilting flowers. A close-up. It was beautiful but disconcerting at the same time. Then Brady realised that the blurred object in the background was a headstone. He leaned in and saw her name at the bottom of the canvas. He realised in that moment that Emily had something about her. She wasn't some prostitute, or heroin addict. Just some statistic from the care system.

Brady turned and looked around the rest of the living room. It was tidy. Shabby but comfortable. Budget stylish even. Unusual for an eighteen-year-old. If Brady had been expecting plates and mugs littered around the place and ashtrays filled high with tab ends and empty cans, he would have been bitterly disappointed. He walked through into the small kitchen. The window over the sink looked out onto the backyard below which was filled with rubbish, including a sodden, grubby double mattress and a sofa. He cast his eye around the kitchen worktops. For what it was, a seventies throwback, the place was immaculate. He opened the small fridge. It was virtually empty, aside from milk that was now two days out of date and a yoghurt, also past its best. The contents of her fridge exemplified student living. She was broke.

Brady double-checked to make sure there were no notes or letters lying around. Anything that would give him an idea of why she had disappeared. But there was nothing. He then made his way to her bedroom. It was pretty much the same as the rest of the flat. Run-down and damp. But again, she had made it hers. A single bed was positioned against the wall with a battered bed cabinet and lamp on one side. He noticed that she had left a book half read. It was the only book he had spotted in the flat. He went over and picked it up. It was Harper Lee's *To Kill a Mockingbird.* He wondered whether she was reading it because the acclaimed and notoriously reclusive writer had been in the news lately. He skimmed through the opening pages to see whether it had been a signed gift from someone. It wasn't. He put it down and looked around. The room was tidy. No clothes thrown down in a hurry. No struggle suggestive of being forced out the flat against her will. Nothing. Even the bed had been made. He pulled open the cabinet drawer. It was filled with expected paraphernalia. Nail polishes, lipsticks, cheap jewellery. Nothing out of the ordinary.

He walked over and opened her wardrobe. She didn't have many clothes, but what she did have had been arranged neatly. He glanced down at the black Vans trainers on the floor of the wardrobe. He then moved to the chest of drawers under the window. Pulled open the drawers. Underwear, knickers and bras. The next drawer down had one pair of short linen pyjamas. Three pairs of black socks lay neatly arranged beside them. The bottom drawer was empty. He turned and took in the room. What struck him as odd about the flat and in particular her bedroom, was that there was nothing of *her* here. Not that he had expected to find anything from her childhood. There were no tacky stuffed toys or other sentimental paraphernalia. After all, she had spent her childhood shunted from one foster carer to another until she had eventually ended up in a residential children's home. However, what did surprise him was the fact there were no personal items – not really. No photographs – not even recent ones.

The only item that she did have was an acoustic guitar in the corner of the room. It was maybe worth sixty quid, if that. He shook his head. He had no idea who Emily Baker was or what she looked like. Apart from the fact that she was a talented photographer. Ironic given the fact that apart from the canvas in the living room there were no other photographs in the flat. He had expected to find a laptop. There wasn't one. He assumed she would have taken it into college. He glanced back across at the bed. Crouched down on the floor. Looked underneath. Nothing apart from clumps of hair and dust. He went over and lifted the mattress. Nothing. Then he noticed her phone charger – an iPhone – left plugged into the socket down by the bedside cabinet. He was now certain that something had happened to her. That she was missing – and not through choice. Otherwise, she would have taken her phone charger.

He checked the bathroom. Her toothbrush, make-up bag and deodorant were still there. Undisturbed. He felt the bristles of the toothbrush. Dry. As were the towels. From the look of them, neither the sink or shower had been used for a few days.

He had no choice but to chase up one of her tutors at Newcastle College. He needed a photograph of Emily and he needed her last known whereabouts. He walked out the flat making sure the door was locked behind him. He couldn't shake the feeling that something had happened to this girl. That it was no coincidence that Hannah had said her name repeatedly. But what had also made him feel uneasy was the fact that he recognised a bit of himself in her. The lack of personal items – of family photographs and childhood memorabilia – had hit a chord. The flat belonged to someone who been institutionalised. Someone raised in care with nothing to really call their own. No identity. No past – aside from an ugly, violent one better left alone. But what had jarred was the intense feeling of isolation. There was no indication of any friends in Emily Baker's life. She seemed very much alone. And that worried him. If he was right, then there was no one in her life to know whether she had gone missing. Aside from the ex-inmate in the flat below, whose interest in the teenager was unhealthy but didn't place him high on Brady's suspect list. He made a mental note to get Harvey to bring him for questioning all the same. First, he had to establish that the girl was definitely missing. For that, he needed her mobile number.

He took his phone out as he walked towards his car. He scrolled down until he reached DC Daniels. Then pressed call.

Chapter Sixteen

Sunday: 2:38 pm

Daniels had managed to source Emily's mobile number. And her social worker's contact details. Quicker than Brady had expected. He called the mobile. But the phone had been switched off, adding to the overwhelming feeling that something was wrong.

He then rang the first contact number he had for her social worker. It went to voicemail. He tried the second one. He was in luck. Sandra Campbell answered.

'Hi, Sandra? Detective Inspector Jack Brady here. Apologies for calling you on a Sunday but it concerns a client of yours. Emily Baker.'

'Is she all right?'

Brady could hear the muted concern in her voice and wondered whether her colleague Siobhan Reardon had talked to her about Hannah Stewart.

'That's what I am trying to find out,' Brady answered, honestly. He didn't see any point in pretending otherwise.

'Have you checked her flat?' she asked.

'Yes. She hasn't been seen there since late Friday

morning. And I've tried ringing her mobile but it's switched off.'

'Oh . . . Maybe she has gone off for the weekend with friends?' Sandra suggested. But she didn't sound that convinced.

'That's why I am ringing you. What do you know about her personal life?'

Brady watched a young man get out of a car next to his while he waited for a response.

'Well . . . I've been her social worker since she was nine. She was placed into emergency care at the age of two. Sadly, she remained in care from then on. Her mother, who was just sixteen at the time, had spent most of her life in care herself and found herself pregnant at fourteen. She was given as much support as the system could offer but . . .'

Brady waited. He knew that whatever support that had been well-intentionally meted out had not been enough. No surprise really. So, Emily Baker's mother herself was a victim of the system.

'I'm sorry. I'm just hoping that she's all right. Her phone is definitely switched off?'

'Yes,' Brady answered.

'That's really unusual for Emily. She always answers her phone. You see, I set her up in her first flat in Whitley Bay. I saw her get her A-levels and then, I was the first person she contacted when she got accepted into college . . . Whenever I've rung her she's always answered my calls. But if I'm honest it has been a few months since I talked to Emily. You see, she is no longer within North Tyneside Council's care . . .' Sandra Campbell faltered.

'I know this must be difficult,' Brady sympathised. 'But I don't know if anything has actually happened to Emily. I just need to verify her whereabouts.'

'Yes . . . of course. I . . . well there's not a lot I can tell you . . .'

'What about any family?'

'No. She had no immediate family.'

'Her mother?'

'Died of an overdose when Emily was four years old.'

'I see,' answered Brady. 'What about the biological father?'

'Unknown.'

'Any stepfathers?' Brady already knew that her mother had had a boyfriend at the time of Emily's removal from her care. That he had significantly abused the two-year-old on her sixteen-year-old mother's watch.

'Yes. Give me a minute, will you? I need to double check.'

'Sure.' Brady gave her three minutes, to be precise.

'Sorry about that,' she apologised when she finally returned. 'Mark Sadler was his name. He was forty at the time of his conviction. So that would make him fifty-six now. He had been living on the Meadowell estate before he was arrested and charged with abusing Emily.'

Brady knew it well. It was the council estate he had grown up in. Known as the Ridges then. Located on the outskirts of North Shields, it was an infamous rundown estate that had had its fair share of problems. Some more public than others, such as riots in the early nineties.

'Thanks,' Brady said. He would check the name out. 'Do you know if he had any recent contact with Emily?'

'I don't believe so. At least not when she was in the care of North Tyneside. When she left, I can't say for certain, but I highly doubt it. Unless he somehow tracked her down but I can't see why he would. Or more to the point, why Emily would even agree to see him. I mean, what he did to her then was unimaginable. I'm surprised she survived some of the injuries if I'm honest with you. If it hadn't been for a neighbour reporting her mother and boyfriend for an unrelated crime— God! It's just not worth thinking about.'

There was nothing Brady could add to that statement. He understood that Emily was one of the lucky ones. She had survived. Somehow. But now? He thought of Hannah. What had been done to her. They knew it was a male they were looking for, which was no surprise. Forensics had come back with shoe prints from the crime scene. Size eleven. But, as yet, they still had no other forensic evidence – biological or trace. The laboratory had the victims' hair, clothing and jewellery in an attempt to find DNA evidence. Brady was hopeful. But it just took time. A luxury he wasn't sure they had – at least not for Emily Baker. If she was the *Puppet Maker*'s latest victim, then the odds were stacked heavily against her. The media was filled with garish reports about the twelve murder victims. If the perpetrator was unaware that his collection had been discovered, it would not be long before it came to his attention. That in itself could be the death of Emily. Or any other victims he was holding hostage.

'What about friends? Or a boyfriend? Did Emily ever mention any?'

'No. Not really. Emily's not that sociable. She was very quiet at school and sixth-form. She kept herself very much to herself. She had trust issues. Still has, I believe. Not that I can blame her. And as for boyfriends, no. She has never had a boyfriend to my knowledge. Or a girlfriend.'

'I see.'

'Have you contacted her tutor at Newcastle College? They will have a better idea of her friends than I have.'

'Yes, I was just about to do that,' Brady said as he looked over at Newcastle College.

'If you find Emily, let me know will you?'

'Or course,' Brady replied. He was about to cut the call when he suddenly remembered something. 'Sandra? There was another girl called Hannah Stewart who was also in North Tyneside Council's care. She's a few years older than Emily. Do you think they would ever have met at all?'

'Maybe . . . Why?'

'Hannah Stewart was found seriously injured last night and I need to know if there could be some kind of connection between them.'

'Oh God!'

Brady waited.

'Is she all right? Not that I ever dealt with her but one of my colleagues would have worked with her.'

'She's in the RVI in a critical condition.'

'Can I ask what happened to her?'

'She was attacked. I'm afraid that's all I can tell you.'

'And you think whoever attacked Hannah Stewart could be a threat to Emily?'

'Maybe. At this point, I can't say for definite. So, I would ask you to keep this to yourself.'

'Yes . . . Yes, of course.'

'So, if you find some connection between Emily and Hannah, no matter how small, let me know?'

Brady had just called Conrad and instructed him to check out the whereabouts of Emily Baker's stepfather – Mark Sadler. Emily's social worker had promised that she would cross-reference both Emily and Hannah's records from when they were in care. He was aware that Hannah Stewart's social worker had said that they had not shared the same schools, foster carers or children's homes. But Brady was hoping that there was a cross-over. Otherwise, why would Hannah be repeating Emily's name? The alternative was not worth thinking about. First, he needed to establish whether or not, Emily had been abducted, or whether it was just a coincidence.

But that was Brady's problem; he did not believe in coincidences.

He got out of the car and walked over to the entrance. A security guard was behind his desk watching a TV. Brady knocked on the glass door and flashed his warrant card. A moment later and he was buzzed in.

'Here to see Michael Philips?'

Without looking at Brady the guard checked a list on a board beside him. 'Photography department. First floor. Room 106.'

Brady headed for the first floor. He had been in luck. When he had rung Emily's tutor's office number to leave a message the guy had picked up. He had decided to come in that day to collect a pile of students' essays that he left behind on Friday evening. As soon as Brady explained his concerns he agreed he would wait there to meet him. He said he would rather deal with whatever questions Brady had at work, rather than back at home.

Brady found his office. Knocked and waited.

Michael Philips opened the door. 'Detective Inspector Brady?'

'Yes.' Brady couldn't help but notice Philips' surprise at his appearance. It happened. Often. He didn't look like your typical detective. At least not the stylishly suited and groomed ones on TV nowadays. 'I appreciate you waiting for me.'

Phillips shrugged as he walked back into the cluttered office. 'We have a teething four-month-old at home. Having an excuse to catch up on my workload somewhere quiet suits me,' he replied.

Brady hazarded a guess that he was in his late thirties. Tall, dark-haired and good-looking. He imagined that Philips would be popular with his students.

'Sit down,' he offered.

'Thanks.' Brady sat down.

'I believe this is what you requested,' he said, handing over a sheet of paper that he had picked up from his desk.

Brady took it. There was a small student ID photo clipped at the top corner. He stared at it. He felt sick. She looked familiar – too familiar. Young, pretty with rich, chocolate-brown coloured eyes and long, thick dark hair. He realised that he could have been staring at a photograph of any number of the suspect's victims before they had been abducted.

'Quiet student. Doesn't like to talk a lot in seminars. Just keeps herself to herself,' volunteered her tutor. 'Her contact details are all on there,' he added.

Brady scanned his eyes down until he came to the next of kin details. There was nothing. Nor were there any emergency contact numbers. Only her mobile number, home address and her doctor's practice.

'I know,' her tutor agreed, noting the disappointment on Brady's face. 'It's highly irregular. The admin staff said she refused to explain why so they had no choice but to leave it blank.'

Brady looked up at him. Resisted the temptation to defend Emily by stating that she had grown up in care. That she had no one. And that he imagined she sure as hell wished she had someone to put down as an emergency contact.

'What about friends here?'

He shrugged dismissively. 'Nobody that stands out. Don't get me wrong, she's a lovely girl. Polite, always hands her assignments in on time. Great student in those terms but as for her social life, well she didn't seem to have one. Her peers socialise together. Student parties, drinking in town. What you'd expect. But she has no part of that. Prefers her own company. Comes to college. Works. Goes home.'

Brady nodded. 'Why do you think that is?'

'She's different. Seems more mature than the other students. I think the fact that she lives out on the coast makes a difference. Most of her peers live in either college accommodation or in town.'

'Can I talk to the students in her year?' Brady asked.

'If you like. But I honestly don't believe you'll find out anything more than I can tell you. They will be around in the morning if you want to have a chat with any of them.'

'Thanks,' Brady said, standing up to go. 'I really appreciate your time. Hope you can get caught up with marking those assignments.'

'More chance of it here than at home,' he said, standing up to see him out of his office.

Brady stopped. He hadn't noticed the other coffee cup. It was sat on a filing cabinet behind Brady's chair. Philips had one on his desk. Half-drunk. The other one was identical apart from the dark brown lip gloss around the rim.

Philips caught Brady's eye. 'Personal tutorial. I decided to make the most of my time here.'

'Do you often see your students out of hours?'

'Sometimes. There's no crime in that, is there?'

'What about Emily? Did you see her after college hours?' Brady asked.

Philips narrowed his eyes. 'I don't like what you are suggesting, Detective Inspector Brady.'

'I'm not suggesting anything. All I am trying to do is establish whether you had any contact with Emily outside of lectures or tutorials.'

Philips looked at Brady, clearly annoyed at the question. 'No. I had no contact with Emily Baker other than scheduled lectures or seminars.'

'Anyone else at the college who might have seen her outside working hours?'

Philips sighed heavily as he ran a hand over his designer stubble. Brady couldn't help but notice the wedding ring. Not that Brady could judge. After all, he had been guilty of having an affair with a junior colleague. One that resulted in the end of his marriage.

'She . . . she was interested in one of our lecturers here. Julian Fraser. He's an internationally renowned artist and has a placement here for this academic year as our "artist in residence". I do know that Emily had requested some personal tutorials from him.'

Brady looked at him.

'I only know because she asked me first whether it would be possible. Different departments you see. She is in the photography department and Julian works in the art department. It all comes down to budgets and who pays for whose time.'

Brady nodded. 'Emily was last seen leaving her flat for college late Friday morning. Did you see her that afternoon?'

Philips shook his head. 'No. I didn't but I do believe that Julian had a personal tutorial with her booked in for Friday. Do you want me to give him a call?'

'Better still, give me his contact details.'

Five minutes later and Philips had a print of his colleague's address and contact numbers. 'You might catch him at his studio over in the art department. I passed him in the corridor about an hour back. He said that he was heading over to his studio to finish some work.'

'Thanks,' Brady said taking the information. 'I'll be back tomorrow to have a chat with the students in her year.'

'Fine,' Philips said heading for his office door. He held it open for Brady. 'I really do hope nothing has happened to Emily.'

'So do I,' Brady stated. 'One last question? Friday night, I take it you have an alibi?'

'What exactly does that mean?' Philips asked as his eyes flashed with anger.

'It's just a question.'

'An impertinent one, at that.'

'Well?' questioned Brady, unable to ignore the tutor's terse response.

'I don't see that as any of your business,' Philips replied.

'It will be if I take you in for questioning.'

'And why would you do that?'

'If I find that something has happened to Emily Baker.'

'Don't be ridiculous. You have no grounds to even consider me a suspect in any alleged disappearance. She may be a student, but that is as far as it goes. I have no idea what she gets up to in her free time.'

'But the difference is you see your students in your own time,' Brady said as he looked over at the stained half-drunk coffee cup.

'Christ! That is ridiculous! I already told you before you arrived that I had scheduled a tutorial with a student who is having personal problems.'

Brady nodded. 'I can see that from the traces of brown gloss on your lips. I would think about wiping that off before you head home.'

Philips glared at Brady.

'I saw your student. The one with the personal problems sat downstairs reapplying her lip gloss. Pretty young thing. How old? Eighteen, if that? Whatever pep talk you gave her obviously worked. She looked very happy with herself.'

'Right. If that's all, I have work to do,' Philips concluded as he turned his back on Brady and walked back to his desk. 'Feel free to call in for a chat anytime.'

'Believe me, I will do,' Brady answered as he walked out.

Brady found the art department. He was heading for Julian Fraser's studio. He had already tried his office and he wasn't there.

He knocked on the door to the studio. Waited. Knocked again. He then tried the door handle. It was locked. He turned as he heard footsteps.

'Can I help?' the man asked as he approached Brady.

'I'm looking for Julian Fraser.'

'Can I ask why?' he asked, frowning.

Brady pulled out his warrant card. 'I have a few questions I need to ask concerning a student registered at the college.'

'I'm Julian,' he said extending a hand out for Brady to shake.

Brady took it. He had a firm, assertive grip.

'How can I help?'

'Is there somewhere we can talk?' Brady asked.

'I'm afraid I was just leaving. I am picking my wife up from town. How about we talk as I walk to my car?'

Brady accepted his offer. He had a relaxed, friendly manner about him. He was roughly five foot ten with short blond hair and warm hazel eyes. Slim build. He was wearing faded jeans and a T-shirt. A casual, comfortable look that he pulled off.

'Can I ask who you want to discuss?' Julian questioned as he walked along the corridor.

'A photography student by the name of Emily Baker.'

Julian continued walking. If he had recognised the name, it didn't show.

'What's happened?' he asked as he turned to Brady.

'We don't know yet. From what we can gather she has been missing since Friday afternoon.'

'Really?' Julian said, surprised. He stopped walking. 'I did see her for a tutorial on Friday for half an hour. It had been booked in for a fortnight. She left my office at three-thirty.'

'Did she seem upset at all when you saw her?'

He shook his head. Smiled at Brady. 'Not at all. She was rather excited about a project she was working on. Had lots of ideas that she wanted to run by me.'

'Such as?' Brady asked.

He shrugged. 'Usual stuff you would expect from an eighteen-year-old. Not that interesting. But they are young. Still learning. So my job is to encourage them.'

'Did she say if she would be working on her photography project this weekend?' Brady asked. He was still hoping her disappearance was something innocent.

'No. She didn't say.'

'What about anything personal? Such as plans to visit friends for the weekend?'

Julian continued walking as he thought back. 'No. I can't say she mentioned anything. I don't really know Emily that well. But she seems like a popular girl. Well-liked by the other students. She is one of many young people I see here. My job is to discuss their work. Not their personal lives.'

'I understand,' Brady answered as they reached the double doors leading out into the main reception area. 'If you think of anything, give me a call,' Brady said as he gave him a card with his contact details.

'I will do. I'm sure she'll turn up tomorrow after a weekend of partying. You know what students are like. I would check with her friends though. I'm sure they will be more help than I have been.' He searched in his jeans pocket for his car keys. 'Look I've got to dash. Sorry. Wife and all that.'

'No problem. Thanks for your time,' Brady said as he watched Julian Fraser walk briskly out the building. But it was clear that he didn't really know Emily. Otherwise, he would have been aware that Emily had no friends to speak of. Otherwise Brady would have already talked to them.

* * *

Brady took a swig of water from the bottle he had bought out of the vending machine.

He had a bad taste in his mouth after his talk with Michael Philips. But the water seemed to be making no difference. Brady took another drink. He had his phone pressed to his ear, waiting for Conrad to answer.

'Where the fuck have you been?' questioned Brady as soon the call was picked up.

'Dealing with the press, sir.'

Brady took a deep intake of breath. He needed to steady himself. Public opinion of the Northumbrian force – and Brady – was low and consequently, the press counted. Time had to be spent placating them, which was why Brady had asked Conrad to act in his place. Brady's reaction would have been short and succinct. And one that they wouldn't have liked. But it would have made great headlines.

'Emily Baker is definitely missing. No sign of her at her flat and she hasn't been seen since Friday afternoon when she left college. I just talked to her tutor who said that he last saw her at three-thirty p.m. when she left his office after a tutorial. Her phone has been switched off.' Brady breathed out, trying to steady the rising panic he felt. He couldn't rid himself of the grotesque image of the murder victims. Each one wearing masks of their own faces. Their own scalped hair. And identical Victorian-style long, white nightgowns. The macabre nature of it made it seem unreal. But it was very real.

He heard Conrad breathe in. As if preparing himself for what was about to follow.

'I checked out Mark Sadler, Emily Baker's mother's old boyfriend. He's back inside.'

'Shit!'

'Why were you so interested in him?'

'He was charged and convicted of abusing her when she was two years old. She's suddenly disappeared. We know he is more than capable of hurting her. Past behaviour is a good indicator for future behaviour.'

Conrad didn't reply.

'Anything else?' Brady asked.

'DNA results have come back on eight of the victims, sir. All with identical backgrounds. Young, vulnerable women, all prostitutes. No family to mention. Each one has been arrested or charged with soliciting. Their custody photos are identical to the face masks each victim was found wearing. The Christian names inscribed on each necklace also matches the victims' actual names.'

Brady instantly felt sick. The reality was too much. 'What about the others?' If they had been abducted years ago, even if they had also been prostitutes and arrested for soliciting, DNA swabs would not have been taken. The UK national DNA database was created in 1994. However, DNA samples were only taken from convicted criminals or those awaiting trial. Then in 2003 it was changed to allow DNA to be taken on arrest. Only the victims arrested after April 2004 when the law came into force would have had their DNA taken and stored in the database – regardless of whether they were charged, or convicted.

'Nothing.'

Brady was disappointed, but not surprised. 'Of the eight victims we know of, were any reported missing?'

'None of them, sir. Not one. I've checked their police records and none of them had an actual contact address. It seems they lived and worked on the streets. I have tried to go back over twenty years, considering that one of the victim's remains could date that far back, comparing reported missing young women who fit the type taken by perpetrator with the face masks found on the victims. But . . .'

'But what?'

'Thousands of young people go missing every year. Roughly two hundred and fifty thousand people go missing every year and one hundred thousand are children under sixteen years old. A high proportion are reported to have run away from care. A high percentage are found within forty-eight hours but that still leaves a significant number unaccounted. But it is the people in the fifteen to seventeen age group who go missing most often.'

Brady was staggered. He knew from Wolfe's findings that the victims' skeletal remains were in keeping with young women between the ages of late teens to early twenties. The question was, how old were they when they were abducted? He couldn't believe that twelve young women, teenagers even, could just disappear and no one would notice. Or maybe they did, but they just didn't care. Plenty more to fill their spot on the street corner.

'The eight you've identified, were they arrested locally?' he asked.

'Yes.'

Brady realised that he could have processed any number of these arrested women. He would have released them back onto the streets. Homeless, with no place to go. They would have been easy targets. It didn't bear thinking about. And then there was Emily Baker.

'Emily—' Brady began.

Conrad cut him off. 'I have to say, she doesn't fit the suspect's type.'

'Physically she does,' Brady replied with an unmistakable edge to his voice.

'But she's in full-time higher education and she has an address. The other victims were homeless and jobless. They weren't integrated at all into society. The reason the suspect has selected them is because they are guaranteed to cause minimum, if any police attention.'

Brady remained quiet. He knew exactly what Conrad was getting at.

If no one knows you're missing, how will they know to find you?

To Brady, Emily Baker fitted right into that type. He wondered how long it would have been before someone reported her missing. She had no friends to speak of, no family. Her college peers might have noticed that she had disappeared but would not have thought anything about it. As her college tutor had remarked, she was a student who kept herself to herself. It could have been weeks before the college lecturers realised that she was missing lectures and seminars. And then, it could have been even longer before someone actually realised that there was a problem.

Too little, too late.

Brady felt plagued by the thought that whatever he did was not enough. Or that he had acted too late. Again, Annabel Edwards came to mind.

'Trust me, Conrad. He has her.'

Conrad's awkward silence was enough.

'For fuck's sake! I know a lot of shit has happened and I'm being blamed for most of it by the media but I haven't lost my fucking mind! Maybe my job – but not my mind. So when I tell you that he's got her I expect you to take me seriously.' Exhausted, Brady breathed out. He noticed someone walking down towards the college campus giving him a strange look. Realised then that his car window was down.

'Yes, sir.' The reply, terse.

Brady didn't give a fuck. Not anymore.

'What do you intend to do?' asked Conrad.

'Find her. Before it's too bloody late!'

'What do you want me to do?'

'Get Daniels and Kenny to check out the CCTV footage from Newcastle College leading down to Newcastle train station will you? She went somewhere after her tutorial on Friday afternoon. It's our job to find out where.'

'Yes, sir.'

'What about the CCTV footage around St George's? Have Daniels and Kenny found anything?'

'Nothing yet.'

'Have they checked to see whether the Autumn Residential Care Home behind the woods has any security cameras covering the car park and grounds? What if he parked in the car park there? No one would notice. Staff would think that the car belonged to a visiting relative.'

Brady knew that the police dogs had tracked Hannah Stewart's scent across the field and down through the woods to a small layby where it was believed the suspect had parked his car. The scent had ended there. Ainsworth's team had examined the parking area and found nothing. But Brady was wondering if they were looking in the wrong place. For all they knew, Hannah Stewart could have wandered off from the suspect and his car down the track that led to the lay-by. He knew it was a long shot. But he was prepared to consider all possibilities.

'I'll get on to it,' Conrad assured him, eager to go.

Brady knew why. 'What happened after the raid this morning? Have they got any new leads?'

'All I know is that the team still believe he is in London.'

Brady didn't say what he wanted to. Instead, he kept quiet. But what was worrying him was all the time and energy Gates was expending searching for Macintosh and the abducted girl in the wrong place. The problem was, DCI Gates wasn't crediting Macintosh for the highly intelligent psychopath that he was and always had been. Brady knew by the time he did, it would be too late.

Too little, too late.

Chapter Seventeen

Sunday: 6:01 p.m.

Brady was back at the station. Sandra Campbell, Emily Baker's social worker, had called him earlier. She had said that both Hannah and Emily had resided with the same foster carer. Not at the same time. There was a two-year gap between each girl being placed there. Both had only stayed for a short time before being placed into different children's homes; one in North Shields, the other in Wellfield. They had never met. But what did interest Brady was the fact that Joyce Seaman had a twenty-six-year-old son who had been eighteen at the time of Hannah's placement. When Emily, who had been twelve at the time, had been placed in the foster home, he had still been living there.

Brady grabbed a coffee and a sandwich from the basement cafeteria. His plans after he had eaten were to interview Ryan Seaman. He had had contact with both young women when they had been in foster care. Whether inappropriate or not, Brady could not say. At least, not yet. But it was enough for Brady to have him brought into the station for questioning.

Ryan Seaman interested Brady. A lot. He now lived in a flat in Whitley Bay and was employed as a full-time labourer for a local building firm. But what interested Brady were the charges that had been made against him four years back. He had been arrested and charged with rape. The victim had barely been above the age of consent. Not that there was consent when it came to rape. The sixteen-year-old in question had been placed in Joyce Seaman's foster care. At the time, Ryan Seaman had still lived there. He had protested his innocence. And it had never gone to court. The teenager, for whatever reason, had dropped the charges.

Brady didn't know the reason why Hannah had run away repeatedly from Joyce Seaman's house. Or why Emily refused to stay there after only one week. But he thought he was about to find out.

'Look, I ain't done nothing. I didn't touch the fucking cow! Anyways, that was four years back. Stupid slapper that she was! Caused me no end of fucking bother!'

Brady looked at Ryan Seaman. Resisted the urge to give him a smack to teach him some respect for women. But he knew he would be wasting his time. Scrotes like him would never change.

'Ryan, do you remember Hannah Stewart?'

Ryan Seaman shrugged. 'Dunno. Should I?'

'I need a straight answer. Yes or no,' Brady stated.

'Fuck do I know!' Ryan answered. He turned to the appointed Duty Solicitor sat beside him. 'I've got nothing to say.'

Brady looked straight at the Duty Solicitor. He was new. But it was clear from his attitude that he didn't give a damn. He was here simply for the extra cash.

'My client has nothing else to say,' he reiterated flatly.

'Yeah. We heard,' Brady answered. 'Hannah Stewart,' he continued. 'She was twelve when she was placed in your mother's foster care. That was eight years ago. Would have made you eighteen then. Why did she keep running away?'

Ryan shrugged. 'Fuck knows. No doubt shagging around. Most of them foster kids are a handful. Drinking, taking drugs and fucking whoever and whatever,' he replied with a sneer.

It took some willpower for Brady not to punch the smirk off his face. 'Is that what happened with Janine Rogers? You're saying she was sexually promiscuous?'

He shrugged again. 'If you mean was she a slapper? Then yeah.'

'What was it about her? Did she remind you of Hannah Stewart and Emily Baker? Was that it? All three were petite with long, dark hair. All a type. But Janine fought back, didn't she? Difference was, she wasn't twelve years old like Hannah and Emily. She was sixteen. She had a bit more about her than two pre-pubescent girls. Couldn't be so easily silenced.'

'Fuck you!'

'What about Emily Baker? She managed to stay for a week before she asked to be removed. Why?' Brady asked. 'Was it because you liked to go into her bedroom and touch her? Just like you did with Janine?'

'Fuck you!'

'Can I ask exactly where you are going with this line of questioning?' interrupted the Duty Solicitor.

'Of course,' Brady answered, his eyes still fixed firmly on the suspect. He watched as Ryan scratched at a scab on his upper right arm. 'Hannah Stewart was found last night. She had been savagely attacked and left for dead. And Emily Baker, also known to Ryan, is now missing.' Brady shoved the student photograph of Emily towards him. He watched as Ryan glanced down. Then away.

'Don't recognise her.'

'Are you sure?' Brady asked.

He scratched at his arm again, making it bleed. 'Nah. Told you me mam has had countless strays through her door.'

'But Emily remembered you.'

Ryan slouched back against the chair. 'That's shite!'

Brady shook his head. 'Her social worker told me that you were the reason that she would rather be in a residential children's home. What did you do to her to make her want to leave?'

Ryan's eyes darted back down to the photo of Emily Baker.

Brady could see that he had hit a nerve. Not that her social worker had actually said anything of the sort, but he had a feeling that Ryan Seaman had played a big part in Emily Baker's refusal to stay. 'Must have been great. No one to stop you doing what you liked to these young girls. No one ever listened to them. Did they?' He paused as he caught Ryan's eye. 'No. Why would they? Troubled kids from even shittier backgrounds than yours. No surprise your mam thought they were lying. Trying to cause trouble.'

'My client has nothing to say,' interjected his solicitor.

Brady continued. 'Where were you on Friday, Ryan?'

'My client has already answered that question.'

Irritated, Brady stared at the Duty Solicitor. Then turned to Ryan. 'Yeah, we checked out your alibi. Work said you left shortly after three p.m.'

Ryan slouched even further down in his seat as he stared at Brady.

'The building site where you're based is a five-minute walk from Newcastle College.'

'So? Not against the law to leave work early,' Ryan muttered.

'Emily Baker was last seen leaving Newcastle College around the same time you left work. Had you been watching her? Waiting for the right moment to talk to her? Persuade her to go somewhere with you? Did you decide to finish off what you had started when she had been twelve? Is that what happened to Hannah? You found her and decided to sort her out.'

'Really DI Brady, this is pure speculation. My client does not know these young women.'

'He knows them. Got to know them very well. Didn't you, Ryan?' Brady questioned as he scrutinised him.

'No comment,' muttered Ryan.

'So, this weekend? You went on a bender? Is that right?'

Ryan stared at Brady. 'No comment.'

'Late Friday afternoon to Sunday morning?'

He shrugged. 'No comment.'

Brady looked back down at the file in front of him. Opened it and checked the four names listed. He was waiting for confirmation of Ryan's alibi. Granted, he did smell like he had spent the past thirty-six hours in a brewery. That had been his alibi. That he had gone on a stag night in town. Left work early to go home, shower and then headed out with the lads. It had been a two-night bender. The problem for Ryan was that his mates hadn't materialised yet.

Brady turned and caught Conrad's eye. His deputy didn't look that convinced that Ryan Seaman was responsible for the abduction and torture of Hannah or the disappearance of Emily. Brady was feeling the same. Then there were the other victims. Ryan Seaman was twenty-six. His age ruled him out. But what if he had an accomplice? Or he was copying someone?

'Can I get a tab?'

'You already know the answer.'

'Fuck you! This is against my human rights. I'm a fucking addict with a forty-a-day habit!'

Brady was starting to get tired of Ryan Seaman. Very tired.

'When was the last time you saw your dad?' Brady asked. He watched as the suspect shifted in his seat.

'Dunno, like.'

'Yesterday? A week back? Two years ago? When?'

'He disappeared when I was little.'

'Why?'

Ryan shrugged. But Brady could feel the hatred emanating from him. Hatred at Brady for poking around in his life.

'People don't just disappear, Ryan. Not for twenty years.'

'This is ridiculous. What's the relevance of this?' interrupted his solicitor.

'It has every relevance,' Brady answered. He turned back to the suspect. 'You see, Ryan, someone has been abducting and murdering young women like Hannah Stewart and Emily Baker for what we believe could be as long as twenty years. You personally knew Hannah and Emily. Too personally, by all accounts. You were in the same location and at the same time that Emily Baker disappeared. You have already have a track record of sexually assaulting women—'

'The charges were dropped, DI Brady,' interrupted the Duty Solicitor.

'Do you believe in coincidences, Ryan?' Brady continued, ignoring his solicitor.

Ryan didn't reply. Instead he waited.

'I reckon he's been in touch. Hasn't he?'

Brady watched as Ryan shifted his weight again in his seat.

'No comment.'

'You see, we can't find him, Ryan. He doesn't exist. Or at least, hasn't existed for twenty years. Why? What would make him disappear like that?'

Ryan stared at Brady.

'Where is he, Ryan?'

Brady waited. Nothing. 'You two have a lot in common, don't you? Your father was arrested and charged for raping a barmaid who worked in his pub. Did two years for that.'

Ryan shrugged. 'Stupid bitch tried to blackmail him. Me mam told me all about it. When he refused to pay her she went to you lot. Made a false claim just like that fucking slapper Janine.'

'But he did time for it, Ryan. Suggests there was concrete evidence against him.'

'Yeah? Her word against his is what I heard.'

Brady shook his head. 'No. He didn't just rape her. He beat her. Left her with a broken nose and two broken ribs.'

Brady studied him. If Ryan was surprised by the revelation, he didn't show it. Then again, given the suspect's attitude to women, Brady imagined that he would have little or no empathy for his father's victim. It was clear from the look of cold hatred in his eyes that he did not care.

'Your dad served two years inside. Then when he came out he stayed with you and your mam for two months before he disappeared. Why was that? What happened to make him go like that? Was it you? Your mam?'

'No fucking comment!' he retaliated.

'I've got all night, Ryan. So, we can sit and wait this out as long as you want,' Brady said folding his arms and sitting back.

The stalemate was disturbed a minute later by a knock at the door.

Brady turned and looked up as Harvey opened it. 'Sir? A word?'

'Can't it wait?'

'No,' Harvey replied.

'This better be worth it.'

Brady stood, arms folded behind Daniels and Kenny. He was still in a foul mood over Ryan Seaman. He was really hoping that they might have had a positive lead. But his alibi had finally been verified. Harvey had been the one to break the news to Brady. Not that he had been too impressed at the time. It transpired that Ryan Seaman had been telling the truth and had spent the weekend drinking with his mates. Consequently, he had been released without charge. However, his father, Geoffrey Seaman was still an enigma. There had been no trace of him for the past twenty years. Whether something had happened to him, or he had just wanted to distance himself from his past, Brady couldn't say. Nor it seemed, could his son or wife.

'It is, sir. Wait . . .' Daniels said pointing at the screen. 'Here . . . here it is.'

It was CCTV footage taken from the residential nursing home behind the bluebell woods.

Brady looked. 'No . . . I don't see anything.'

'Just here, sir. Look!' Daniels ordered, pointing to the screen.

Then Brady saw her. A young woman walking. Alone. 'Are you sure it's her?'

'One hundred per cent, sir. That is Emily Baker. If you wait you'll get a clearer image.'

Brady watched. It was hard to see at first as the figure was caught walking up the road that turned off into the care home. But then he saw that she was wearing the same clothes and carrying the same backpack over her shoulder, which Brady assumed contained her camera equipment. Daniels and Kenny had done as instructed and methodically followed her movements on Friday afternoon from Newcastle College to Newcastle train station. She had then surprised them all by catching a train to Morpeth. Her movements had been tracked by CCTV camera walking through the small market town's centre. The direction she had been heading in was Bluebell Woods.

'I don't understand why she was going there,' Brady mused as she continued walking on and then disappeared from sight. The road was a dead end. The only other place she could be heading was the derelict psychiatric hospital through the woods and then across the field. The time was 6:01 p.m.

'It gets better,' promised Daniels, excited.

Kenny nodded. 'Yeah. This is where it gets interesting.'

Brady looked at them both. Sat there with their arms folded. Proud of themselves. If Brady was honest, he had to admit that the pair had surprised him. They had persevered until they had found something conclusive. He watched the fast-forwarded footage. And waited. Then he saw it. Realised the reason they were so impressed with themselves. It was a shot of Emily Baker coming back down the road, past the residential care home at precisely 10:19 p.m. But she wasn't alone.

'Freeze it!' ordered Brady. He stared at the grainy image. She was definitely with a man. He was significantly taller than her which immediately ruled out Ryan Seaman who was five foot three – if that.

Brady scrutinised the suspect. It was difficult to make any identifying details apart from the fact he was wearing a long coat.

'Can you enhance it?' Brady asked.

'Yeah. But it's still not that good,' Daniels replied.

Brady waited to make that decision for himself. But Daniels was right. The footage was of the back of the suspect's head. At no point did he turn round. But what did intrigue Brady was the intimacy between Emily and the suspect. He definitely wasn't a stranger. It was evident from the way they were chatting in a relaxed manner that they knew each other. If anything, Emily was animated. She was using a lot of hand gesturing as she seemed to be describing something in detail to the suspect.

But it struck Brady as odd. The intimacy. Emily had no friends. No boyfriend to speak of. Or girlfriend. Harvey and Kodovesky had managed to expedite her mobile phone records. They had the details of all the calls she had made and received. But none were personal. They consisted of companies cold calling or texts alerts about her next phone bill. No other texts. Nothing. She kept herself very much to herself. Brady had also checked out Facebook. She didn't have a profile. That had surprised him. He had assumed everyone would be on Facebook. Nor did she use Twitter. Whether she had been trolled on Facebook and had left the social site was worth considering.

'Get a copy of this film out to the media. I want her face out there as well as this footage of her with him. For all we know someone might recognise the suspect,' Brady said.

'She's definitely missing, then?'

Brady turned around. Conrad had walked in to the small room. 'Take a look at this, then decide. Last seen walking away with an unknown man at ten nineteen p.m., Friday evening.'

Conrad looked mildly surprised at this news. 'Where?'

'Road leading off from Bluebell Woods. Roughly half a mile down from the old hospital. She and the suspect look to be heading to the lay-by at the bottom of the woods. The exact place where Hannah Stewart's scent ended. It suggests he drove Hannah there and then, from the scent followed by the dogs, he walked her up through the woods and gained access to St George's across a field that leads directly to the extensive grounds at the rear of the hospital.'

Conrad looked at him. 'And there's nothing caught on film?'

'No. Absolutely nothing. Bluebell Woods backs onto a field and beyond that the grounds at the rear of the hospital. There are no security cameras at the back of the hospital. I've had all the security footage scrutinised and it is possible to get in that way without being detected. Also, there is a barbed wired fence at the edge of the woods leading into the field that has been cut for easy access. We've found multiple footprints there but we did get a match of the size eleven prints that Ainsworth's team found at the crime scene. I would say that the suspect parked his car at the lay-by at the bottom of the woods on Saturday evening and then walked up with Hannah across the field, gaining access to the rear of the hospital.'

Brady didn't need to say anymore. He could see from Conrad's reaction that he now realised that Brady's suspicion about Emily being abducted was fast becoming a reality. The question that concerned Brady now was who had taken her. He was certain it was the same man who had murdered the twelve young women found in the old furnace in the old hospital's basement. And who had lobotomised Hannah and left her, locked inside with the other victims, to share the same fate.

Brady realised the crucial role that Emily's abduction now played in solving these macabre killings. None of the victims they'd been able to identify had had registered phones, including Hannah. They were not active on Facebook or any other social media site. It was no surprise, given their homeless status. If Emily Baker had been abducted by the same killer, then the man caught on the CCTV footage was the suspect who had gone unnoticed for twenty or so years – until now. There was a chance that Emily had met him at the hospital.

Brady doubted it was prearranged. Otherwise he would have expected to see some communication between them. But there were no texts, phone calls or emails. Nothing. Which led him to suspect that she had been in the wrong place at the wrong time. He suspected that the perpetrator had been revisiting his collection of victims on the Friday evening. He knew for definite that Hannah had been left on the Saturday evening. The doctors' opinion was that Hannah had been lobotomised approximately a few hours before she was found by Brady. That would mean that her captor had left her there sometime on the Saturday evening, under the cover of darkness. Forensics had also established that she had not been lobotomised at the crime scene; she had been mutilated somewhere else. That tied in with Brady's theory that it would make her more amenable. More compliant. So when he came to walking her through the woods to join his other collection of women hidden away, she would not try to escape. Or shout for help.

Brady thought of Emily. Had she just been in the wrong place at the wrong time? Coincidence? But Brady didn't believe in coincidences. There was one element which stood out. Emily knew her abductor. Brady hoped that they would identify the suspect and find her in time. Before . . . He stopped himself. Couldn't let himself think about it. Not yet.

Time was eluding them. Fast. The news of the serial killer was now overshadowing James David Macintosh's murders and the abduction of Annabel Edwards. That worried Brady. Macintosh wouldn't want to share the media spotlight; let alone have it stolen. But the media were fickle when it came to news coverage. Unfortunately, the aptly named *Puppet Maker* and the sadistic nature of the injuries he inflicted upon his victims had created a media circus.

His worst fear had been realised. The CCTV footage of the missing teenager walking along the woods down from the old psychiatric hospital with an unknown male convinced him that they now had a fourteenth victim – Emily Baker. Also, that the unidentified suspect walking down the isolated road alongside her had abducted her. If he was the serial killer they were trying to apprehend, then the odds were stacked heavily against her. The media attention could drive the suspect to kill her to avoid being caught. And they still had no idea about the identity of her abductor.

Camera crews and journalists from around the world had set themselves up outside the old psychiatric hospital, unable to get enough footage of the crime scene. They were also camped outside Whitley Bay police station in a bid to glean more information on the case. But the police had nothing to offer them. Or to be precise, Brady had nothing.

DNA evidence had been retrieved from the victims' clothing and hair and it did not match the security guard's DNA sample. Neither did it match with the other three guards employed by the same security company, or Ryan Seaman. Not that it came as much of a surprise. Brady's team, which consisted of whoever Gates could spare, were doing their utmost to go through everyone and anyone associated with the hospital. There was a backlist of employees who had worked for the security company since the hospital closed in 1995.

Slowly but surely, each person was being ticked off. But it just wasn't enough.

Brady ran a hand back through his hair. Frustrated. He looked around the room. There were only a handful of them: Harvey, Kodovesky, Daniels and Kenny. Conrad was on his way. The one person missing from the team was Amelia Jenkins. Brady had never wanted her as much as he did now. He could have used her expertise. They all could. But she was still in London with Gates. Brady had already updated Gates regarding the CCTV footage. The Puppet Maker's crimes now dominated the media, overshadowing the Macintosh investigation. Gates had informed Brady that he would be returning from London within the next day or so, but wanted to be updated, regardless of the hour, of any new developments.

Brady had held a briefing – despite the lack of numbers. But no one was much in the mood for talk. They were all exhausted and running on empty. He had attempted to bribe them by buying a Chinese takeaway but it had not had the desired effect. They had eaten and now simply wanted to go home. To forget for a couple of hours what some psychopath had done to thirteen women. But the problem was, they couldn't forget. Because he had a new victim. One whose likelihood of survival was diminishing with every passing hour.

'Someone has been accessing the building from as far back as 1995 when the first victim was dumped. Someone knew about that building. Had an attachment to it. His signature tells us that. He has a psychological and emotional need to return to the bodies. To attend to them.

Adorn them. Then there's his modus operandi. It's beyond anything I've ever seen . . .' Brady faltered. 'What he does to them before he kills them.' He shook his head in disbelief. 'But I guarantee it's all tied up with that hospital.'

He shot a glance at Harvey. He was grim-faced.

'Harvey? Kodovesky? What have you got?'

He had set them the task of investigating everyone who worked or resided as patients at St George's when it was still a hospital.

Tom Harvey cleared his throat before answering. 'Nothing. Most of them are either too old or dead to have committed these murders. Or they've left the area. Lots were admitted to other psychiatric hospitals.'

'Not good enough, Tom! The suspect's not just dumped one body there. He's dumped *thirteen*. Then he goes back. Dresses them. Arranges them. Spends time with them. So, we're looking at someone who has a connection with the place. I mean . . .' Brady shook his head as he turned to the crime scene photographs on the whiteboard. Thirteen victims. Twelve dead. One alive – just. 'He lobotomises them for fuck's sake! So, we have to do our damnedest to find this suspect, which means narrowing down whatever impossible list we have to try and nail this bastard.'

'Yes, sir.' Harvey answered through gritted teeth.

Brady resisted the urge to reprimand him for his belligerent attitude. They were all running on empty. Exhausted and overwhelmed by the magnitude of the job before them. He watched Conrad make an unapologetic entrance.

'Hope it was important!' Brady snapped.

Conrad looked at Brady. 'I think you'll agree that it is, sir.'

'Go on,' Brady ordered not in the mood for games.

'One minute,' Conrad said opening up his laptop. 'Take a look at this,' he instructed as he displayed the footage from his screen onto the whiteboard.

Conrad remained standing as he watched the CCTV footage. 'The black Volvo Series 200 that the security guard mentioned, the one that can be seen on the CCTV footage sporadically driving around the hospital grounds?'

He suddenly had the room's attention.

'Approximately ten minutes after the CCTV footage of Emily walking down from the woods with an unidentifiable male, this car can be seen exiting Morpeth town heading towards the A1 North.'

'Did you get the registration plate?'

'Working on that. You know how poor CCTV film can be. Give me time, I'm sure I'll get something. Or at least, Jed will. I've already sent it over to him to clean it up.'

Brady nodded. Jed was Northumbria's computer geek. Overworked, underpaid and one of the best computer forensic officers in the force.

'Did you see how many people were in the car?'

Conrad nodded. 'Two. Driver and passenger. And just like the security guard said, there is a dog on the back seat.'

'Can you make out if it's her?'

'Like I said, the quality of the film makes it really difficult, but this shot here? See? I would say that it is her,' Conrad stated. 'It's Emily Baker.'

Brady stared at the frozen image on the screen. There was no mistaking it. Emily was in the passenger seat of the Volvo. The driver sat next to Emily – her abductor. His identity unknown. His face obscured by a baseball cap, the peak pulled down low over his eyes. But Brady was certain that this was the man responsible for the barbaric mutilation of one woman, and the cruel deaths of twelve others. The driver of the eighties black Volvo 200 was the *Puppet Maker.*

DAY THREE
MONDAY

Chapter Eighteen

Monday: 11:31 a.m.

Brady had talked to all of the students in Emily Baker's year. He looked up at Conrad as he came back into the room. They had been given someone's office within the photography department to conduct the interviews.

'One more,' Conrad said.

Brady checked the names off against the list. Realised that Conrad was right.

'Bring her in,' he instructed. He reached over and picked up his coffee from the table in front of him. He looked around the spacious office. It was more than comfortable. A large desk with chairs either side was positioned under the window. A desktop computer, books and other personal paraphernalia covered it.

The walls had various leaflets and other college information attached to various boards. There were also some dramatic pieces of photography – not surprising since they were in the photography department. Brady stared at the imposing photograph opposite. A black and white abstract piece that looked unnervingly familiar. He couldn't quite make out the subject matter. But whatever it was, it left him with a feeling of disquiet.

He took a much-needed drink of coffee and then leaned back against the leather couch. He assumed whoever occupied the room used this space for tutorials. It was informal. Relaxed.

The door opened and Conrad returned with the final interviewee.

Brady smiled. 'Hi, Lauren?'

'Yes. Lauren Smith,' she answered. Nervous. It wasn't every day that the police turned up to question them about a fellow student's disappearance.

'I'm Detective Inspector Brady and this is my colleague Conrad,' he gestured towards Conrad. Smiled again. 'I'm sure he's has already introduced himself.'

She nodded.

'This won't take long,' Brady reassured her. 'Why don't you take a seat?' he asked, gesturing towards one of the two chairs opposite him.

She sat down.

Conrad stood back. By the door. Less intimidating having to face one officer, than two. But it also prevented anyone from accidentally walking in.

'You know what this is about?' Brady asked.

She nodded. Her blond hair falling across her face as she did so. She pushed it back. Embarrassed. Chewed her lip for a moment. 'I don't think there is anything I can tell you about Emily. At least nothing more than my friends have told you.'

'That's all right, Lauren. We're just trying to build up a picture of Emily. Trying to get an idea of who she was and what she liked to do.'

Her cheeks suddenly flushed. 'I didn't know her. Not really. She . . . she kept to herself.'

Brady nodded. Glanced at the notes he had already made. Same story. No one knew anything about her. Despite the fact they were all studying the same course. Some had said that she was 'a loner'. Others, that she was 'weird'. All very politely phrased of course. Apart from one female student who clearly didn't like Emily and had made no pretence at hiding it. She had described her as a 'pervy lesbo'. Brady didn't even bother to argue why it would make the student dislike Emily. He didn't have the time or inclination to challenge a small-minded eighteen-year-old. But it had surprised him to hear that kind of homophobic talk on a campus. He had perhaps naïvely expected a more liberal attitude.

'So you have no idea where she would have gone when she left college on Friday afternoon?' Brady asked Lauren.

She shook her head. 'No.' She then frowned. 'Have you asked Julian? Julian Fraser? He was one of her personal tutors. He's in the art department.'

'Why should I ask him?'

'Well, Emily was obsessed by his work. I mean . . . really obsessed. It was weird, like.'

'How so?' Brady asked, leaning forward.

'Julian is a really nice guy. Everyone likes him, yeah? But his art is sick. And I don't mean in a good way. Like, really sick. I had a look in his studio once. He wasn't around and I heard all this talk about what a great artist he was and I thought I would sneak a look.' She seemed to shudder as she thought about it.

'What was it about his work that you found so disturbing?'

She looked at Brady. 'He did all this work about insane people . . .' she paused, shaking her head. 'Like really gross stuff. Women tied to chairs being tortured by doctors.'

'How were they being tortured?' Brady asked.

She swallowed as she looked at him. 'I dunno. Medical stuff. Being injected with syringes by doctors in white coats. I couldn't understand why he was so celebrated in the art world for this kind of stuff. Or what it was about him and his work that fascinated Emily. I saw a couple of photographs from this project she was working on last Friday and it was really similar to Julian's work. I mean embarrassingly so. I didn't tell her that of course. You just wouldn't.'

Brady looked up and caught Conrad's eye. It was clear his deputy was thinking the same as him. That they needed to talk to Julian Fraser – now.

'One last question,' Brady asked. 'Do you know where her portfolio would be? I asked the office this morning but it seems that no one can find it.'

'Try Julian,' she answered. 'If it's not in Emily's locker then he might have it. I know she had a tutorial with him on Friday afternoon. That was the last time I saw her. It was just the two of us in the photography studio. She was busy organising her portfolio. That was when I caught a glimpse of what she was working on. She said she wanted to show Julian some new photographs and ideas she had.'

'Right. Thanks for that, Lauren,' Brady concluded.

'I can go now?' she asked.

Brady nodded. 'You've been a great help.'

She didn't look that convinced. 'I hope you find her. You know . . . Emily. From what I heard she'd had a really hard time growing up.' She stood up. Turned to leave. Stopped. She looked at the black and white abstract photograph on the wall. 'That's one of Emily's,' she said as she turned to look back at Brady.

'What is it? Do you know?' Brady asked, standing up and walking over to it.

'If you look closely you can make out a window with bars on it. It's really creepy. It was taken at that old mental asylum in Northumberland.'

'St George's in Morpeth?'

She shrugged. 'Could be. But Emily won a national award for it. That's part of the work she was doing with Julian. It was one of the reasons that she's not that popular with the other students . . . I don't know if you picked up on that?'

'I did get that impression,' Brady answered. 'Why was that? Because she won the award?'

'Partly. But mainly because she only won the award because of Julian's help.'

'What do you mean?'

'Julian took a special interest in Emily. Tutored her in his own time. Just her. None of the other students.'

Brady stared at the photograph. He needed to have another chat with Julian Fraser. He recalled his conversation with the lecturer yesterday afternoon. One in which the artist had clearly distanced himself from his student. He had lied. Now that interested Brady. A lot.

Brady was pissed off. Big time. He hadn't managed to track Fraser down at the college. Seemingly he had phoned in sick. Brady was convinced his sudden illness was connected to his visit yesterday. The problem he had was proving it. Aside from Fraser's inconvenient absence he had returned to find journalists and TV crews camped outside Whitley Bay police station. He had had to force his way through. Heckled and shouted at like some criminal.

When they had pulled up and saw the media crews waiting, Conrad had suggested that he use the back entrance. Brady refused. Feelings of anger and frustration had overwhelmed him. So Conrad's well-meaning, untimely remark had nearly resulted in Brady's fist in his face. Instead, he had told his deputy to, 'Fuck off!' He got out the car, slamming the door as he did so, and marched straight towards them.

Brady took a sip of coffee. It was the last thing he needed considering how wound up he was, but the alternative was a bottle of scotch. He was sorely tempted but he didn't have the time to sit and feel sorry for himself. There were two victims' lives at stake. Two serial killers still at large. His hands were tied when it came to the

Macintosh investigation. He had asked around to see if anyone had an update. Seemingly, no one did. Or if they did, they weren't telling him.

He had been back for over two hours and had got nowhere. He looked down at the notes in front of him. They were on Julian Fraser. He had assigned the team to dig around into Julian Fraser's background. Brady knew that he was linked to the old St George's hospital. Could feel it. But he had to find the evidence to prove it. He needed more than the feeling that Fraser had minimised his relationship with Emily. Or the fact that he had called in sick to work. Then there was Fraser's artwork. All Brady had to go on was what the student, Lauren Smith had told him, so he needed to see the work for himself. The last thing he wanted to do was knee jerk. Not when he was already under the media spotlight.

He picked up the file that Harvey had dropped off earlier. It was a list of all the patients dating back from 1950. Fraser's name had already been eliminated. But Brady thought that maybe a family member of his had been institutionalised there. If he was obsessed with mental illness in his art, maybe it was personal. Then he found out what the connection was . . .

Harvey had finally traced Fraser's parents for Brady. His father was Dr Nigel Fraser. He had been an eminent neurologist in his day. Between the 1950s and 1960s he had performed over 10,000 lobotomies. A staggering number. One that had left Brady numb. The last lobotomy had been performed on a sixteen-year-old girl at St

Mary's Hospital in Dundee in 1972 when he was fifty-five. Julian's father had died four years ago.

Brady was forcing himself to accept that Fraser had 'father' issues and his artwork questioning society's attitudes to mental health was his way of struggling with his father's extraordinary work. His father had received many accolades for his work that mainly involved lobotomising depressed housewives. It still staggered Brady when he thought about it.

Brady had been surprised that Fraser's father was fifty-five when his son was born. His mother, Susan, had also been older than the norm; forty-seven at the time. He found this odd for a first child. But then, he had no idea what they had gone through to get Julian. He thought of Claudia for a moment and the heartache they had gone through with IVF in an attempt to have a child. It was the first time he had been grateful that it had never happened. Realising that the last thing he would want to do would be to bring a child into a world where the likes of James David Macintosh existed. Or a serial killer like the *Puppet Maker*.

He tried to shake off the disquiet he felt about Fraser. Maybe he had overreacted. Brady was no psychologist, but it was clear that Fraser had 'issues' and these were around his father's choice of vocation. He then thought of Emily. He wondered whether she had simply shared Julian Fraser's interest in mental health and its representation in society. Nothing more. He had nothing that tied Fraser to the murdered women, aside from the fact that his father was a neurologist who performed lobotomies.

And all thirteen victims had been lobotomised. Coincidence? Brady sighed heavily. He didn't believe in coincidences.

He dropped the file and took another gulp of coffee. The suspect had completely evaded them. If Brady was honest, he now had no idea who the suspect could be – let alone where he could be hiding Emily.

There was a sudden knock at the door.

'Yeah?' called out Brady.

It was Kodovesky. She looked awkward. More so when she saw Brady's surprised reaction.

'Can I speak with you for a moment, sir?'

'Sure. Take a seat,' Brady offered.

He watched, intrigued as she closed the door behind her. She was clutching a file to her chest as she walked over to his desk. She then sat down opposite him. Her face was flushed. Her eyes hesitant.

'Is everything all right?' he asked, worried that she wasn't coping. Either with the workload, or the gruesome nature of the case. After all, she was the only female detective on his team and they were dealing with a misogynistic serial killer who literally took away his female victim's cognitive abilities.

The latest medical update on Hannah was a cruel testimony to that face. When Brady had returned to the station, it was to the unwelcome news that Hannah would never fully recover. Doctors had carried extensive tests and had come to the conclusion that she would have to be institutionalised – for life. Unable to look after herself. Let alone talk coherently. Or walk.

Brady waited. But Kodovesky seemed reluctant to talk.

'Look . . . whatever it is, I'm sure I can help,' he reassured her, smiling.

She nodded. Chewed her lip for a moment as she thought over why she was there. 'I . . . I wanted to bring you something. I know I shouldn't have been working on it but . . .' she gave Brady an apologetic shrug as she handed over the file she had been clutching.

Brady opened it up. There was one sheet of paper inside. It concerned details regarding a Kathleen Fitzgerald. Seventy-six-year-old retired nurse. Her address was a suburb of Sydney, Australia. He looked up at Kodovesky. 'Is this who I think it is?'

She nodded. Mildly apprehensive as she tried to gauge his reaction.

'You know I'm not allowed to deal with this? That it has to go to DCI Gates?'

'Yes, sir. I have already sent it to him. But I don't believe they are going to do anything about it. DCI Gates made it clear that they didn't have the time to follow up some woman living in Australia who may or may not be the suspect's mother.' She waited for his reaction.

'Tell me your thought process here. Why do you think this could be Eileen Macintosh?'

'She disappeared in 1977. Vanished. I assumed that she had gone to Australia. I heard Conrad talking to you on the phone about the statement you had taken from the Macintosh's neighbour yesterday,' she explained, blushing an even deeper crimson.

Brady nodded for her to continue.

She did. Relieved. 'So, I then researched her maiden name. It was Taylor. So I thought she would return to her maiden name. I also knew her date of birth and that she was British. So then I just spent hours searching. I narrowed it down to a few women and then figured she had chosen the name "Kathleen" as it was close to "Eileen" and would feel more natural for her.'

'So, I take it she remarried?' Brady asked.

Kodovesky shook her head. 'I'm not sure yet. I don't know whether she was scared someone would trace her maiden name and connect it with James David Macintosh and so she changed it again. Or whether she did remarry. I'm still working on it.'

'You're absolutely certain this is . . . was Eileen Macintosh?'

'Yes. I believe so.'

'Have you contacted her?'

'No, sir. After DCI Gates said not to bother following it up I thought I would see what you wanted me to do. I know I have no authority to be working on this but I can't let this lead go, which is why I've come to you. I . . .' She faltered for a moment, unsure whether to risk continuing.

'This is between us. It won't go any further,' Brady assured her.

She nodded, nervous. 'What if . . . if DCI Gates is wrong? What if we should be trying to track her down?'

Brady sat back. He knew that if he ordered Kodovesky to contact Eileen Macintosh aka Kathleen Fitzgerald he would be a crossing a line. It would be tantamount to asking for his P45. He thought of Annabel Edwards. *Fuck it!*

'Do you think he's in London?' Brady asked. 'Macintosh?'

Kodovesky shook her head. Her dark brown eyes said it all. She had the same feeling as Brady that he was definitely still in the North East.

'All right. Contact Kathleen Fitzgerald. But whatever you do, don't scare her. If this woman really is Eileen Macintosh, we need her help. No one will know James David Macintosh better than his mother.'

'Do you think she will help?' Kodovesky asked.

Brady shrugged. 'I don't know. But it's worth a shot.' He was certain that the reason Macintosh had abducted Annabel Edwards and Ellen Jackson in 1977 was to do with his psychological and emotional need to resolve whatever had happened to his three-year-old sister, Lucy. A little girl who one day disappeared. And like the *Puppet Maker*'s victims, no one reported her missing. The significant difference here was that this child had two parents and a brother.

He looked at Kodovesky. 'We need to find her before she hears the news about her son. She went into hiding once before. There is no reason why she wouldn't do it again. I imagine she will be scared that someone will uncover her true identity.'

Kodovesky stood up. She had a determination about her that told Brady she would get to her before that happened.

Chapter Nineteen

Monday: 11:33 a.m.

Her body felt heavy. She couldn't move. Could barely open her eyes. She looked at him. Something was wrong. She moaned as he slumped her into the old wooden psychiatric chair.

'No . . .' She resisted, realising what was happening.

He deftly shackled her wrists first. Then her ankles. Finally her head.

'Please . . . No . . . No . . .' she objected.

He ignored her.

'Please don't hurt me . . . Please,' she begged as she tried desperately to make eye contact.

'It's me . . . Emily. Emily Baker. Please? Emily . . .' Again. And again. And again.

'SHUT UP! Do you understand? Shut the fuck up!' he screamed, spraying her face with spit.

Silence.

He bent down and opened the bag on the floor beside the chair. She couldn't see what he had taken out. What he was holding. Her head was fixed straight ahead. Staring at the wall of Polaroid photographs he had taken of the others.

She felt sick.

'Please? Please? I won't talk. I won't tell them who you are.'

'Shhh . . .' his voice was sad. Reluctant. He switched the clippers on and started shaving the side of her head.

'No . . . no . . . NO!'

Chapter Twenty

Monday: 12:39 p.m.

Brady had gone looking for DS Tom Harvey. Something hadn't felt right about Julian Foster's parents. From the details on his parents' ages they had seemed too old to be having a first child. So Brady had done his own digging.

He walked into the Incident Room. Harvey was sitting with his arms folded behind his head having a laugh with Daniels and Kenny.

The two young DCs saw Brady walk in first. Then they saw the expression on his face. They quickly dropped their heads and focused on whatever they were supposed to be doing.

'What the fuck's got into you two?' Harvey questioned.

'Me! That's what!' Brady thundered as he came up behind Harvey.

Harvey swung round to face Brady. 'What's wrong with you?'

Brady threw the notes that Harvey had given him on the table. 'This!'

Harvey picked it up. Read a few lines and then looked back up at Brady. 'I don't get it?'

'That's my problem! You don't get anything, do you? He was bloody adopted, you stupid bastard. Adopted! These aren't his biological parents.'

Harvey looked back at the paperwork he had given Brady. 'I didn't realise . . . I thought they were a bit long in the tooth.' He looked at Brady and gave a half-hearted shrug. 'I thought, well, shit, women have babies in their sixties. I was just reading about that woman who gave birth to twins at the age of sixty-six!'

'IVF you idiot! She would have conceived through bloody IVF!'

'Well . . . maybe they did as well?'

Brady resisted the urge to pull Harvey to his feet and give him a good shaking. 'Fraser was born in 1972. IVF wasn't invented until 1977. The world's test tube baby wasn't born until 1978.'

'How was I supposed to know that kind of shit? Come on, Jack!'

'You're bloody paid to realise this shit! Paid to question when something doesn't feel right. So, if they're too old, your job is to actually trace the birth certificate. You checked against Fraser's amended birth certificate. The birth parents' names have been replaced by the adopted parents. And as for his original birth name, it was James Donald McBride.'

Harvey looked up at Brady. 'I . . . I don't know what to say.'

'Why does that not surprise me?' He suddenly turned to Daniels and Kenny. 'You two, check for a Shauna

McBride against the list of psychiatric patients at St Georges. Just in case she was there. Born in 1958.'

'Who is she?' asked Daniels.

'Julian Fraser's biological mother. That's who!'

'Come on . . . We all make mistakes. Even you!' Harvey retaliated, trying to calm Brady down.

It didn't work. Brady glared at him, eyes flashing with anger. His face suddenly dark and menacing. 'What the fuck does that mean?'

Harvey shrugged, realising too late he had crossed a line. 'Nothing.'

'If you've got something to say, then say it. Or anyone else in this room for that matter!' Brady shouted as he looked around the room. There were only a handful of people. But it was enough for an audience. 'I'm serious. If anyone has something to say, then say it now!'

An awkward silence filled the room. Suddenly everyone was extraordinarily busy. No one dared look up.

'Look, Jack—' Harvey began.

Brady cut him off. 'Forget it! I need you to go to Newcastle College and interview Julian Fraser's colleagues. I want to know everything we can about him. Even the kind of art he paints. And in particular, his relationship with Emily.'

He then spotted Conrad in the room. 'My office. Now!'

He poured himself a scotch. Knew he shouldn't but at that precise moment didn't give a fuck. He heard Conrad come in. Didn't turn around. Instead Brady knocked the scotch back in one. Put his mug down and walked to his desk.

He sat at his chair and looked up at Conrad. 'What are that lot saying?'

Conrad frowned. 'About what?'

'About me! The papers. "Police Incompetence" and all that crap. Macintosh being released and then going on to . . .' Brady couldn't say it.

'Nothing, sir. Nothing that I've heard, anyway,' Conrad answered, looking uncomfortable.

It wasn't enough. Brady still felt like crap. He might be working on a new case but he was very aware of the fact that the media was claiming that he had released Macintosh knowing that he was a danger to society. Worse still, that he had the evidence to prove it. That by default, he was responsible for the murder of Annabel Edwards' family, and her abduction.

'Do you want an update on the CCTV footage I've been looking at?' Conrad tried.

Brady remained silent. He realised that he shouldn't have lost it in the Incident Room. That word would get back to DCI Gates that he wasn't coping. *Fuck it!* He couldn't continue in the job if he worried about every bloody thing he said – or didn't say.

'Sir?' Conrad prompted.

Brady nodded. Distracted.

'I've just run a check on cars registered in Julian Fraser's name.' Conrad shook his head. 'He only has the one. And it's not a black Volvo series 200. It's a BMW estate.'

Brady sighed. It was the same car he had watched Julian Fraser head towards when he had met him at

Newcastle College. He had been silently hoping that the black Volvo caught on surveillance footage at the old psychiatric hospital would have been registered to Fraser. Since he'd learned who Fraser's real mother was, he was increasingly sure Fraser was their suspect. But they still had no real proof. Nothing that actually tied him to the victims.

He sighed. 'All right. Take a seat. This will interest you.'

Conrad did as instructed.

'Julian Fraser was born in 1972 in St Mary's Hospital in Dundee, Scotland. His mother, Shauna McBride, was sixteen years old. Father of the child, unknown. The first lobotomy in the UK was performed at St Mary's Hospital in 1946. The last in 1972. In that period 17,000 people were lobotomised in the UK,' Brady said. He thought about it for a moment, absorbing the number. It was hard to believe that it wasn't that long ago.

'Do you know who the last lobotomy patient was?' Brady continued.

'Fraser's mother?'

'Correct. Shauna McBride.'

'What was wrong with her?' Conrad asked.

Brady looked at him. He didn't like the answer and he sure as hell knew Conrad wouldn't. 'She was gay. Her parents wanted her "sorted". At least that's what was reported in the article I read. "Fixed" was another word that was used.'

Conrad was silent for a moment. He frowned. 'Where did you find that out?'

'Internet. Articles in the press. Someone wrote a book on the history of St Mary's and Shauna McBride is mentioned in there.'

Conrad looked surprised.

'There was a lot of controversy around her lobotomy and the psychiatric hospital was closed down shortly afterwards,' Brady explained.

'Was it closed down because of her?' Conrad asked, his voice strained.

Brady shook his head. It was wishful thinking on Conrad's part. And Brady could see in his deputy's eye that he knew it. 'No. Sadly not. There were two reasons behind its closure. Obviously, this is conjecture.'

Conrad waited.

'The article I read said that Shauna had been raped whilst an inpatient there. That was how she got pregnant. Her parents were interviewed by the author in the late nineties and explained that the psychological effect on her was devastating. No one knew about the sexual abuse until she was seven months' pregnant. Her mental health had radically deteriorated over that time.' Brady looked at Conrad. He knew what his deputy would be thinking. Could see it on his face. That this girl was institutionalised because of her sexuality. Then found herself being raped. Presumably, repeatedly. And who would listen to her? After all, she had been confined to a mental institution, known in those days to be draconian in their treatment of patients, to say the least.

Conrad remained silent.

Brady accepted that there was nothing he could say.

'From what I read, Shauna was an exceptionally bright girl who suffered extreme bouts of dark depression when she hit adolescence. Understandable when you consider she was trying to cope with her sexuality and her parents' homophobic values.'

'So why did the press suggest the hospital had been closed down?' asked Conrad.

'Her parents signed the legal document for her to be lobotomised when she was eight months' pregnant.'

'What?' Conrad said, unable to keep the shock out of his voice.

'I know. It's unprecedented. But then . . .' Brady shrugged. 'Christ only knows what other malpractices went on. They were effectively self-governing.'

'What happened to her afterwards?' Conrad asked.

Brady could see from his expression that he was struggling to comprehend what he was hearing. 'Well, a caesarean section was performed on her a month later. By the same doctor who lobotomised her.'

'Julian Fraser's father?' Conrad asked.

Brady nodded. 'Yes.'

'How did the Frasers adopt the child? Surely the girl's parents would have wanted him?'

'Who knows?' Brady replied. 'Even in 1972 it was a stigma. A sixteen-year-old unmarried mother in a psychiatric hospital gives birth to a child who is the product of rape? If I've assumed correctly that the Frasers couldn't have children, then this might have been an ideal situation for them. It's not as if the birth mother was in any fit state to object.'

'I suppose not, sir. What happened to her after the birth of Julian?'

'The articles I read reported that St Mary's closed down in 1972, shortly after McBride's lobotomy. She was then transferred to Lennox Castle Hospital in Glasgow. It closed in April 2002.'

'Is she still alive?'

Brady shook his head. 'But this is the interesting part. She died twenty years ago.'

Conrad frowned. 'Wolfe said that he believed the earliest victim was murdered twenty years ago?'

Brady nodded.

'But that doesn't necessarily make Julian Fraser a suspect. Yes, it could be a trigger. But did he know about it?' asked Conrad.

'Shauna McBride was transferred in 1980 to St George's Psychiatric Hospital and remained there until she died in 1995. Just before the hospital was closed down.'

Conrad shook his head in disbelief. 'Are you certain?'

'Of course I'm bloody certain! I checked her death certificate. I don't know why she was transferred to St George's. Perhaps her parents had her moved? We'll never know, because they're both dead. Or maybe Dr Fraser had her moved?'

Conrad looked at Brady. 'He worked at St George's?' His voice was unable to hide his incredulity.

'No. He wasn't a member of staff, which is why our team missed him. He was on the board of directors. Remained on the board until the hospital closed down.'

'And you think Julian Fraser somehow found out about his birth mother? That she had been lobotomised and was a resident at St George's Psychiatric Hospital?'

Brady nodded. 'Definitely. And he definitely lied to us when he said he had never been to St George's.'

Conrad shot him a quizzical look.

Brady turned his laptop to face Conrad. 'See here? Old photographs of when the hospital was still open. All very civilised, of course. Here, standing outside on the grounds is Dr Fraser. See? Below it states that Dr Fraser was on the board of directors.'

Conrad nodded as he looked at the man listed as Dr Fraser. Beside him was a young boy, smiling, holding his hand.

'That's his son? That's Julian?'

Brady nodded. 'It was a public holiday and some charity event was being held there. The press were there. It was good publicity for the hospital.'

'Christ!' muttered Conrad. He shook his head in disbelief. 'What are you going to do?'

'I don't know. It's all circumstantial. Fraser could easily argue that he had no memory of St George's because he was a child when he visited. It is clear from what we have heard about his artwork that he has issues around mental health treatments. Does that make him a serial killer? No. Does it make him suspicious? Yes. One hundred per cent.'

Conrad nodded. 'But there's nothing tangible here, is there? DCI Gates wouldn't authorise you bringing him in for questioning. Not with this evidence. It doesn't mean Fraser's a murderer. It just tells us what a tragic background he had. Or should I say his mother had . . . And he's clearly not hiding the fact he has issues around his father's neurological practices. He's made that very public. So, I wouldn't be surprised if he did know about his biological mother, that there is a history of mental illness in his family. But I don't believe it would make him a murderer. His art could be a direct reaction, a rebellion if you like, to the fact that his father was a neurologist who practised lobotomies.' Conrad shook his head.

'I know what we have is tenuous, Conrad. But don't forget he is the last known person to have seen Emily before she disappeared. I think that gives us grounds enough to bring him in for questioning.'

'Not with all the media interest. If we make a wrong move we will be crucified by the press.'

Brady looked at Conrad. It wasn't the answer he wanted to hear but he knew his deputy was right. The media were camped outside the station. One wrong move and Brady's career could be over. *Fuck it! He had no other choice.*

'I want a briefing with the team first. Then I'm bringing him in for questioning. He was the last person we know to have spoken to her. That's significant enough for me, Conrad.'

Chapter Twenty-One

Monday: 2:16 p.m.

He had found it all too easy. Smiled. Looked around the bedroom. Breathed in the air. Breathed his smell. Detective Jack Brady. He wasn't here. Not that he had expected him to be. He could feel the stirring sensation in the pit of his stomach. His smile widened as he thought of what he had planned for him.

Not yet though . . .

He still had work to do. He thought of his mother. The smile gone. Anger coursed through him.

That fucking bitch! That lying fucking bitch!

He had tracked her down. He knew it would not be long before Brady did the same. He was aware he was running out of time. He had been following the news. All the false leads he had put in place had been swallowed. Gullible fools. But not Jack Brady. The police believed he was in London. Apart from DI Brady who he had seen sniffing around Mill Cottage. Taking things that he had no right to remove. *Her things.*

But he was disappointed with Brady. It seemed that he had forgotten him. And her. Maybe he needed to remind him to get his priorities in place?

He walked over to the bed. Pulled open the bedside cabinet and found what he expected. A photograph of Jack Brady and his wife, Claudia. He removed the photograph from the frame. Stared for a few moments at the picture. It was clear that Brady had loved her. He touched her face. It was tilted up towards him, laughing at something he had said. Her long curly red hair was wild. Her green eyes filled with joy. He felt a stab of envy. The only love he had ever truly felt was for Lucy. But she had been taken from him. The pain had never left him. Instead of lessening over time it had intensified. So much so that at times it was unbearable.

He snapped himself out of it. *Not now. Not yet.*

He put the photograph of Brady and Claudia in his jacket pocket. He removed a Polaroid photograph he had taken of Annabel and placed it in the frame. She looked so much like Lucy, dressed like that and holding Lucy's favourite doll.

Fucking bastard. You stole her doll. And the photographs of her. Everything I had saved, you took ... You went through my house and you found all I had left of her. And you took it from me.

Macintosh reined in his anger. He needed to keep it under control. For now. He still had a plan to exact. For now he was focused on making DI Jack Brady suffer as much as he suffered. Brady had taken from him so now it was time to take from Brady. Something that would destroy him.

He placed the frame on the bedside cabinet. He knew Brady would see it as soon as he walked into the room.

He wanted him to have a choice to make. One that would affect him every day for the rest of his life.

He left the room. Walked down the dark corridor. Passed Claudia's room. Then passed the bathroom. The cabinet where he had seen her medication. Left behind. In a hurry.

Just like Lucy . . .

No! Not like Lucy. Claudia, Brady's ex-wife was still alive. Wanting Brady back. To make amends. Start again. He had heard her words. Sweet. Sickly . . . Begging Brady to visit her. To wait for her.

Then he heard his father's voice. Screaming at him. Admonishing him.

What have you done, you little shit? What have you done to her?

NO! He slowed his breathing down. He had a job to do. Focused, he walked down the stairs. He looked at the answer machine. He had silenced the flashing light. The irritating beeping noise. He memorised the number that Claudia had left for Brady. Then he had pressed delete. Eradicated her pathetic message.

Brady wouldn't know until it was too late.

Then . . . then he will know what it feels like.

Chapter Twenty-Two

Monday: 3:21 p.m.

He turned around as Conrad walked into the Incident Room. 'Anything?'

'No, sir,' Conrad answered.

They still had nothing on Emily's whereabouts. The ageing druggie from the flat below her on Whitley Road had been interviewed. Harvey had given him a hard time. But it was clear that he knew nothing. He had an alibi. One that covered him for all of Friday and Friday night. Not that it had surprised Brady. He was convinced, as were the rest of the team that she had been taken by the same suspect who had killed twelve women and left Hannah Stewart brain damaged. But where was she?

Where are you hiding her? She has to be close. Close enough for you to abuse her ...

Brady caught Daniels and Kenny sniggering over something. He snapped: 'If you two haven't found the registration of that black Volvo 200 yet, then I don't see why you're both sat there with your fingers up your arses doing nothing!'

Conrad caught Brady's eye.

Brady ignored him. He would be the first to admit he was in a foul mood. He was tense. Time was running out for Emily. The suspect would feel backed into a corner. He would worry the police were on to him. It would just be a matter of time. His crimes were all over the media; national and international. Brady thought about Julian Fraser. He had a gut feeling about the man that he couldn't silence. But, as Conrad had pointed out, they did not have enough to charge him. However, he could bring him in for questioning which was exactly what he was about to do. Whether it would bring him any closer to Emily and her whereabouts, he couldn't say.

The nationwide police hunt for Macintosh was still the main focus – after all, a three-year-old girl had been abducted. Brady had been left with the dregs. Not that he could complain. Annabel Edwards was the priority. He glanced around the room. There were ten people in here. But still – ten people. Six uniform, four CID. The four detectives were his old team. Apart from Amelia Jenkins, who was still in London helping Gates and the Met with the Macintosh investigation. He hadn't talked to her since yesterday afternoon when he had been outside Mill Cottage. That was before they even realised that they had another sick bastard on their hands. That was when all Brady could think about was James David Macintosh and finding three-year-old Annabel.

And bring her home ... But she had *no home. No family. Nothing.*

The parallel with the latest *Puppet Maker* victim hit him hard. Both missing. Both potentially dead. Brady swallowed. Had to clear his throat. He was struggling to cope. Terrified of failure. That he would lose Emily to him. That Brady would find her too late. After all, he had released her information to the press. Had claimed that she was another potential victim of the *Puppet Maker*. He had wanted to see a result. Had hoped that someone would ring the police with crucial evidence. Details of when she had last been sighted and with whom. Details of the car Brady believed she would have been driven away in – the Volvo 200. She would have climbed into the passenger seat willingly. *Why not?* She knew the man. Of course she did. Otherwise, why did she walk with him down the road from the nursing home? Why did she look so animated, so enthralled to be in his company?

Brady knew the answer. As did Conrad. They just needed to prove it.

'This is the best I could get,' Conrad said as he connected his laptop to the interactive board.

Brady turned and looked at the board. Conrad had put up a frozen image of the suspect walking away with the victim, alongside one of Julian Fraser that they had found from the college website.

Conrad turned to him. 'What do you think?'

Brady shrugged. 'Could be him. Then again, could be anyone. His hair roughly looks the same. Height the same. But that big coat he's wearing is disguising his build. And he has his back to us. What about the suspect's face?'

'No good. In every shot his face is obscured by the baseball cap. It's impossible to say whether it's Fraser or not,' Conrad answered as he changed the image of the suspect to a close-up of his head.

'Shit!' cursed Brady. The suspect had pulled the baseball cap peak down low enough to make it impossible to see any distinguishable features. 'All right. Let's see if Jed can do anything with it.'

If anyone could find something conclusive from these images, it would be Jed.

Brady looked over at the wall that had the twelve victims' faces covering it. Some mug shots from when they had been arrested. Four of them still remained unidentified.

He shook his head. Brady didn't want to think about what *he* had done to them. How Hannah Stewart had been left, barely alive.

'All right, Conrad. Let's go bring Fraser in for questioning,' Brady conceded. He had nothing on Julian Fraser. Aside from circumstantial evidence. Did that make him a serial killer? No. But what he did have was one glaringly obvious fact – he was the last known person to have seen Emily before she disappeared. And that was what Brady was banking on. Simply because that was all he had.

'Yes, sir,' Conrad answered as he started to get his things together.

'Meet you outside,' Brady instructed as he headed towards the door. He had wanted to have more leverage on Fraser. But they had nothing but circumstantial evidence.

Suddenly Harvey came barging through the door, red-faced and out of breath.

'What the fuck has got into you?' Brady demanded, barely avoiding being run into by the DS.

'You need to see this! Now!' he insisted thrusting his phone at Brady.

'Why? What is it?'

'There's two photos on there, just look at them will you?' Harvey wheezed as he tried to catch his breath.

He looked at the first photo. Then the second. 'Shit! Conrad, upload these will you?' Brady demanded as he handed the phone to him.

He stared at the whiteboard as Conrad uploaded the first photo, and felt the hairs go up on the back of his neck. Realised that the room had taken on a deathly silence. Everyone had stopped what they were doing and were staring at the image on the board.

'Christ!' muttered Brady. He looked at the painting. A study of a woman in a psychiatric chair. Naked. Starved. Tortured.

'Tell me you are seeing what I'm seeing?' Harvey asked, as he stared at the work.

'A woman about to be lobotomised,' Brady answered. He swallowed hard, as he stared at the brutal, sickening images on the board. The woman's face was jarringly blank. Mask-like. Disturbing. She was shackled to a psychiatric chair while a faceless doctor – male – studied her. Leaned over her with . . .

An ice pick . . .

Brady walked over to the board. Examined the instrument. He was correct. The white-coated male figure was holding an ice pick in one hand and a small hammer in the other.

'What is that?' Daniels suddenly interjected.

Brady turned around. Daniels' mouth was open in shock. His partner, Kenny opposite him, looked sickened. As did the others in the room.

'An ice pick,' Brady answered, turning his attention back to the board, to the man in the painting. Brady stared at him. He looked unnervingly like Julian's father, Dr Fraser. The hands poised over the patient's eyeball . . . Waiting to take the patient's identity away.

Brady turned to Harvey. 'This is by Julian Fraser?'

Harvey nodded. 'Yeah. I sped down the coast road to get this to you. Needed you to see it before you brought him in for questioning.'

'Why didn't you call me?' Brady demanded. 'Or even just send it to me?'

'Because I wanted you to see it in person first. And as for sending them to you, fuck Jack! It's me you're talking to. You know I'm crap with technology. You're bloody lucky I figured out how to take the photographs on that bloody thing!' he stated, gesturing over at his phone.

'Where did you find them?'

'Newcastle College. I've been trying to find someone there who had any images of Julian Fraser's artwork. These two paintings were being stored by the caretaker. Fraser had cleared out all his work yesterday afternoon. Had loaded it into a hire van with the help of the caretaker. These two pieces didn't fit. So Fraser had asked him to store them until he was able to collect them. Last the caretaker saw of him was when he drove off late yesterday afternoon.'

Brady realised that he had inadvertently warned Fraser that the police were after him. He assumed Fraser had returned to the college to get rid of any evidence. Or was it just coincidence? He turned back and looked at the painting on the screen. Admittedly, it was disturbing, but that was all. Nothing tied it to the twelve murder victims, or Hannah Stewart. All it told Brady was that Julian Fraser had issues with his father. Issues that he committed to canvas. That was it.

'Good try, Tom,' Brady replied, shaking his head. 'But I need more than that to charge him. Come on, Conrad. Let's go.'

'No. Wait!' Harvey called out after Brady's retreating figure.

Brady stopped and turned.

'The other painting. You need to see it blown up on the screen. Trust me here,' Harvey said. 'I recognised something and I think you will too.'

Brady nodded at Conrad to upload the second painting.

'Fuck!' Brady muttered as he stared at the new image on the white board.

The rest of the room was shocked silent.

The image had been too small on Harvey's screen to see the detailed features of the patient – *victim*. But now Brady could see that she looked uncannily familiar. She was a young woman shackled to a psychiatric chair while a male figure in a long white coat shaved the side of her head.

'Her face, Conrad. Zoom in on the face.'

The sudden disquiet in the room was deafening.

'That's one of our victims,' Brady muttered as he looked at the tortured face in the painting.

There was no disputing that the painting was of one of the unidentified victims whose face – *death mask* – was on display with the rest of the crime scene photographs on the other wall. This victim was believed to be the earliest one. The one that Brady had seen on the mortuary slab when he had visited Wolfe. Even checking dental records with local dentists had failed to come back with a positive ID. Not that he had expected to find a match. It had been a futile stab in the dark. One that hadn't paid off.

Brady stared in shock at the painting, not quite believing what he was seeing. The mask that *he* had made of the victim was indistinguishable from the young woman Julian Fraser had painted. The thick scar in the left eyebrow where the hair had never grown back. The large black mole on her left cheek. Her nose, flattened. Broken, he presumed by a punter. Or her pimp. It didn't matter. She was inconsequential. So much so, no one even noticed that she had disappeared. Twenty years ago she had been murdered. And for two decades no one had known. Or cared. But nothing had changed. She would remain unknown . . .

But it was there in front of him. The face of a young woman who had died at the hands of a psychopath. Someone who had drilled into her head and altered her brain – permanently. And had then locked her up to die.

It was conclusive evidence. Julian Fraser had painted

this victim. There were no two ways about it. And that meant that he had to be . . . *Shit!*

'Get a warrant for Julian Fraser's arrest, NOW!' Brady ordered.

Suddenly, everyone in the room were on their feet.

'Don't you think we should clear this with DCI Gates first?'

Brady looked at Conrad as if he had lost his mind. 'Are you crazy? And tell him what? That this artist is painting his victims for posterity? He'd have me committed!'

Conrad shook his head. 'Not if he saw the evidence.'

'Well, he's not here and I haven't got time to wait for a decision,' Brady said, as he picked his jacket up off the back of one of the chairs. He turned back to Conrad. 'Are you coming or what?'

Conrad nodded. 'Let me just close this down,' he replied as he shut down his laptop.

'For fuck's sake, Conrad! Get a move on!'

Brady didn't have time. *Emily Baker didn't have time*. 'I saw him yesterday, for fuck's sake. I alerted him to the fact that Emily was missing. What would you do with that information? You'd bloody get rid of the evidence. So come on. Move!'

Chapter Twenty-Three

Monday: 4:33 p.m.

Brady banged on the door of number 39 Grosvenor Drive, Whitley Bay. He had called backup. They would be here within minutes. But he didn't have minutes.

Just like before … Jonathan Edwards' house. Queens Road. Banging on the door. Shouting. No one answering …

The door opened suddenly.

'Police!' Brady flashed his warrant card at the startled Annika Fraser, Julian Fraser's wife.

'What?' she asked, shocked. She pulled her cardigan protectively around herself, hands trembling as she did so.

'Where is he?' demanded Brady as he pushed past her.

She stepped back. Flattened herself against the wall as she stared in disbelief

Fast approaching sirens could be heard. Flashing lights followed as cars screamed to a halt in the street.

'I'm sorry about this,' Conrad said. 'We need to talk to your husband.'

'Talk? This is talk?' she spluttered incredulously as she gestured outside at the chaos in the street.

'Where is he?' shouted Brady as he made his way down the corridor.

'In his studio. Why? What has he done?' she asked. Her tanned face had lost its healthy vigour. She turned and stared, numb with shock as bulky officers wearing protective body armour ran up the path towards her house. One of them was armed with a battering ram. 'I . . . I . . . don't understand!'

She stumbled back. Out of the way of the officers. Confused. Scared. She looked for the detective who had flashed her his warrant card. Wanting answers. But he had gone. Disappeared through the house and out in to the back garden, followed by ten or so heavily armoured officers.

'We need to open this,' Brady urged as he threw his body against the double wooden doors. It didn't budge. He knew Julian Fraser was in there. Had locked himself in. Brady had seen someone through the large windows on the side of the single-storey brick building. But the glass was frosted to prevent anyone from clearly seeing in. The lights were on. Brady held his ear against the wooden doors. He could hear banging in there. As if Fraser was rearranging his art studio. No. Smashing everything up.

He needed in. Needed to get to her before . . .

He stopped himself. Turned, as officers in black protective gear came running down the large back garden. One ready with a battering ram. The studio, which looked like it had originally been constructed as a double garage at the bottom of the large garden, was a decent size, with a pitched, tiled roof. A driveway gave access from the street through double wooden doors to the side of the house. The garden was secluded, not overlooked by the neighbours. It was the perfect location to hide someone.

'Open it!' ordered Brady as he stood out of the way. 'NOW!'

'POLICE!' yelled the officers as they stormed the building.

Brady watched them force their way in. Had decided it was better to let them check out the situation. After all, Julian Fraser was cornered and Brady had no idea how he would react. It seemed like an eternity, but was in reality only a minute or so, before two officers emerged.

They shook their heads at Brady. 'There's no one else inside, sir. Apart from the suspect. The first part's a garage. Car parked up. Then a door leads into an art studio. Nothing else.'

Brady made his way in. He saw the car. A BMW estate. There was no Volvo Series 200 parked up here. No black Labrador. For a moment Brady wondered if he had got it wrong.

Could it all just be coincidence?

He walked over to the door, which hung, smashed and crooked. He walked through into a brightly lit, deceptively spacious studio. Paintings had been ripped and smashed beyond recognition and thrown in disarray around the room. A large leather couch sat against the far wall. It was clear from the cushions and blankets thrown on it that Fraser used it to sleep on. Two easels stood at the side of room. Both works in progress. But both canvases had been shredded into pieces by a knife.

He turned. Nothing.

He scanned the room. Looking for signs of Emily. But the officer had been right. There was nothing. He ignored Julian Fraser who had been restrained by two officers, holding him back. Ignored his outraged shouts claiming police brutality – and the rest.

Brady walked around the large space. He was looking for a hiding place. Couldn't see one. The exposed floor had been laid with polished concrete. His eyes glanced over at the small kitchen. A sink, cabinets and a work-top. A kettle and a couple of paint-covered mugs. He opened the cupboard doors with latex gloved hands. Nothing.

He could hear Julian Fraser's shouting. Getting louder and more aggravated. He continued his search.

'She's not here, sir,' Conrad quietly informed him. 'I've checked the bathroom back there. There's no sign of her. Walk-in shower, sink and toilet. That's all.'

Brady didn't respond. He refused to accept that she wasn't here. The alternative was too hard to face.

If she's not here and he's hidden her somewhere else, I'll never find her. She'll die . . .

'She has to be here. Keep looking!'

Brady turned and looked across at Fraser. Brady swore he saw a trace of a smile on his face. His hazel eyes were steady, calm.

'What were you doing in here?' Brady asked as he walked over to him.

'I could ask you and your armed gorillas the same question,' Fraser said, gesturing with his head at the grim-faced officers flanking him on either side.

Brady got right in to his face. 'What the fuck were you doing in here?'

'Painting. That's what I do for a living.' he replied.

'Looks to me as if you were destroying evidence.'

Fraser shrugged.

'I know you've got her.'

'I have no idea what you are talking about.'

Brady lunged at him. 'If I find her too late, I'll kill you. You hear me!' he yelled, his face contorted with rage.

'Sir!' cautioned Conrad.

Brady ignored him.

The other officers kept out of it.

'I'm fucking serious, you little psychotic shit! I have enough evidence to lock you up forever!' Brady spat at him. He raised his fist. 'Are you going to tell me where she is or do I have to beat it out of you first?'

'Sir!' Conrad shouted.

But Brady didn't care. Not anymore. He would rather have the satisfaction of hitting Fraser than walking away, knowing that he had won. That they had no way of finding where Emily was hidden.

He pulled his arm back.

Fraser winced. Shut his eyes. His forehead glistened with perspiration. He raised his hands to protect himself.

Brady stopped. Suddenly. No matter how good it would feel, it wasn't worth losing his job.

Startled, Fraser opened his eyes to look at Brady. His gaze filled with pure murderous hate. The look in his narrowed eyes told Brady he was right. Fraser had taken Emily and all the others. She was here. She had to be. But where?

'Arrest him!' Brady ordered.

He watched as Fraser was read his rights. Handcuffed and taken away.

He could hear his wife running down the garden towards them. Screaming and shouting at the officers. Demanding to know what he had done. Why they were arresting him. No one said a word to her as they walked past.

Chapter Twenty-Four

Monday: 7:01 p.m.

Brady looked at Fraser. He had been arrested. His home and garden had been searched. But there was no sign of Emily Baker. No evidence to suggest that she or any of the victims had ever been held captive there. Nor were there any paintings. Nothing. Nothing to suggest that he was involved in abducting, lobotomising and then murdering young women over a twenty-year period.

It was clear from the outset that Fraser wasn't going to talk. Brady had tried every form of coercion and nothing had worked. He simply refused to talk. But they had him. It had taken time but biological evidence had been recovered from the victims' nightdresses and hair. The forensic evidence found matched Fraser's DNA. It was the conclusive evidence that Brady had needed.

But Fraser had Brady by the balls. And he knew it.

Time was running out for Emily, if she wasn't already dead. Brady breathed in slowly. Steadied himself. Resisted the urge to throw Julian Fraser against the wall. His eyes automatically looked up at the camera in the corner of the ceiling filming the interview. It wouldn't look good on his CV.

Brady turned to Conrad, who looked as frustrated as Brady felt. He nodded at Conrad. It was all they had left. It was clear that Fraser was not going to talk. This would be Brady's last-ditch attempt at trying to break him. Whether it would work was yet to be determined.

Brady turned his attention to the file on the desk in front of him.

He took out the photograph that he had downloaded from the press article in 1972. 'Pretty girl, your mother,' he said, staring at the image. He turned to Conrad. 'Wouldn't you say?'

Fraser kept his eyes on Brady, refusing to look at the photograph of Shauna McBride that Brady had now placed directly before him. His face was filled with anger and disdain.

'Why do you think your adopted father lobotomised her?'

Fraser didn't respond.

Brady sat back and folded his arms. He was exhausted. Mentally and physically. The last place he wanted to be was in front of Julian Fraser – the *Puppet Maker*.

'Did you visit your mother when she was at St George's? Must have screwed with your head when you realised what your father had done to her.'

Again, Fraser didn't say anything.

Brady had had enough.

He pushed his chair back and stood up. Leaned over. 'Where the fuck is Emily Baker? Where the fuck are you keeping her?'

Fraser shook his head. 'No comment.'

'I'll give you no fucking comment!' he threatened as he banged his fist down on the table.

'DI Brady, I must object to this behaviour!'

Brady ignored the Duty Solicitor. He didn't need her telling him how to do his job.

'Where is she?' he hissed, his face inches from Fraser's.

'You're not that clever are you? You don't even know about my adoptive father, do you?'

Brady sat back down. Whatever surprise he felt at Fraser's sudden decision to talk, he hid. 'Go on.'

'He was my biological father,' said Fraser. His voice thick, filled with loathing.

Brady stared at him.

'Didn't know that did you?' Fraser laughed. Brutal. Cruel. 'Not that smart after all?'

'So why would you lobotomise those women? Why do what he did to Shauna?'

He didn't answer Brady. Not directly. But he did start to talk.

'My father persuaded Shauna's parents to have her lobotomised. Not that there was anything wrong with her. She wasn't mentally ill. She just wasn't what her parents wanted her to be. My grandparents were . . . very much of their generation. My mother was an embarrassment to them. Sexually active. But with the wrong sort, if you get my drift. They thought she would grow out of it. But when my grandmother caught her with a friend in a compromising position, well they had no choice but to deal with it. With her,' he smiled at Brady.

Brady didn't react.

'So, she was committed and put under the care of my medically esteemed father at St Mary's, who took the opportunity to abuse her. Then she got pregnant. When he realised, he naturally worried that she would talk. Not inside. Nobody listened to them on the inside. But once she was out. She would have exposed him. So, he used his expertise. The ultimate power he had to keep her quiet permanently. A month later he delivered me. Wanted to see if I was healthy. Then he told her parents, my grandparents, that I was "mentally retarded". He recommended they forget that I was ever born.' He suddenly stopped.

'How do you know all this?' Brady asked.

'I checked my birth certificate when I graduated from university. Had this feeling that something wasn't right. I was definitely my father's son. I never doubted that. But I did doubt that she was my real mother.' He shook his head. 'She never liked me. You see, she could see that I was his child. I looked just like him.'

And he did. Brady had seen the photograph of Dr Nigel Fraser. He understood why Harvey wouldn't have questioned the suspect's parentage. Julian Fraser did look just like him.

'You know how I found out about Shauna McBride? That bitch who raised me! The one I was forced to call Mother. She told me. She had put two and two together. Knew my birth mother was a young patient of his. She was happy to begin with, and then I started to grow up. Started to have this uncanny resemblance to my adopted father. Then that bitch somehow found out my father had had Shauna McBride transferred to St George's. He had that power. He could do whatever he liked and he did. But she would take me there. My adoptive mother. To humiliate me,' he said staring Brady straight in the eye. 'Point at her and tell me that she was my real mother.'

Brady remained expressionless. There was nothing Fraser could say that would shock him. Or provoke him. Not now. Not after he had seen what this man had done to women as vulnerable and helpless as his own biological mother. Julian had copied his father. He had taken it to a perverse and sadistically inhuman extreme. But there were parallels. And that was what Julian Fraser was explaining. That he was really no different from his critically acclaimed, neurologist father. Yet here he was, charged with kidnapping, torturing and murdering the women he lobotomised. Unlike his father who, when he retired, received the British Medical Journal Lifetime Achievement Award for his work.

'You know, Shauna wasn't the only young woman my father sexually abused. There were others. All lobotomised. All locked up under his authority. Waiting, strapped to a chair or a bed, for Dr Fraser's visits.' He suddenly shook his head and laughed.

Brady could hear the pain in the guttural laugh.

'I saw him once. I wasn't supposed to. I was there on a visit. My father had taken me. I was ten years old. He had said he had a meeting with the hospital's board of directors.'

Brady thought back to the photograph taken on the grounds outside the hospital. The one where Dr Fraser stood holding his son's hand, surrounded by medical staff and a few, specially selected patients.

'I went looking for him. Found him in a patient's room. She was strapped to the bed and he was doing things to her. And then she turned her head and looked at me. Stared with blank eyes. As if . . .' Julian faltered, lost in the moment. 'As if she was already dead. Or wishing she was dead.'

Brady looked at him. Felt no pity. Nothing but contempt. Whatever had happened to Fraser as a child could never justify the heinous crimes he had committed against women. The most defenceless women in society. Just like his mother.

'What about Emily Baker? Have you . . .' Brady couldn't say it.

Julian Fraser smiled at him. 'Lobotomised her?' He studied Brady. Considered whether it was worth telling him. 'They were all the same as my mother. They were diseased. Their minds crawling with filth. Whores. All of them. What I did to them was for their own good. I cleansed them. Took away their obsession with sex. Cut it out of them, so to speak.'

Brady had had enough. He felt sickened. He knew that Fraser would never tell him where he had hidden Emily Baker. Let alone whether he had lobotomised her. He turned and walked out of the interview room. He imagined that Fraser's artwork would command a high price now. A killer painting his victims as he tortured them. It would be priceless to some people.

'I'm just like my father, Detective Inspector Brady. That's what that bitch would taunt me with. But you know something? She's right! You tell her from me that she was right! I am my father's son! You tell that fucking bitch of a woman what I did for him!' Fraser shouted after Brady's retreating figure. 'Do you hear me? You tell that fucking bitch!'

Brady continued walking. Slammed the door behind him. To block out his voice. His taunts.

Tried to focus. He had to keep it together – for Emily's sake, Brady could not let go of the eighties black Volvo. If he found the Volvo, he would find Emily Baker. He knew it had to have been Fraser who had walked Emily down past Bluebell Woods. Presumably he had offered her a lift home. After all, what was there to be fearful of? She knew Fraser. And Brady was certain that Fraser knew of Emily's plans to visit the old hospital to take photographs. An assignment that was heavily influenced by Fraser's own work on mental illness and psychiatric hospitals. If Brady had not been looking for old patient files on James David Macintosh, he would never have come across Hannah and the others. And Hannah's repetition of Emily's name had led him to Fraser.

The car had to be how he could find where Julian Fraser had hidden her. He just hoped to God he was right.

'Conrad!' Brady shouted down the hall. He could feel the tension building. He didn't have time to wait around. 'CONRAD!'

Moments later his deputy came running down the corridor.

'You got it?'

'Yes, sir,' Conrad said, red-faced.

'About bloody time. Come on, we'll take my car,' Brady instructed as grabbed his jacket and keys. 'What's the address?'

'It's about three miles from Wooler. Remote place by the looks of it.'

'Sounds about right,' Brady replied.

Brady would not have expected anything else.

Brady sped up the A1 North heading for the countryside on the outskirts of the Northumberland town of Wooler.

'I don't understand . . . Fraser's paintings. The doctor with the ice pick?' Conrad questioned.

Brady shook his head as he thought back to the painting. 'Yeah . . . most people don't realise that a simple kitchen implement like the ice pick advanced modern lobotomies.'

'You are serious?' Conrad questioned.

'Yes. An American doctor named Walter Freeman was the first surgeon in 1945 to use an ice pick. Taken from his own kitchen as a means of lobotomising his patients. He popularised the operation to the extent that it was still being practised in the United States and the UK until the seventies,' Brady stated, pausing for a moment as he thought about it. 'He even travelled around the United States in a coach offering the operation. No anaesthetic needed, so consequently, no operating theatre. A simple ten-minute procedure that involved inserting the ice pick behind the eyeball, followed by a few firm taps to break through the skull. Then a few more taps to sever whatever neurons were malfunctioning in the brain and there you are . . . Lobotomised.' Brady shook his head again. The practice beyond his comprehension. 'Depressed housewives . . . disobedient children. Fixed in ten minutes,' he stated.

'Homosexuals . . .' Conrad added.

Brady nodded. 'Lobotomies were seen as a positive cure for extreme schizophrenics, violent patients and,' he looked at Conrad, 'people seen as socially deviant.'

'Do you think he has already—' Conrad faltered. Unable to say it.

Brady turned and looked at Conrad.

'What? Lobotomised her?' Brady shook his head. 'I don't know. I just don't know.'

He drove in silence for the rest of the journey. He didn't feel much like talking. Nor it seemed, did Conrad.

'There!' Conrad pointed over to his left. 'That track there must lead up to it.'

Brady looked up at the detached stone house. It was built on a hill overlooking Wooler. 'Looks like it's been abandoned for a few years,' Brady commented as he drove towards it.

He parked his black 1978 Ford Granada Ghia in the drive next to the black Volvo Series 200. The registration plate was 1985. Brady got out and walked around the car. The partial registration they had caught on the CCTV surveillance footage at the nursing home matched. But Brady already knew it would. 'It's in good condition.' He peered in through the windows. He knew that forensics would find conclusive evidence against Julian Fraser. His

DNA would be all over the car. Fingerprints, strands of hair. He was equally certain that forensic evidence would place Emily in the car as well.

Brady called in backup. He had waited. He had wanted to be certain first. But he had been right.

'Sir!'

Brady looked over at Conrad's concerned expression. Then he heard it. A dog barking. It was coming from within the house.

'Come on. Let's go find her, shall we?'

Conrad followed Brady up the stone steps to the large wooden door. He knocked. The dog's barking intensified. Brady waited. He knocked again. Waited. Nothing.

He tried the handle. The door was locked. 'Reckon we need the "big red key". Get it out my boot will you?' Brady instructed. He went over to the living-room window and peered into the gloom.

Conrad came back with the battering ram.

Brady took it and after three hard blows the heavy wooden door gave way.

The smell of decay and stench hit them. The place had not been lived in for years. Brady walked into the dark hallway. He flicked a switch on the wall. A light overhead came on illuminating the dismal, worn decor and threadbare Axminster hall carpet. He immediately noticed the pile of unopened mail piled at the bottom of the stairs. He walked over and picked up an envelope. It was addressed to a 'Mr D. McBride'.

When Julian Fraser had mentioned his grandparents in the interview room it had struck Brady that he had a relationship of sorts with them. That was when Brady started to wonder whether the Volvo could have belonged to the McBrides. After all, they would have been in their sixties when they had bought the car new. So, after finishing the interview with Julian Fraser, Brady had researched vehicles registered to Dougal McBride and his wife. The Volvo that had so eluded his team had been registered to Julian Fraser's biological grandfather. Brady had found out that the couple had retired in the mid-eighties and had moved from Dundee to Wooler. Brady seriously doubted that it was to be closer to their daughter in St George's. But if they had found out that Dr Fraser and his wife had adopted Julian, and that he was healthy, then maybe that was a good enough reason to relocate. Brady doubted he would ever find out. But Julian had a relationship with them – or at least his grandfather. One that had allowed him to use his grandfather's Volvo to abduct his victims. But his grandparents had both been dead for over ten years.

Brady just hoped that they were not too late. Unwittingly, Brady had warned Fraser that they were looking for him. For Emily. Fraser had already attempted to get rid of anything that tied him to the crimes – primarily his artwork. Brady was no fool. He realised that the likelihood of finding his abductee alive was remote. Easier to destroy all evidence.

Brady dropped the envelope and turned and looked at Conrad. 'Where's the dog?'

It had stopped barking as soon as they had entered the house. The noise had been replaced by frantic scratching. Wherever the dog was, it had been locked in.

'Down there,' answered Conrad as he gestured towards the closed door at the end of the hallway.

Brady nodded. He walked down the corridor. 'EMILY?' he shouted as he approached the door. 'Emily, it's the police!'

He knew the door would be locked before he even attempted to turn the handle. 'Stand back,' Brady ordered.

Conrad did as instructed as Brady ran at the door throwing his weight against it. But to no avail.

'Shit!' muttered Brady.

The scratching behind the door had become even more furious.

'Do you want the battering ram, sir?'

'No,' Brady answered. 'Just in case she's directly behind the door.' He then rammed his shoulder hard against the door, succeeding in forcing the lock to give way.

Brady opened it, not sure what he was going to find. 'Emily?' he called out.

But she wasn't there. Instead a dog was anxiously clawing and digging at something in the corner.

'God that is foul,' Conrad complained as his eyes watered.

Brady looked around. It was a small, windowless room. The plaster walls scratched and chewed. He realised the black Labrador was clawing furiously at what seemed to be a metal door. It was covered in scratches, telling Brady the dog had been kept in here for years. *Why? Unless the dog was a deterrent in case anyone tried to escape?*

'I bet that door leads to a basement of sorts. Remember all the victims sustained injuries from being thrown or pushed down from a height?' Brady said as he turned back to Conrad. 'Grab hold of the dog, will you?' Brady asked. 'I don't want him going down there.'

Conrad pulled the dog back by its collar, allowing Brady to pull the metal door open.

It screeched as it dragged across the stone floor.

'Turn on that light switch, will you?' Brady asked as he peered down into a chasm of bottomless blackness.

Conrad reached up with his free hand and flicked the light on.

If Brady thought the smell from the trapped dog had been bad, it was nothing compared to the stench emanating from the basement. The air foul with the smell of sweat. Urine. Faeces.

Brady tried not to react. Or gag. All he could think of was her.

Brady looked down into the underground room. A basement. A cell. He saw a mattress in the corner. It was empty. It took a moment for his eyes to adjust to the light. Then he saw her. Tied to a chair identical to the ones he had seen dumped in the basement of St George's. It was the missing eighteen-year-old. They had found her.

'Oh fuck!' he muttered. 'Emily? Emily?' he shouted as he ran down the steps. 'It's the police! Emily? Emily Baker?'

No response.

He realised then how the other victims had suffered such injuries. The stone steps were steep and slippery. He imagined they were pushed through the door at the top of the steps and fell, shattering and twisting whatever bones they landed on. Brady jumped the last few steps, landing on the dirt ground.

'Emily?' he called.

Nothing. *Shit!*

She had her back to him. The chair was positioned directly under a naked bulb. He walked over. Stopped. Stared at the wall of Polaroid photographs ahead of him. *God* . . . He looked away. Had to. Turned his attention to the victim.

'Emily? It's the police. Emily?' Brady called out as he crouched down in front of her.

She didn't move. Didn't react.

Fuck!

He noticed her hair. The sides of her scalp had been shaved.

He breathed out. Slowly. Steadied himself.

Brady looked up at her face. It was pale. Her eyes were closed. But she was breathing. He touched her. Gently. 'Emily?' he whispered. 'What has that bastard done to you?'

Fraser had left her dressed in a white Victorian-style nightgown. Identical to the others.

'Sir? Is she alive? Sir? Can you hear me?' Conrad yelled down over the dog's howls.

Brady heard him. Heard the pitiful yowling from the dog. But didn't answer. He couldn't. He just kept willing her to open her eyes. To look at him. To let him know she was going to be all right.

Oh God . . .

Chapter Twenty-Five

Monday: 10:10 p.m.

Brady sat there with her in silence. They didn't need to talk. She was too exhausted after her ordeal. And Brady was too relieved to spoil it with words. But just being present was enough.

She was one of the lucky ones. Unlike Hannah and the others. He tried to focus on the positive.

She's going to be all right. You got to her in time ...

But it was hard to feel positive. Emily would recover. Physically and psychologically. He was sure of that. But as for Hannah, the young woman who had effectively saved Emily's life, her outcome could not have been more different. She was alive. *But ...*

Brady thought about the ones who didn't make it. The ones who even in death had no dignity. Four of Julian Fraser's victims remained unidentified. Nameless. And would continue to do so. *How do they know you're missing, if they don't even know you exist?* It was a question that would haunt him. But he had to be grateful for this one victory.

'Jack?' asked Emily, turning to look at him. 'You won't leave, will you?'

Brady smiled at her. 'I'll stay until you fall asleep. As promised. But then I have to go back to the station. Fill out some paperwork and then go home and crash myself. I'll come and visit you tomorrow.'

Emily's dark brown eyes studied him. Serious. Distrustful. It was clear that she had never had anyone to rely on. Not really. Yes, she had a social worker. But that wasn't the same. And now that Emily was out of North Tyneside's care her social worker had no need to keep in touch. But Brady knew that Sandra would. He had called her as soon as Emily had been admitted to hospital. She was coming to visit Emily first thing in the morning. Her gratitude was immense. As was her relief. But Brady did not feel the same elation. For Emily's freedom had come at a price. He thought of Hannah again. She was still in ICU. It was touch and go as to whether she would pull through. Brady had planned to visit her after Emily had fallen asleep. Not that he had told Emily that. Nor had he told Emily the full extent of her injuries. That could wait. He didn't have the strength to tell her. And she didn't have the strength to process it. Not tonight. Tomorrow he would explain to her how Hannah had saved her life.

He had already taken Emily's statement. Made her relive her abduction by a man she had trusted – her tutor. A man she respected as an artist and lecturer. A man who had suggested that she break into St George's at night and photograph the building. Then, to her surprise, she had met him walking Henry, his black Labrador, in Bluebell Woods just as she was making her way back down through the fields. He had singled her out. Her background in council care fitted his type. As did her looks. The difference was, she wasn't the stereotype. She wasn't living on the streets. She hadn't turned to drugs, alcohol or prostitution to feed a habit that kept her from facing the harsh reality of her life. A childhood bandied from one foster carer to another. And then a dumping ground of a children's home until she reached an age where she was not the responsibility of the local authority. Or anyone else's.

Brady knew this life all too well. He understood what Emily had survived. After all, he had been separated from his younger brother Nick and placed in countless foster homes across North Tyneside. But he and Nick had been lucky. They had made something of their lives. Brady had had Detective Superintendent O'Donnell looking out for him when he was Emily's age. O'Donnell had been a DC back then. He had given a damn about a kid who had grown up with every disadvantage that life could throw at him – and more. Now it was Brady's turn to repay the gesture by looking out for Emily.

'Jack?' she muttered, yawning.

Brady leaned in towards her. She was lying on her back with her head tilted in his direction. The distrust had gone from her brown eyes. Now, they were filled with sadness.

'Why didn't he do to me what he did to the others? The ones whose photos were on the wall . . .' Her tone was plaintive.

'I . . . I don't know, Emily. I honestly don't know why.'

'The last time he visited me, I thought then he was going to do what he had done to her. To . . .' she shook her head as she tried to blink back the tears.

'Shhh . . .' Brady consoled.

She shook her head. 'No. I can't stop asking, why me Why did he let me survive?'

Brady didn't have an answer. Or at least one that h wanted to share. He hadn't told her that if he had nc made the connection between the black Volvo 200 an Julian Fraser's grandparents, then she would never hav been found. She would have starved to death down ther in that basement secured to that chair.

And as for Julian Fraser, Brady knew he would nc talk, let alone admit to Emily Baker's abduction an torture. He had said all he had wanted to. It was over. Bu they had his paintings in custody. He had removed then from both his studio at home and at work and had hidde them in his grandfather's house in Wooler. Countles macabre paintings that depicted the dehumanisin torture of young women – most of whom matched wit the murdered victims. And questions, like the one Emil was asking, would have to be left unanswered. Life wa arbitrary. Unimaginable acts happened.

'I don't know why, Emily . . .' Brady finally answered.

'Those noises I would hear. The ones that used to terrif me. The scratching and banging. That was really his dog?'

Brady nodded. 'I believe so. He had locked the dog in the small room that led down to the basement. From th looks of it, the dog had spent hours and hours scratchin at that metal door. As for the banging, the dog migh have even been throwing his body at the door in despera- tion. With it being metal, the sound would have boome around the basement.'

'Henry . . .'

Brady waited.

'The dog. He's called Henry. He was in the back of the
ar. The night he . . .' Emily closed her eyes.

'Henry's a good name for a dog,' Brady said, smiling.

She opened her eyes again. Then returned the smile.
Yeah . . . I reckon it is. What will happen to Henry?'

Brady shrugged. 'I don't know. The PDSA will get him
ehomed.'

She nodded, thoughtful. Sad. 'Bit like waiting to be
adopted then?'

'Yeah. I suppose,' Brady agreed.

'He's too old,' Emily said.

Brady didn't understand.

'To be adopted,' she explained. 'People like them when
hey're cute. Puppies, kittens, babies. You know?'

Brady knew. A childhood in care taught you some hard
acts about life. Not necessarily ones that you wanted to
earn.

'Maybe I'll home Henry?' Emily suggested. Her voice
was starting to slur as exhaustion took over.

'Maybe . . .' Brady replied softly.

He watched her start to drift off. Her eyes eventually
closed. Her breathing finally relaxed. Steady. Slow. Safe.

In that moment Brady felt an overwhelming sense of
peace. Something he had not felt for a long time.

He headed down the corridor towards his office. He was
going to collect his car keys and jacket and go home. He
was exhausted. All he wanted to do was crawl into bed

and forget. To block out all the sadistic images that kept going through his mind. He had hoped that by finding Emily alive he would exorcise the demons that had been tormenting him. And he had done. But it was brief. And he knew the reason why – *Annabel Edwards.*

You failed her . . . You saved another victim. But at her expense.

The station had breathed a collective sigh of relief. Julian Fraser had been arrested and charged. Emily Baker had been found. It had become a media sensation. Journalists were gorging themselves on the grisly nature of the case. The public's appetite for gore was insatiable.

DCI Gates had even called him. He had just returned from London. He had praised Brady for apprehending Fraser, and for finding Emily – alive and physically unharmed. Psychologically was a completely different matter. Brady wondered how long it would take her to get over her abduction. Her torture at the hands of a serial killer. Knowing that at any minute he could kill you. And worse.

But Gates' words of commendation were hollow. The underlying fact was that Brady had still fucked up. In the media's eyes. The public's eyes. And in Gates' mind. He might not have articulated it, but Brady could hear it in his voice. His name would always be associated with Macintosh's. And not in a good way. Gates had asked to see him the following morning at 8:00 a.m. sharp. Whether it was connected to the on-going Macintosh case he couldn't be sure. All he knew was that a three-year-old girl was still missing. The likelihood of finding her alive now was fading – fast.

Brady knew that whatever leads there had been in London had turned cold. Not that he was surprised. Nor did he feel any satisfaction in being proved right. He just wanted that little girl back. Safe. But as the hours blurred into days, the likelihood of finding her alive was becoming more and more remote. The investigation was again focusing on the North East. The question was, were they too late? It was something that Brady couldn't bring himself to think about. Not now.

He needed to go home. But even there he felt a failure. He thought of Claudia. His ex-wife. The woman he had spent the last five months living with trying to make amends. She had been held in a hostage situation. Beaten, tortured and . . . He stopped himself. But it was all his fault. He had been a shit husband. Maybe if she hadn't left him then none of it would have happened. The abduction. The brutal murder of her boyfriend. But Claudia *had* left. And she had had every reason to. And now she was gone again. She had admitted herself to a private psychiatric hospital and Brady had no idea where.

He reached his office. Walked in. He could hear someone running down the corridor. A few seconds later Kodovesky was standing in the open doorway.

'Sir?' she panted, out of breath.

Brady turned to her. 'Kodovesky? What the hell are you still doing here? It's past midnight?'

'She's dead,' she said. Flustered. 'His mother, sir.'

'Macintosh's mother?'

She nodded quickly. 'Yes. When I did some more

research into the name I then found her death certificate. She died this year.'

Brady sighed. It was another false lead.

'But I did find out that she had a son from her second marriage. In Australia. You need to talk to him. There's something his mother had told him before she died.'

'Did he tell you?'

'No. Donald Fitzgerald said he would only talk to whoever was in charge. Wasn't sure if he even believed it himself. He hadn't been aware that he had a brother until I talked to him. Once I mentioned James David Macintosh's name he insisted he talked to you.'

Brady frowned. 'Gates is in charge.'

'I . . . I told him you were in charge when I initially talked to him. I didn't know DCI Gates would be returning from London tonight. But, whatever it is, he said it was urgent. That it related to Annabel's abduction.'

Brady had tried the number Kodovesky had given him. But no one had answered. He had left a voice message asking him to return his call ASAP. He accepted the time difference could be the reason why he couldn't get hold of him. There was nothing he could do but try again once he got home.

As soon as Brady walked through the door and flicked the lights on, he knew. Someone had been inside his house. The unopened mail on the hall table had been moved. Not much. But enough. The answer machine was no longer flashing. Whatever messages he had not bothered to listen to had been erased.

He walked from room to room. Nothing had been aken. He climbed the stairs. He was trying not to think it.

Had Claudia come back?

He glanced across at the bathroom. Nothing unusual. Ie continued on, heading for the guest room. Nothing. Ie then turned to the master bedroom.

Maybe . . .

He walked towards the closed door. He was certain hat he had left it open.

He reached out for the handle. Stood there for a noment. Unsure. Then he swung the door open. Nothing.

He breathed out slowly. Shook his head as he stared round the room. Then he saw the frame on the bedside abinet. The photograph. It had been removed. Replaced.

He walked over. He didn't think to protect whatever ingerprints could be on it. He already knew who had een here. The photograph was evidence enough. He icked the frame up. Hands trembling as he stared at the hild in the photo – at Annabel's pale, unresponsive face. Her body awkward, unnatural. She was sitting in a chair, Victorian-style doll on her lap. The old-fashioned lothes she was wearing were identical to the ones that Ellen Jackson had been found in. Brady took a deep reath in.

Hands still trembling, he removed the photo from the rame. Macintosh had scrawled something on the back. He read it. It meant nothing to him. He still had no idea where he was. Or where he had hidden Annabel.

Was he too late?

His phone suddenly rang. He answered.

'Yes. Detective Inspector Brady . . .' He listened to th
caller.

It was Donald Fitzgerald. And he gave Brady th
answers he needed. It all made sense now. He remem
bered when he had first visited Mill Cottage. What h
had found in the woods.

Without hesitation, Brady grabbed his keys and jacke
and ran.

He jumped in his car. Turned the engine on. Reverse
out from between two other vehicles, swung the ca
around and sped down the road, driving like his lif
depended on it. And it did. If he didn't get to Annabel i
time then he would never be able to live with himself.

He tried to keep his mind clear. Focused on the road
Not on Macintosh. Not on what he could have done
Then it hit. He fumbled around for his phone. Found i
Tried to keep his eye on the road at the same time as cal
ing Conrad.

He put the phone on speaker and waited for Conrad t
pick up.

Fucking pick up, Conrad! Come on. Come on!

'Sir?'

'Where are you?' Brady demanded, ignoring hi
question.

'At home. Why?'

'Where's Claudia?'

'What's going on?' Conrad asked, worried.

'For fuck's sake, Harry! Where is Claudia? Is she sti
in the North East? Tell me she didn't fucking book int
somewhere in Northumberland?'

Conrad's silence confirmed his worst fears.

'Fuck!' yelled Brady as he thumped the steering wheel.

He had a choice to make. And he had to make it fast. The next decision would affect the rest of his life.

'Where is she Harry? Where the fuck is she?'

'Rothbury. She's in a hospital in the hills up there.'

Brady did the maths. Both locations were in the same irection but Rothbury was thirty miles further north.

He pulled out at the next junction and put his foot on he accelerator and sped north.

'Conrad, I need you to get to Rothbury . . . To Claudia. ASAP. Get as much backup as possible,' Brady ordered.

'Why?'

'Because Macintosh has gone after Claudia. The astard's gone after her.'

'He can't have done. How would he know where she s?' Conrad asked.

'For fuck's sake I don't know. It's Macintosh! All I now is that he has been in my house. He took a photo-raph of Claudia.'

'Is that where you're heading now?' Conrad asked.

'No.' His voice was strained. Strangled.

'Sir?'

'I need you to get to her. Now!'

Brady cut the call. Threw the phone down. Thumped his fist against the steering wheel again. Anything to take he raging pain that consumed him, that squeezed and queezed the air out of his lungs.

Fuck it! Keep it together. For her. You've got to keep it ogether for her. Otherwise . . .

Macintosh had given him a choice. He had chosen.

He thought of the photograph of Annabel. Sitting stiffly in a chair, dressed up in an old dress. In her hands an identical doll to the one Brady had found in the old suitcase in the eaves of Mill Cottage. On the back of the Polaroid, Macintosh had written something. For Brady. After all, this was personal.

Look at you, sullen in yielding, brutal in your rage – you will go too far. It's perfect justice: natures like yours are hardest on themselves.

Macintosh was taunting him.

He had to make a choice. Macintosh had seen to that. And it was one that he knew he would struggle to ever accept.

He willed the Armed Response Unit to get to Rothbury. Conrad could warn Claudia. Warn the staff. He hoped to God he wasn't too late – that they weren't too late.

He continued. Speeding in and out of traffic. Heading towards Annabel. Had he made the right choice? He didn't know. Wouldn't know until he got there. He ignored the panic. Tried to. Blocked the guilt. The '*what ifs*' that were trying to unhinge him. He had to keep focused. Not let Macintosh beat him.

But he understood now. He understood the quote – '*natures like yours are hardest on themselves*'.

Whatever choice he had made, the outcome would destroy him. Slowly but surely. Macintosh would make certain of that.

Chapter Twenty-Six

Monday: 11:37 p.m.

Brady raced up the dark, secluded overgrown drive. Braked. Got out the car, leaving the headlights on. He opened the boot and grabbed the bolt cutters he had thrown in. He picked up the torch. Then he ran. Ignored the boarded-up cottage. Already knew no one would be inside. What he was looking for was in the woods. Knew in his gut that Macintosh had been – *and gone.*

He ran through the long grass and weeds round to the back garden and then as fast as he could to the woods. He needed to find her alive.

Then Claudia. He would drive to Rothbury. Hold her. Kiss her. Tell how much he goddamn loved her. Whisper that he would never let her go. Never again.

He found it. The steps down to the bunker. Someone had been here. The wild foliage, the climbing ivy had been ripped. Torn as someone had forced the metal door open. Someone – *Macintosh.* Then they had locked it behind them.

But the rusted padlock remained in place. Brady cut it open, then dragged the resisting door back. A dank, musty smell of earth and decaying leaves hit him. The air was heavy. The room, black.

'Annabel? Can you hear me? Annabel!'

He shone the torch into the dark space. He had been right, it was an old air-raid shelter. Ten foot by ten foot. Enough. His eyes scanned the room. For signs. Anything that told him she was here. It was filled with debris. Wooden chairs. Shelves stacked with tins of outdated food. Newspapers. Books. Candles. He knew she had to be here. *Had to be . . .*

'Annabel?' he called out as he stabbed at the darkness with the torch.

Then he realised. In the corner. Someone had been here. Someone – Macintosh – had left a handful of bluebells on top of a small mound of freshly dug-up soil. Brady ran over and started digging with his hands at the disturbed earth. The dirt was loose. The hole in the ground shallow. Then he felt something. A blanket. Something was wrapped inside.

Shit!

He dug his hands into the dirt and scooped out the blanket and its wrapped contents. There was barely any weight to it. Just enough for it to be the body of a very young child. He laid it gently in front of him and unfolded the wool blanket. As he did so a lock of blond hair fell out. Knew then, it was her. Macintosh had buried her.

Oh God please . . . please . . .

He felt numb. His mind blank. Hands trembling, he pulled the remaining blanket away.

* * *

Brady sat in his car. An ambulance had been dispatched. He could hear it in the distance, along with backup.

He had wrapped her in his jacket, was holding her tight against his chest. Her curly knotted blonde head lay still against his thundering heart. He sat there. Numb. Waiting.

Waiting for Conrad to tell him that everything was OK. That everything was going to be all right. To tell him he could breathe. Could continue to keep breathing.

Behind Brady, sirens shrieked and blue lights flashed as police cars, followed by an ambulance, pulled up the lane. He felt her stir against him. Unsettled. She could feel it. The chaos that was about to ensue. He held her even closer. Didn't want to let her go. He had saved her – *just*. Any later and she would have suffocated to death. Macintosh hadn't touched her. Had not harmed her. She was severely dehydrated. If she hadn't suffocated, she would have died from organ failure. She had hours left to live.

Why? Why leave her for me to find? Alive?

But he knew the answer. He had made a choice. For Annabel, it had been the right choice. *But what about Claudia?* He shut his eyes. Forced himself to think of something else. Anything, rather than what might or might not have happened. She was in a private clinic in Rothbury – an expensive one that dealt with depression, eating disorders and alcohol and drug-related addictions. In other words, security would be at a minimum. These were not high-risk patients: either to themselves or to society. The clients had voluntarily checked themselves in after paying a substantial fee for the privilege. Brady was aware that someone as Machiavellian as Macintosh would have no trouble gaining access to the clinic's grounds, or building.

He opened his eyes and dragged a shaking hand back through his hair as he stared out at the all-consuming blackness. The thoughts assailing him overwhelming. He needed to distract himself. Anything to stop himself from going crazy.

He thought of the air-raid shelter. What he had found. Annabel had not been alone. Another small body had been buried with her. Brady assumed it was Lucy Macintosh's remains. Brady had no idea whether Wolfe would be able to determine the cause of death. But he was certain the little girl had been murdered.

Had Macintosh lived with this knowledge? Had he been blamed for the death of someone he idolised? Demonised and abused by the very man who murdered her – his own father. Her body buried in the grounds of a disused air-raid shelter. Hidden for years and years. Forgotten. Her death unreported.

He thought of his phone call with Donald Fitzgerald. Eileen Macintosh's second son. James David Macintosh's younger half-brother. Of the death bed confession his mother had made. Blighted by guilt. The choices she had made. Like Brady, she had been forced to make choices that had haunted her to the day she died. She had confessed that her husband had told her that their son James had killed his sister. Her husband, a respected officer in the army, had insisted that it could not be reported for fear of the scandal. That James would be taken from them – permanently. So, they upped and left.

Locked up Mill Cottage. Locked up their son in St George's Psychiatric Hospital. But . . .

Ellen Jackson's injuries came to mind. She had been strangled. Had Macintosh been trying to recreate what happened to his three-year-old sister? Trying to awake a memory. To see whether he had actually killed his sister – accidentally, or otherwise. For he had lived with the tortured belief that he had. His parents had seen to that. Her last words to Donald were that James had never murdered his sister. That she had suspected all along that it was her husband. That she had watched him bury her three-year-old daughter in a disused air-raid shelter at the back of Mill Cottage. That her six-year-old son had witnessed *everything*. Her husband had chained and padlocked the door of the air-raid shelter so no one would ever find their daughter. *Until now . . .*

But Eileen Macintosh had told the wrong son. If only she had told James what she had confessed to Donald, then maybe none of this would ever have happened . . .

Brady accepted that he would never actually know. No one would. Only Macintosh.

The same could be said of Fraser. Only he knew why he had committed those atrocious acts. Had Fraser too been trying to recreate something in his past? His biological mother had been lobotomised by the man who had systematically raped her. He had done the same thing to his victims.

Both killers had come from disturbed backgrounds. Childhoods blighted by psychiatric hospitals and dominant, abusive fathers. By mothers who had stood back and witnessed unspeakable horrors. Macintosh's mother had

had her own son committed for an act carried out by her husband. Fraser's adopted mother had forced him as a child to face the reality of his lineage: a father who abused his position of authority and a mother lobotomised for being what her own parents deemed as sexually deviant.

Had that made them into the psychopaths that they were? Brady would never know the answer to that. What these men had experienced in their childhoods had influenced the choices they had gone on to make in adulthood. *But* they had chosen to act upon whatever compulsion they felt driven by. It had been their choice. And theirs alone.

His phone rang. He clicked answer. Didn't say anything. The fear crippling.

Please God . . . Let her be OK.

He squeezed his eyes shut. Held his breath and waited for the words that would change his life. He had made a choice. Now he had to live with it. His hand stroked Annabel's curly hair as he held her close. It threw him back to Claudia's wild red curly hair. Her Scottish ancestry. He bit his lip. Waited.

'Sir . . .'

He didn't answer. Couldn't.

'We got him. He was shot in the grounds of the hospital. He's dead . . .'

Brady didn't respond. He wasn't interested in Macintosh. All he wanted was to know that Claudia was safe.

He waited.

Then heard the words.

'Sir? Sir? Are you still there?'

Epilogue

Brady had kept a respectable distance between himself and the mourners. In particular, Claudia's parents. They had made it clear that he was not welcome. They openly blamed him for their daughter's death. Her blood was on his hands.

Not that Brady disagreed with them. He had made a choice. He had sacrificed Claudia in exchange for Annabel Edwards' life. He would never know if he could have got to Claudia in time. Maybe that was the point. That he was supposed to try to get to Claudia first. Only to find that by the time he got there, Macintosh had already . . .

Brady could not bring himself to think about what Macintosh had done to Claudia. Too horrific to even comprehend. Maybe that was the point, too. Macintosh had wanted Brady to discover Claudia's murdered body. At the expense of his sanity. And then Annabel's tiny body. For she would have suffocated to death.

Brady felt no satisfaction in Macintosh's death. Instead, he felt cheated. Cheated out of the chance to find out why. Why he had wanted Brady to suffer so. That, and rage. The rage was so intense. He wanted revenge.

Wanted Macintosh to experience the pain he felt. His body, every muscle, every thought screamed in agony at the reality of what he had lost. Of what he could not bring back. At what his life was without her.

He blinked back the tears as the anger coursed through his body. Threatening to unhinge him. He focused on the mourners. On the reason he was here.

He watched as Conrad left the mourners stood by the graveside – *her grave* – and walked towards him. Head down. Brady realised how easy it was to forget that other people felt her loss. That he was not the only one who was being tortured with every breath he took. Thoughts of Claudia assailed him. He was reminded of her everywhere he looked. A constant torment.

'Hello,' Conrad greeted him.

Brady didn't reply. A look was enough.

'I'm sorry . . .' Conrad began.

Brady shook his head. He didn't want to hear it. Didn't want to ever hear that word again.

'Amelia has been asking after you,' Conrad added, unsure of the right thing to say.

Brady nodded, as he continued to watch the funeral.

'What are you going to do now?' Conrad asked.

It was a good question. From the moment he knew he had lost her, he had done nothing else but wonder what he was going to do with his life. He still hadn't found the answer. All he knew was that he needed to get away from the North East. To get some distance from everything that had happened. There was only one person he wanted to be around right now. His younger brother, Nick. He knew him. Understood him. After all, they had survived a horrific childhood together. Brady had looked out for Nick. Protected him. And Nick had done the same for Brady.

He turned and looked at Conrad. He knew he would miss him. Had spent too long working with him not to. 'I need to get my head together. You understand that?'

Conrad didn't say anything. He didn't need to. Brady could see in his eyes that he didn't want to hear what was coming.

'I'm thinking of taking a couple of months' leave.'

'Where will you go?' Conrad asked, unable to disguise his concern. Or sadness.

'Anywhere but here.'

Brady looked over at the mourners. They were starting to disperse. For a second he caught Claudia's father's eye.

'Look, I've got to go,' Brady said. He didn't want a scene. Not here. He turned and headed towards his car.

'Sir,' Conrad called out after him. 'Keep in touch.'

Brady didn't answer. He did not want to commit himself – because right now, he was not sure whether he would ever return to the North East again.

Acknowledgements

I would first like to thank my family for all their constant support; especially Janette Youngson and Paula Youngson. Also, Betty Dand and Natalie and Scott Ritchie. Thanks to Eliane and Professor Pete Wilson and Dr Barry Lewis – you have been there for me from the beginning. Thanks also to Clare Usher and Amir Assadi whose skill and expertise enabled me to finish this book. I would like to thank Keshini Naidoo for all her editorial help. Thanks also to Andrew Potts and Jill Potts. Thanks to Suzanne Forsten and Tina Scrafton for their continuous support. A heartfelt thanks to Pamela Letham and Gill Richards for everything they have done for me to ensure that I kept writing and, kept my sanity. Finally, Francesca, Charlotte, Gabriel and Ruby, you are the reason I write – always.

Thanks to my literary agent, Euan Thorneycroft of A.M. Heath to whom I am eternally grateful for all his support and his straight-talking.

Special thanks to all at Mulholland, Hodder & Stoughton for being such an extraordinary team. Finally, I am indebted, as always, to my exceptional editor, Ruth Tross. Thank you – you truly are one of a kind!

If you've enjoyed THE PUPPET MAKER,
why not try another Jack Brady book?

Read on for an extract
from the gripping BLIND ALLEY, out now.

Chapter One

Thursday, 24th October: 10:23 p.m.

He watched her as she came outside. She couldn't see him – he had made sure of that. He sat back in the dark and waited. It was the anticipation of what was about to follow that he savoured more than the event itself. He licked his bottom lip. The location was perfect. Rundown and deserted. If anyone heard anything they wouldn't get involved. People here minded their own business. She couldn't have chosen a better place for what was about to happen to her. *If only she knew . . .*

He smiled to himself. He clenched and unclenched his hands as mentally he walked through the various scenarios he had meticulously planned.

Trina McGuire pursed her bright red lips and sucked on her tab as her cold, hard eyes scanned the shadowy street corners. It was second nature for her. A silver saloon car turned slowly off Saville Street West down onto Borough Road, casting its harsh beam over her. Blowing out smoke seductively, she looked in the direction of the driver. The silver car was now parked directly opposite her with the engine idling. The driver's face was in shadow but she knew he was watching her. Before she had a chance to walk over, he drove off. She was no fool. She was aware that the glare of his headlights had done her no favours. The roots of her long, straggly, bleached-blond hair and the uneven fake-tan smears on her arms and legs would be all too visible.

'Fuck you!'

She was getting too old for this game. And she was cold, despite it being mild for late October. She wrapped her thin, bare arms across her low-cut vest top in an attempt to keep warm.

She rested her back against the wall and listened to the dull thump of U2 on the jukebox inside as she smoked. Anything to calm her nerves. She had never known the streets to be so dark and quiet. Business was virtually non-existent. Even the Ballarat pub was empty apart from the hardcore regulars. She shivered again. She could feel the small, prickly hairs on the back of her neck standing up. She didn't know what it was, but something felt wrong. Maybe it was just her nerves getting the better of her, but she couldn't shake the feeling that someone was watching her. She glanced up and down the badly lit street. She couldn't see anyone. *Or could she?*

'Fuck this!' she muttered as she threw away what was left of her cigarette.

She turned on her three-inch red heels, about to go back in.

Before she had a chance to realise what was happening, he had already dragged her into the alley behind the pub where the rubbish bins were kept. A large leather-gloved hand covered her mouth, preventing her from screaming. Panicking, she struggled to get free but it was futile. He had the upper hand. He was at least six foot one and built like a Rottweiler on steroids.

Suddenly his other hand was tearing at her vest top. He found her breasts and started twisting and pulling at them roughly.

She felt physically sick. She wanted to vomit as his hand mauled her. But she knew that no matter what he did to her she had to keep focused. Her mind was racing. She was trying to process what was happening to her and at the same time trying to figure out how to get free.

Was he a punter? No . . . no. She'd been roughed up before but this was different. He *was different . . .*

Then it hit her. The news. It had been all over the news. There was a rapist in the area. *Shit! Shit! Shit! How could she have been so stupid?*

The police had put up photofits of the bloke throughout the local pubs. There was even one pinned by the toilets in the Ballarat. He had attacked three women in the past two months. And from what she'd read in the local paper that evening, the third one had been hurt pretty badly – enough for the poor cow to need reconstructive surgery.

Shit . . . shit . . . shit . . .

Tortured thoughts tore through her mind.

She was confused. She was sure he had only struck in Whitley Bay. She had been relaxed about the story because this was North Shields. How wrong could she have been?

She had to get away from him. Fight . . . Anything to stop him hurting her . . .

She used all her strength to prise his hand from over her mouth. Her long manicured nails snapped and split as she scratched and tore to no avail at the gloved hand. If she could scream it might be enough to scare him off. Desperate, she took her chance and bit as hard as she could through the leather to the flesh underneath.

His reaction was sudden and swift. He raised his knee and rammed it as hard as he could into the small of her back to make her let go.

It had the desired effect.

She was too winded to realise what was about to happen.

The first blow was a surprise. It split her nose clean open. She heard the sickening sound of snapping bones as his fist connected with her face, followed by the hissing of escaping air and blood. She was stunned. She had no chance of protecting herself against what was to follow.

The second punch was harder than the first. It smashed into her face with such force that her left eye socket imploded. Her head snapped violently backwards as her teeth ricocheted off her bottom lip, bursting it open like a swollen dam. Her legs gave way beneath her as everything went black.

Minutes passed as she lay on the ground, her body consumed with a blinding agony. Nothing made sense. All she knew was that she hurt so badly she was certain she would die. Slowly, the hazy fog started to lift. She remembered that she'd been attacked. He had dragged her into the perilously black alley behind the pub. She was aware that she was lying on something cold and hard – the ground. She must have collapsed after he'd punched her.

She could feel the panic overwhelming her.

She looked around in the darkness for him.

Where are you, you bastard? Where the fuck are you?

Her left eye had swollen shut and her right eye was nothing more than a slit. But it was enough to see the glow of a cigarette in the blackness by the large waste bins.

She realised with sickening clarity it was him. That he hadn't finished with her – not yet.

'Where is he?' he asked, throwing his cigarette butt away.

His voice was seamless and flat, devoid of any emotion.

It was this that scared her. It was the voice of someone capable of murder.

Her mind spun as she tried to figure out who he was after.

Realising he wasn't getting anywhere with her, he decided to jolt her memory. He walked over and bent down.

She waited, expecting him to hit her again, but he took her by surprise when he started caressing her bare thin legs with his gloved hand.

She trembled as he touched her gently. He slowly moved his hand further and further up her legs until it was under her skirt.

She tried to struggle, to get his hand away from between her legs. But he had her pinned down.

'I said, where is he?'

He stopped caressing her. His hand had become a ball of tension, waiting to explode.

She attempted to shake her head.

It wasn't the answer he wanted. He rammed his fist as hard as he could between her legs.

The pain was unbearable. She was certain she would pass out. Instead she retched.

He stood back and watched while she vomited, until eventually only bile was left. His stomach was turning at the sight of her. Vomit combined with blood trailed down the seeping, swollen mess that was her face.

'Nick. Where is he, you fucking slag?'

He was starting to lose his patience.

The question jolted her.

'What?' she mumbled through swollen, bloodied lips.

But the word she uttered made no sense.

Irritated, he bent over her, bringing his face close to hers. She was terrified. The look in his eyes told him he wasn't just going to rape her – he was going to kill her.

'No . . . please . . . no . . .'

But the words were inaudible. The only sound was a gargling, hissing noise.

'I said, where the fuck is NICK, you stupid bitch?'

He rammed a hand deep under her ribs to make sure that she was lucid.

She gasped in agony.

When she managed to breathe again, she mustered all the strength she had and spat at him.

Blood, vomit and spit hit his face. He took a tissue out of his jacket and wiped his cheek. He then took off the jacket and rolled up the sleeves of his shirt.

'Maybe it's time to teach you some manners,' he suggested as he began to unzip his trousers.

She tried to get up but her body refused to move. She willed herself to make a run for it. But something was wrong. Her legs wouldn't work.

Move . . . come on, Trina . . . Fucking move, girl! Move it before it's too late!

Desperate, she tried shuffling backwards on her elbows, dragging herself towards the entrance of the alley.

He was more than ready. He had been anticipating this moment for some time. He took his time stretching a condom over himself. He knew he couldn't take a chance with this disease-riddled bitch. He kneeled down and grabbed her by the legs as she tried in vain to scramble away from him. He leaned over and flipped her onto her stomach.

She groaned in pain at the sudden, violent movement.

Her reaction had the desired effect. It made him even more excited. He pulled up her faux leather skirt, exposing her black thong.

She attempted to struggle but was unable to move under the crushing weight of his body. She felt him yank her thong to one side before he forced himself into her. The pain was excruciating. But it was more the humiliation that hurt. Hot, furious tears slipped down her face as he succeeded in violently thrusting himself deep into her. One hand restrained her head, forcing her damaged face into the hard concrete, while the other held his phone as he filmed what he was doing to her.

She couldn't breathe. Dirt filled her bloodied mouth as she choked and gasped, desperate for air.

She could feel her body beginning to convulse as the lack of oxygen took effect. She prayed for unconsciousness. She was lucky. She blacked out before he started to really lose control.

Once finished with her he felt nothing but disgust and contempt. He gave her lifeless body another hard kick. Nothing. Satisfied, he picked it up and dumped it into the pub's industrial waste bins where it belonged.

Fucking bitch. Deserved everything she got. He had bigger problems than some has-been prostitute. He still had to find Nick Brady. And when he did . . .

He smiled at the prospect. He had what he wanted safe in a plastic bag: evidence that he had dealt with her. He felt no emorse. She was a used-up prostitute who was better off dead. Jo one would miss her.

He threw the business card with her name scrawled on the ·ack into the alleyway before turning to walk back to his car. Ie doubted the police would be able to identify her. Not n the condition he had left her in. But he was more than ıappy to point them in the right direction. After all, he had a ɔb to do and he had to be sure that the police didn't fuck verything up.

Chapter Two

Six days earlier:
Saturday, 19th October: 3:07 a.m.

Hidden in the shadows, he waited as she staggered on ahead of him. She made a sudden turn off the road into the alley behin the boarded-up Avenue pub, her body lurching from one side another as she did so. She seemed oblivious to the fact that th streetlights were out in the alley. Too drunk and too intent o getting home to care. He followed, making sure he didn't get to close.

She stopped.

He pushed his body flat against the wall, obscured by blacl ness as he held his breath and waited.

Had she seen him? No . . . He was sure of that. She had no ide that he was there. Or of what was about to happen.

'Shit!' she cursed, nearly falling over as she bent down t undo the straps on her black heels.

Successfully removing them, she yanked her dress up an crouched down.

He watched with stirring excitement as she relieved herself.

She was different. His tongue snaked slowly across his bottor lip as he thought about touching her. If he was honest, it was he tattoo that aroused him. It fascinated him.

Unlike with the others, he had waited for this moment – reli giously following her movements on Facebook and Twitte Even tonight she had updated her status:

'*Out to get as drunk as I can. Are you up for it?*'

He was 'up for it' all right. And if it was trouble she was look-
g for, she was heading in the right direction.

He studied her with a predatory interest as she managed to
mehow pull herself up without tumbling forward. She even
anaged to drag her dress back down. Not that she needed to
o that; he would soon be ripping it off.

He double-checked his jacket for condoms. Two weeks of
atching her. Fantasising. Planning. Now he was ready, he
anted to savour every detail.

He had his phone with him so he could film her. Not that she
ould object, given the state she was in. She was lucky he'd been
eeping an eye on her. Her friends – if you could call them
iends – had abandoned her. Left her dangerously drunk
utside the Blue Lagoon nightclub while they went on some-
here else.

It couldn't have worked out better for him when she decided
walk home – alone at 2:51 a.m. through the dark, empty
treets of Whitley Bay.

Had she not watched the news or read the papers? Obviously not.

*The police hadn't taken him as seriously as he wanted. But after
night all that would change. She was the one. The one that was
oing to make the headlines. Her name – Chloe Winters – would
oon have the following she craved. She wanted to be famous and he
ould be the one to give her that, and more.*

He would make her newsworthy.

He playfully fingered the Stanley knife safely hidden in his
acket pocket for later. What he was going to do to her would
ake time. He would make sure it was slow and deliberate. The
ain would be delicious. He could feel himself getting hard as he
magined the knife slicing neatly through her delicate, pale flesh.

He was ready to make a move.

He crept up behind her.

Hearing someone, she spun round. She froze for a second as
he tried to register who was behind her – and why. Even through
he hazy blur of drunkenness she could tell that something about

him was wrong. She started to edge backwards, away from him
He scared her. It was his eyes. Something was wrong with the wa
he was staring at her.

Instinct took over.

She made a move and ran as hard and fast as she could.

But he was too quick. That, and she was too drunk to hav
ever stood a real chance of escaping him.

With no real effort he caught hold of her and rammed he
hard up against the alley wall. He then used his body to pin he
against it. He knew she could feel his hardness in the small c
her back. He pushed it against her, wanting her to know hov
excited she made him.

He could hear her breathing – short, shallow gasps of air lik
a wounded animal. She was really scared now. He liked that.

He grabbed a fistful of hair and yanked her head back. H
knew it hurt. He wanted it to hurt.

She cried out from the pain. Stinging tears blurred every
thing around her. She started whimpering.

He breathed in her fear. He could smell it on her skin, emanat
ing from her pores.

'Shhh . . .' he whispered in her ear, enjoying every delectabl
whimpering sound she made.

Her eyes were desperate. Filled with terror at what wa
happening to her.

He knew that she couldn't breathe. He could feel the pani
rising up from within her pathetic body as she struggled desper
ately to prise his hand off her face. It was useless. He completel
overpowered her.

He had trained for this – worked out at the gym for hours o
end. Pumping weights and then working on his cardio. It wasn'
just his body he had taken care of – he also had a place prepared
He had thought of everything. He needed to be certain tha
nobody would find them. Let alone disturb him. What he had
planned for her would take time. Lots and lots of time.